Naked Truth II
The Whip Hand
by
Nicole Dere

Free first chapters of all Silver Moon & Silver Mink
novels at
http://www.silvermoonbooks.com
Decide before you visit the shop or use our postal
service!
Electronic downloads also available

This is fiction - In real life always practise safe sex!

Silver Moon & Silver Mink

HAVE A COLLECTION
OF 61GREAT NOVELS
OF
EROTIC DOMINATION

If you like one you will probably like the rest

A NEW TITLE EVERY MONTH
NOW INCLUDING EXTRA BONUS PAGES

Silver Moon Books of Leeds and New York are in no way connected with
Silver Moon Books of London

If you like one of our books you will probably like them all!

Write for our free 20 page booklet of extracts from early books
- surely the most erotic feebie yet - and, if you wish to be on
our confidential mailing list, from forthcoming monthly titles
as they are published:-

Silver Moon Reader Services

c/o DS Sales Ltd.
PO Box 1100 London N21 2WQ
http://www.limitededition.co.uk

or leave details on our 24hr UK answerphone
0181 245 0985
International acces code then +44 181 245 0985

New authors welcome
Please send submissions to
PO Box 5663
Nottingham
NG3 6PJ

www.silvermoon.co.uk
www.silvermoonbooks.com

Naked Truth II (The Whip Hand) first published 1999,copyright Nicole Dere
The right of Nicole Dere to be identified as the author of this book has been asserted in accordance with Section 77
and 78 of the Copyrights and Patents Act 1988

Naked Truth II - The Whip Hand
By Nicole Dere

Chapter One

Vee turned in the darkness at the bottom of the stairs. She could see the eyes glinting in the black face, the flash of his teeth at his smile. Her heart was pounding with excitement, and with fear. You're mad! her brain screamed. Absolutely mad! He's a boy, for God's sake! Sixteen years old, seventeen at the most. One of your own students!

But already that other, wickeder part of her brain was chuckling that it was too late. Behind his bulk, the front door was shut, securely locked against the outside world. And that hulking shape was far from boyish. That was what had started the whole thing, the sudden vivid reminder of that other towering shape, the rebel sergeant who had plucked her naked form up so easily the night of her capture, in that far off African land, and who had later so potently possessed her body in the narrowness of that stifling tent.

At least, that's what had started things for her, what had led to this seminal moment in this blackness at the foot of her stairs. Though, in her defence, she had to argue that it would never have been, but for the chance encounter with Wayne Grainger, and the breathtaking insolence of his approach to her. She could spread the blame farther - her desolation, the loneliness of this poky little flat, her feeling of being so cut off from every human contact and emotion, and at Christmas, too. The one time of the year when even the most feeble familial ties and relationships were strengthened, however temporarily. And there was no one, no one at all, she could turn to, or be

5

with, in this freezing festive season.

It didn't help to tell herself that was what she had wanted, planned for herself, glad only to escape into anonymous isolation after the glare of world media attention had focused so mercilessly upon her. She recalled the shock of seeing those photos of her, and of the Danish girl, Katya, both naked, staring forlornly into the lens, and the others, in the glossy magazines and the newspapers which Keith, her husband - ex-husband, she reminded herself bitterly - had hoarded away in his sick jealousy.

Those unrelenting newshounds had almost ferreted out the truth, that her marriage was on the rocks before her captivity in the rebel's hand's, but even so, after the trauma of her months of capture, she had clung tot he hope that her relationship with Keith could somehow be saved. When it all fell apart so catastrophically soon afterwards, she had fled back to England like a fugitive, afraid that she would never escape the terrifying publicity. But her brother David had been right. A change of name, of hairstyle, burial in the anonymity of London and the humdrum existence of a schoolteacher, had worked all too well. Until the ache of loneliness and the need for some kind of human contact other than the cautious, guarded role she was forced to play at work, had driven her to this desperate madness.

The heavy hand on her shoulder brought her back with a jolt. "You gonna keep us 'ere in the dark all night then, Miss?" Wayne's voice rumbled with laughter.

She knew that the 'Miss' was far from a term of respect. Quite the opposite. He was mocking the status which had been so comprehensively shattered in the last eventful hour or two since they had met in the launderette. She had been breathless, rigid with shock, at the sight of that great dark hand closing over the delicate little scrap of her underwear, crushing it as he picked it up from her bag, rubbed it savouringly across his smiling lips, so that those other, secret lips of her own, hidden smotheringly under the layers of winter clothing, had twitched and spasmed in helpless thrill. And somehow, fiend-ishly, he had known about it. It had led inevitably to that same hand cradling in her back, steering her out into the garishly lit, steambreathed night, and, in the awful, sneaking intimacy of the under table groping in the coffee bar, those thick fingers outlining the groove of her beating, moist sex through the thick-ness of her woollen tights, the hugging dampness of the body shaper.

She turned, climbed ahead of him up to the flat. The lamp light was discreet, even cosy, hiding the bareness of the rented bolt hole. She hurried across and turned the gas fire on full, though Wayne blew out his cheeks as comment on the heat thrown out by the central heating, which had never been off since the start of the holiday three days ago. "Jesus! You really have come from Africa, incha?" He tossed his fleece jacket onto the sofa, stood there grinning at her.

She blushed fiercely, could not meet his direct, mock-ing gaze. "What we talked about", she stumbled, her voice husky and small. "I don't want any of it to get out. To anyone. It's a secret. I'm sure you can understand. I don't want to have to run away again."

"My lips are sealed, Miss. As long as you promise to be nice to me, that is. And speakin' of lips. How's about a little Christmas kiss, eh? Just to get the ball rollin', as it were." He moved easily towards her, and she glanced up at him, wide eyed.

"Don't you think - " she stammered, her blood ham-mering. "I mean - is it a good idea? I'm your teacher. Older -"

7

"Old enough to be my mother?" he cut in aggressively. "No fuckin' way! How old are you? Twenty four? Five?"

"Twenty six." Her voice shook. She tried a pathetic little smile. "A lot older than you. Ten years."

He shook his head fiercely, closed in on her. He pulled the woollen hat from the back of her head, unwound her scarf, dragged off her beavy coat. He let them fall on the rug. "Forget that shit. Come here!" He grabbed her, pulled her against him. His head bent, his mouth seeking hers, with frank sexual hunger. She was limp. She did not struggle or reciprocate his urgency, but when his lips closed over hers, she felt her blood racing, and eventually, with a smothered whimper, she opened her mouth, and the kiss became mutual, a blaze of raw passion. His tongue drove into her, and she clung, shaking in his tight embrace.

She was panting, half weeping, when he released her mouth. His arms still clasped her to him. "You're all clothes!" he growled. "I want to see you. See what you really look like." He put his big hands on the hem of her sweater, pulled it over her breasts, her shoulders, then her head. The short, fair hair was tousled when he pulled the heavy cloth clear. The thin straps of the body bisected the fragile hollows of her shoulder bones, its thin cotton clung to the rising shape of her slight breasts, whose erect nipples thrust against the cloth. The pale divide showed above the dipping piping of the garment's edge.

All the while, she stood submissively still, trembling, offering no resistance or assistance. His hands fumbled with clumsy haste at her thick skirt, finally succeeded in unhooking it, drawing down the zip, and pulling it down off her hips. It fell with a soft whisper to catch at her ankle boots. The thick black tights came up to just below her breasts. "You are fuckin' wrapped up. It's like pass the parcel, this is!"

8

She stared down at the woolly kinks of his hair as he knelt and lifted her legs, to ease her skirt clear of her ankles. He unlaced the heavy boots, slipped them off. The great fingers reached up, hooked into the high waistband of the tights, rolled them down, dragged them slowly down her thighs, her calves, and she lifted her feet obediently, one after the other, so that he could remove them altogether. Her voice caught on a sob. "My luh - legs! They're skinny!"

He came slowly upright, his hands moving over the curve of her behind, only half concealed in the body shaper. "I like my gals skinny," he said. The fingers plucked at the shoulder straps, pulled them down to where they clung to her upper arms. She could feel her excitement, weakening her now with its need, feel the wetness, the swelling of her crotch, her vagina spasming with her excitement, and suddenly she was both afraid and titillated by her need.

"Wait!" she cried out shrilly. "I want to see you, too." Her fingers went to his chest, where the buttons of his shirt lay, but he thrust her hands roughly aside, and peeled off his upper garment hastily. The muscled sheen of his torso took her breath. She timidly laid her hands on the dark, satin flesh, quivered at the intensity of the contact. Suddenly, she sank to her knees in front of him, and her fingers tore at the flies of his jeans, clawing, fighting, and again his hands were there, undoing himself with difficulty, so that she could tug down the clinging garment until it hung hung about his knees. He wore tiny striped trunks underneath, filled with the huge swell of his genitals. She could see the rounded head of his prick, the dark patch of wetness at its helm. She smelt the yeasty male tang of him, her throat already working as she reached out, gently now, fearfully, and eased the elastic down, to bare his manhood.

She saw the tight, small scrub of pubis, then the long,

writing column of his prick uncoiled, like a live creature, the helm already poking clear of the thick ruff of foreskin. The split was agleam with moisture. It leapt to meet her, the shaft springing forth, jutting proudly. And it was hot under the reverent touch of her fingers.

"What - ?"

She cried at his protest, stilling him. "No! Please!" she begged. Her fingers were stroking, stirring, sliding up and down the hard column, whose giant head bobbed in front of her eyes. Frightened, transfused with her own pounding excitement, she bent forward, let its slimy wetness touch her brow, before smearing it worshipfully across her features, into the depths of her eyes sockets, along the sides of her nose, rubbing it across her closed lips, larding herself in the cloying thickness of his issue, anointing herself in the fluid abundantly seeping from it. Then her tongue poked out, flickered in a paroxysm of ecstatic fear across the slit of that pale dome, tasted the sweetness of his emission before her lips stretched wide, and she strained her jaw to take its massive beat inside her warm, suckling mouth.

Her head turned slightly sideways as she drove herself down, jaws agape, working furiously, until she gagged at its filling shape choking her. She bobbed up, her lips sliding to the dome, then she plunged down again, swallowing him as far as she could, dizzy at the savage swelling thrust of him into her. His hands were twisted in her dishevelled hair, tearing at her scalp in his frenzy. Swearing pungently, he dragged her mouth clear of him.

The breath was buffeted from her at the force with which he drove her back, and then fell on her on the rug. She felt his fingers scrabbling, scratching her tender flesh cruelly as he tried to claw the wet scrap of cloth from her loins. She dove between them, her own fingers frantic as she unsnapped the three pop studs to release the garment, which flew up about her waist, and she was as naked as he. She felt that great prick jab and slide all along her soaking, eager slit, and she fought for him, grabbed him, guided his stabbing strength into her madly welcoming sheath. Their pubic bones clashed at their coming together with a grunt which merged simultaneously from their riveted mouths.

She lifted her legs high, her feet waving in the air around his plunging shoulders. She cried with the pain of his burning thrusts, yet her belly leapt upwards to meet them, to impale herself on his driving invasion, helpless against her clamorous hunger, after all these months and endless months of solitary denial. Her head was back, tossing wildly on the hardness of the worn rug, her long throat exposed, its muscles rippling at the cries drawn from her as the orgasm surged up through her, to every part of her jerking frame, died, came again, and again, a roller coaster of consummation that left her sobbingly exhausted.

She whimpered at her renewed awareness of agony, the lancing nightmare now as he bucked, drove, grunted, battering her, before, at last, she felt the deep spurt of his coming, and that fearsome hardness eased, died a little, and they collapsed together, sweating, quivering, clinging in the lost aftermath of their mutual tempest.

She came through from the bathroom, stood in the doorway, staring at his relaxed, naked frame bathed in the rosy glow of the fire. His prick looked dark, vulnerable, small and curled on his thigh. "You'd better go," she croaked. "It's after two. Your folks. They'll be worried."

"They'll all be pissed." He held out his arms. Wearily, she walked across to him, very conscious of his gaze on her

11

nakedness as she moved.

"God! I can hardly move. I'm sore just about every-where." And that was no exaggeration, she thought. She lowered herself carefully beside him, and he folded her into his arms, so that she half lay on top of him, her head on his smooth shoulder. His hand moved between her thighs and she caught at his wrist, held him from laying it on her vulva. "Please! Not there! It's swollen up like a football. I haven't - done this for so long I've forgotten what it's like."

"I can't believe that." He shook his head in what seemed like genuine wonder. "You - you're fucking gorgeous."

She giggled. 'Thank you, kind sir." Her voice was serious as she resumed. "I mean it, though." She felt herself blushing. "Not since - before I left my husband. A long time before."

"He must be bloody mental."

And so must I be, she acknowledged tiredly, lying here literally shagged out with a school kid. Could I go to gaol for it? she wondered, not really alarmed at her speculation. No. There's nothing kiddish about this hunky specimen of young manhood in my arms. And, oh God, how much I needed him - it - after all these endless, sterile months of trying to satisfy myself each nights. And most mornings, too, and with nothing but the most temporary of reliefs. Well, maybe I've got it out of my system for a good while. Or have I?

She knew clearly that it would not be so. That she had stirred up a whole new hornet's nest of troubles for herself by her crazy action. Wayne was no little pupil, to be patted on his curly head and sent back to his seat with a winning smile. "Thank you, Wayne. There's a good boy. That was very nice. Now go and sit down and behave yourself."

She felt ashamed at the realisation that she did, indeed, just want him out of the flat. Out of her life altogether, until the next time she felt the overwhelming urge for a fuck. It wouldn't be like that. It never was. His next words proved it. "It's Christmas Eve tomorrer. Sorry. Today. I'll come round tea time. I've got a present for you." He gave a broad smirk..

Reluctantly, he stood. Even now, in spite of her aching weariness, she felt a quiver of lust as she stared up from the rug at his towering shape, the ripe hang of his penis, the sweet compactness of his balls, his lithe, muscled limbs and body shining in the fire glow. He drew on his tiny underbriefs, his shirt and jeans. She did not attempt to hide herself in a robe. When he was fully dressed, she went down the stairs, her naked flesh goose bumped and shivering, and clung to his muffled form in a last, wet, tongueing kiss. "You won't betray me, will you?" she whispered, siren like as she could be.

His broad hand was exploring her cold behind, whose cheek he pinched. "Not as long as you're good to me," he smiled.

She closed the door after he had left, and climbed up the stairs, going from the icy cold into the sealed warmth. She could smell the sexual odours wafting about, in spite of the bath they had shared. Not.surprising. They had gone at it again like maniacs as soon as they were back in the living room. A wry smile played about her lips as she realised they had not even made it to the bedroom throughout the long night. On the floor, like the animals they were. Healthy animals, though. Why not?

At least her bed was warm, an insulated nest, thanks to the electric blanket which had been an essential purchase. A cosy nest, but lonely. How may unfulfilled hours of feverish fantasising had she put in here, she wondered, and was shocked to find hrerself even now lightly stroking the puffed and sore

13

lips of her vulva as she lay in the dark. Insidious quivers of sensation sparked again at the recall of the hectic coupling she had shared in. Was it only black men who could turn her on in this special way? She blushed at the thought. Thought of her sergeant, and of General Mavumbi's rutting bulk, as the rebel leader had used her time and again in the nights of her captivity. Tears stung her eyes, brimmed over as she tried to recall the passion she and Keith had known. and was desolated to find that his loving her was only the mistiest of memories.

Chapter Two

She felt curiously detached, like a spectator watching some explicit sex movie, helpless against her own lust to get up and walk out, to switch off. Anyway, she kept telling herself, it was too late for that. She was as much in his hands, his victim, as she had been in the rebel stronghold, when the general, and the lovely black lieutenant, Awina, had used her as their play thing. If she objected, tried to dismiss him, he would ruin her, all over again.

She moved around the flat naked, as usual, unable to keep from touching herself as she waited for him to appear, yet her heart thumped with fear again when the sound of the door bell pierced the air. She grabbed at her full length, black silk robe with the bright flower prints on it. As she hurried barefoot down the stairs, it flowed open to the top of her thigh, exposing her pale limb, and she felt like a whore rushing to meet her client.

She blushed when she opened the door to him, but

she had no time even to complete her shyly muttered greeting before he crushed her to him, and his mouth sealed off hers, his tongue probing deep into her. She smelt the strong odour of alcohol, tasted its sourness, then he had scooped her up in his arms and was carrying her easily up the steep flight to the living room. Her robe slid off, fluttered down from his hands, and she lay back, panting, staring up from the cushions of the sofa as he swiftly tore off his own clothes.

"Wait!" she cried, meaninglessly. Roughly, he pulled her to the floor, again on the worn rug by the fire's heat, fitting her spread limbs about his thick waist. His prick stood out, pole hard and mighty. He thrust it at her without ceremony, and automatically she seized the thick shaft, guided it to her, wincing at its first nuzzling stab at her still sore vulva. But, in spite of her pain, and the shock of his precipitate lunging, she found she was more than ready, her sheath oily with secretions, and he slid deeply, easily, into her clinging passage. At last, he managed to exert some measure of control. He eased his movements, slowed them down, gentled them, so that he was not battering at her but pistoning smoothly back and forth, holding her thighs against him. She watched the rippling play of his muscles on the satiny, deep velvet skin, the clench of the paler, ivory buttocks, and a great wave of sensual pleasure stirred, fluttered, grew at the steady slide of his flesh in hers. She gasped, bit her lip, her fingers dug into the broad shoulders swooping over her. He stared, his eyes widening at the sharpness of her cry, her convulsive shudder. His broad, shining face broke into a slow, comprehending grin as he realised she was coming, recognised the rising cry, the sudden violence of her squirming belly onto his.

"You're hot stuff, incha?" he marvelled. And she was, she acknowledged, even as she sobbed and galloped into the

15

full splendour of orgasm, threshing around under his bulk, kicking, abandoning herself to the power ripping through her. Hot as fire, melting, arching under him, urging him to split her with his potent weapon. Then the climax passed, she endured the buffeting of his rampant prick searing her now, until he too achieved his goal, and spent himself inside her.

He left in the evening, "to meet me mates", and she sat there, in the sudden empty silence, curled up in front of the fire, his fluids drying on her, and in her, her nostrils filled with their combined odour. She was too drained, too stunned by the force of their loving, to rise and take a bath. When the phone jangled, she stood there, naked, enduring the emotional talk of her parents, of her brother, David, who, with his wife, was spending Christmas with them.

"I wish you could have come down here," her mother said, her voice quavering with seasonal sentiment, though Vee knew well enough that both she and dad had sighed with relief when she had told them she couldn't make it.

"Never mind, mum. I'll get down in the new year - soon." The tears were trickling down her cheeks as she stood there. She stared at her creased and tired face, her bare breasts, in the mirror. Her vagina throbbed. From the distended lips of her vulva, she could feel the residue of Wayne's come oozing slimily.

She stayed in, stayed unclothed, through the lonely Christmas Morning, tried to watch the television as she sat and ate her solitary festive dinner for one, fresh from the microwave. Wayne came about half two. He made her kneel in front of the TV set, and she watched the queen speaking, the traffic passing silently behind Her Majesty beyond the windows of the palace. Wayne knelt upright behind Vee, holding her by her slim hips, driving that long column of his prick throught the cleft of her raised buttocks to her throbbing, eager vagina. He moved almost lazily. She felt the wiry scrub of his pubes rubbing across her bottom, thrust back against the drive of him into her. It was the longest fuck they had had. The queen was long gone, replaced by a spectacular Bond film, and still they undulated before the flickering images until Vee suddenly gave a sharp bark of surprise at the strength of the orgasm which caught her almost unawares, and she folded forward, her head on her arms, shuddering so violently that he all but slid out of her, and had to fall desperately forward too, bearing down on her limp, sweating body, to stay in her.

"Why don't you come out with us New Year's Eve? Have a drink with the lads? Be a good laugh."

She stared at him, aghast. "You haven't - told anyone?" she asked faintly.

He was sitting at her dining table, his cheeks pouched with the bacon sandwich she had cooked for him. They were both naked. She felt she had been doing little else but have sex with him for months. They had even managed to get to the bed at last. He had stayed the night with her. She had woken up to find him parting her legs, ploughing that mighty prick of his into her crusted cunt with irrepressible gusto.

"Naw!" he assured her, with his wide grin. "Anyways, when would I have had the chance to tell anyone anything? You've kept me too busy for that!"

"You mustn't," she told him anxiously. "You promised." She blushed. "I could - get into big trouble, if anyone found out. They could - they could call it abuse."

He hooted with laughter. "Not quite, doll! I reckon I can hold me own, don't you? I think I might even have taught you a thing or two, eh?"

For a second, she felt that spark of inner fury, that quiver of rage at his preening masculine ego that was almost like a wicked thrill to her. She remembered that easy assumption so well. It stirred her even now to recall Keith's superiority over her. But this! This was a seventeen year old kid! For an instant, she was choked with disgust with herself, with the whole set up. She moved to kneel between his knees, resting her hand on his thigh. "Listen," she said earnestly, gazing up at him. "It's important to me. I couldn't face it - couldn't go back to school, if I thought anyone had any inkling of us -." She nodded at their naked bodies. "I mean it. I'd have to leave. Straight away."

"Oright, doll, oright! No need to get them pretty knickers of yours in a twist. Not that I've seen you in them much. What about the two of us, then? We could nip out for a drink, early on, like. Before I meet me nates. What you say?"

But she was adamant, she wouldn't be seen outside with him. For a while, he seemed truculent, but she soon distracted him with other pressing matters. When he had gone, she lay back apathetically in the tangled, stained sheets. What would happen when term started again? How could she possibly cope? She had practically no control over the senior pupils as it was. She thought of the bunch of sixteen and seventeen year old yobboes that made up 5C.; the form that Wayne was in. She grew hot and cold at the thought of facing them, with him there in front of her - her lover! She couldn't manage them as it was. She knew their mocking nickname for her. "Miss Pee-Pee."

At first, she had tearfully thought it had something disgustingly urinary in its meaning, but then she realised that it was an abbreviation of their original, fairly innocent epithet for her. "Miss Prim-n-Proper." Perhaps as a reaction to the notoriety which had briefly fallen on her as a result of her being held hostage by the northern rebels out in Makamba, and partly as a result of her inability to exert any proper control over her more senior charges, she had adopted a mantle of old fashioned correctness, thus earning herself an almost mockingly affectionate sobriquet which they had soon shortened to its initials. Pee-pee.

She tormented herself by vividly imagining their reaction, both boys and girls, if they knew of her relationship with Wayne. The havoc it would cause. Worse still was her belief that they must, sooner rather than later, find out. She could not envisage Wayne keeping their secret for very long. What seventeen year old would prove capable of keeping his mouth shut about the fact that he was knocking off his teacher? Especially a stud like Wayne, who, in the hectic hours they had spent together so far, had managed to imply that he had had sex with most of the girls in his class. And a good many others besides. Not that she was jealous of that. Far from it. She just wished one of the little tarts would take him off her hands right now. Then she blushed for shame. As ever, she had to acknowledge how willing a victim she had become. Come off it, girl, she lashed herself. You were as desperate for a shag as he was to get it in you. The thought brought her little comfort. For the umpteenth time, she cursed the fate that had taken her to that launderette during those fateful minutes when Wayne Grainger had walked in.

He came round in the afternoon of New Year's Eve, as expected. "Don't you never wear clothes indoors then?" he grinned.

She blushed hotly, snapped waspishly with guilt, "Not when you're coming round. Be a waste of time, wouldn't it? You'd only ruin then tearing them off me."

"Oh-ho! Gettin' uppety now, are we, Miss? Not complaining, are you?"

She tried hard to look at him as she went on. "Look, Wayne, it's been very - nice" - he snorted at her choice of word and she crimsoned further - "but we really can't go on like this. I mean, you coming round, having sex every day. I think we ought to call a halt."

She was dismayed but not surprised at the strength of his reaction. "Tryin' to give me the brush off now, eh? Had enough black dick? You surprise me! I thought you couldn't get enough of it, especially after what happened to you out in Africa. Well, Pee-Pee, you don't get rid of Wayne Grainger so easy! I know you now, don't I? I've seen through your schoolmarm act, Miss Goody! I know what you're really like, you randy tart, so you better behave yourself. Or there's a few more'll be told about you, Miss!"

As he spoke, he plucked her up and bore her through to the bedroom. She made no effort to put up a fight and lay limp in his grasp. The silk robe fell open as he flung her down on the still unmade bed. Her knees were slackly parted as she watched while he stepped out of the clothing covering his lower body. His prick stood out, ramrod hard, its head nodding as he advanced on her. She drew up her knees and accommodated his lunge onto her belly. She grunted with pain, his massiveness filling her narrow orifice, stinging, yet still the excitement flared swiftly in her, along with the pain, even though he rutted wildly, concerned only with his own hasty pleasure this time. She was on the edge of climax when he came, jetting deeply into her, and she bucked furiously in the last frenetic seconds until she too spasmed at the crisis which swept over her, before his prick slid wetly out of her.

She lay there, exhausted, battered, savouring that special feeling of masochistic pain-pleasure, feeling his fluid oozing out of her, aware of the spread out, used flavour of her sprawling body on the sheete. She drifted, almost dozing, while she vaguely heard his splashing about in the bathroom. She was hurt that he had left her there like that. She had already learnt how much he enjoyed sharing their ablutions, jostling companionably together in the foam of her small bath tub. With a tremor of alarm, she began to realise how much she had angered him with her words, and how dangerous that could be. With a sick feeling in her gut, she admonished herself. She would have to win him over with her compliance.

But when he returned to the bedroom, his mood was uglier than before.

"You got someone else lined up, is that it? Ready to take on somebody new?" He ignored her vehement denial. She struggled up to a sitting position as she realised he was dressing again. It did not take him long. "I bet you're gonna sneak off to some party tonight, incha? Bet you'll have a good laugh with some ponce about the bit of black rough you've been having over the holiday! Well, we'll see about that, bitch! We'll soon put a stop to that!"

"What - what are you doing?" Her voice squeaked with alarm as he seized her by the wrists and jerked her up off the bed. The robe lay like a crushed black snake amid the tangle of the sheets.

He kept an iron hold on her right wrist while he began to pull open her drawers, until he found the bundle of tights, which he hauled out, spilling them all over. He thrust her down onto the rickety, hard chair. "Sit still!" he growled. She could feel the itchiness of the raffia on her bare bottom.

"How dare you? Stop this!" she gasped, but her protest was feeble, shaky with threatening tears, and totally ineffectual against his own anger. She cried out again at his manhandling of her arms, as he positioned them so that he could bind her wrists tightly to the chair back. The tights cut painfully into her sensitive skin. She was trembling. The tears spilt over, she wept. "Please - don't!" She hated herself for the hushed tone, its begging subservience. At the same time, she felt that secret quiver, that spasm of excitement deep in her belly. She did not try to fight as he stooped, and quickly bound her ankles together, then tied them securely to the legs of the chair. "Let me go!" The tears were pouring now, her voice was catchy with her sobs, husky with her plea.

He stood over her triumphantly. "Not so cocky now, are we, Miss? You won't be going anywhere tonight, that's for sure. I'll be back."

"No!" She cried out shrilly, panic setting her heart racing. "You can't leave me - like this!"

"Watch me!" he chuckled. She began to twist against the cutting bonds. It was hopeless and she soon subsided. Her breasts were heaving with her crying now.

"Please, Wayne!" she begged humbly. "I'm sorry - if I upset you. I didn't mean - untie me, please. I'm sorry."

She gasped as he moved behind her. The chair creaked as he picked it up, grunting with effort, yet succeeding in carrying her through into the living room. He placed her where she could feel the warmth of the fire, and where she could see the TV set, which he turned on. "Be good." He grinned at her, came over and slowly fondled her breasts. The small nipples peaked at his touch. He took them between his thumbs and forefingers and twiddled them like knobs on a radio. "I'll be back much later. Unless I'm too pissed to remember. In which case I'll see you tomorrer - some time!"

"No! I'll scream! I swear - "

"Go ahead. Some fucker might even hear you, and

22

send for the police. That'll be a laugh. What'll you tell 'em?"

She sobbed in impotent defeat. "You filthy sadistic bastard!"

He chuckled delightedly. "I love it when you talk dirty. Don't forget to wait up, will you? See you later, darlin'."

She heard him go out, the front door clashing shut behind him. He had a key. But when would he next use it? In a sudden paroxysm of helpless fury, she struggled wildly, until the sweat poured from her and the chair threatened to topple. She sank back, exhausted, and stared through a curtain of shimmering tears at the capering, coloured figures dancing in front of her on the screen.

Chapter Three

Vee jerked awake, her chin lifting from her chest. She had recognised the sounds which had woken her. The fumbling scrape of a key, then the noisy closing of the front door. The heavy, unsteady steps up the steep stairs. With consciousness, the pain flowed back, beginning with the ache of neck and shoulders, where she had slumped in exhausted sleep. She was aware of course of the chafed wrists and ankles. She had from time to time throughout the endless evening and night endeavoured to writhe and twist herself free of the bonds, each effort only adding to her discomfort and leaving her sobbing, sweatily worn out. One of the worst agonies was the imprint of the hard seat on her bottom, which was aching abominably after the long hours she had sat in bound helplessness. She wished she was a bit more fleshily endowed on her buttocks, the way those Baganda girls had been out in Makamba, with their proudly jutting nates. Her backside must look like a page of Braille script now, with the indentations of the raffia patterns on her bum.

At least she hadn't been cold, even though she was naked. She had, if anything, been too warm, what with the gas fire bathing her down one side, and the cental heating full on. She had cried herself to fitful slumber, waking every now and then with a thumping start, only to set off weeping again at her impotence, and his cruelty in leaving her for so long in this state.

She glanced at the clock. Four thirty in the morning! He had left her tied up for more than eight hours, the callous bastard! Well, at last it was over. She heard his heavy tread at the top of the stairs, and let out a groan of tearful relief. The tears started to flow thickly again. She swallowed her anger and humiliation. She had been shocked at what he had done to her, and frightened, too. She knew she must be careful in her approach, she mustn't offend or enflame him. She set her face towards the door in tragic pathos, then her eyes bugged, and her jaw dropped in amazement.

The figure standing grinning at her and taking in the spectacle of her nakedness with evident delight was not Wayne Grainger! This individual was not so tall, nor so bulky, either. He was a good few years older too, she registered in her astonishment. His complerxion was much lighter, the kind of coffee brown similar to the coastal and central tribes out in East Africa. He was much more fashionably and tidily dressed than Wayne. His long, handsome face split into a broad grin, his teeth flashing whitely.

Her face was burning. ":Help me!" she gasped. "Untie me! Please!"

He made no effort to do so, merely stood there, relaxed, dangling her door key from one finger, smiling. And
looking. With clear pleasure.

"Hi. Well well! Young Wayne was right after all, the
crafty little sod! I was sure the toe rag was lying." He shook his
head in disbelief, then advanced into the room, to stand in front
of her.

She put her head down, writhing with shame, her
limbs moving automatically to try to hide herself. "Please,"
she whispered again. "Let me loose. I've been - like this - for
hours. I'm - it's agony."

"Not so fast, teach. Just why are you tied up like this?
What have you and young Wayne been up to?"

"He did this - made me - look, please let me go. I'll
tell you - "

"It's OK. I've got plenty of time. Fancy a cup of tea?
Or coffee? Where's the kitchen? Through here, right? You take
milk and sugar?" He turned back, gave a crudely exaggerated
glance at her body, and grinned. "Or do you prefer it black?"
He chuckled when she didn't answer and turned away again.
She hung her head, cried quietly. She heard him fill the kettle,
switch it on. He came back to the doorway.

"Where's Wayne?" she managed. "He said he would
come back."

"The little sod's sleeping it of. He's had a right skinful.
Spewed his ring up. Serves him right. These kids can't take it,
can they?"

"How did you know - about me?"

He chuckled again. "He was burbling on about you
all night. Once young Wayne's had a few he can't keep his
mouth shut - or his dick in his pants." He came so close that she

cowered against the chair back. "Nobody took any notice of him. We thought he was just bullshitting as usual. Shagging his teacher! I mean - you wouldn't credit it, would you?" His voice sank to a throaty murmur, he knelt, and she flinched as his hand fell on her thigh, moved slowly up it, his clasp warm and firm on her smooth skin. "But bugger me! The little sod was right after all, eh?"

His fingers slid round the curve of her inner thigh, reached the sandy fleece of her pubic hair, the pale nails brushed through it, plucked teasingly at a few tendrils. "How long has this been going on, then? How long have you been shafting our Wayne?"

"It's not - what you - I didn't - it was him - " She gasped, cutting off her words abruptly at the caressive touch, feather light, of his fingers over the lips of her sex. The muscles bunched on her thighs as she pressed them convulsively together, trapping his long brown hand between them. He stroked at her crack, and she shivered. Helplessly, she felt her nipples tingle, perk to erection, and she squirmed on the hard seat. "Don't!" she murmured faintly. The funnel of her vagina was spasming, she felt the seep of fluid at his strokes. Her vulva was opening, blossoming to his stimulation.

His face was close to her, she could feel his breath between her breasts, smell its spirit flavour. "What's wrong?" he purred. His fingers were rubbing up and down the length of her labia now, she knew he could feel their oily pout. "I've heard you're the hottest shag from here to Bermondsey. And the bigger and blacker the dick, the more you like it. Ain't that so? Well, darling, you're finally in luck. I may not be quite as black as young Wayne but where shagging's concerned I'm bigger and better and know more about it than he'll ever know. Even with a shit hot teacher like you to teach him!"

His finger pads were in her now, prising apart the outer lips, playing along the greasily lubricated inner surfaces nearer and nearer the sensitive nub of her clitoris, until her hips and belly were twitching, she was unable to hold herself still, no matter how hard she tried. That maddening chuckle rumbled, scourging her with its knowledge of her arousal. "You're up for it all right, ain't you, darling? I bet it's been a long old night for you, hasn't it?" She gasped, bit at her lip, shuddered at the play of a finger tip over the pulsing trigger of her need.

She sobbed, her head hanging down, as he withdrew his hand from between her clasping thighs, and instead let his damp fingers toy with her right nipple.

"Please untie me!" she sobbed, humbly, begging him. "I really can't stand it. And - I need the bathroom. Please!"

His hand moved to her other breast, hefting its soft outline in the cupped palm.

"Not a lot on top," he teased. "But all of it raring to go, I reckon." Now the other hand seized her chin, lifting her mouth, and she stared hypnotically at the smiling lips descending to spread over hers like an octopus's tentacles, sucking the breath from her, forcing her to open her mouth, and to admit his tongue, which explored deeply, possessively. Her pulse raced, her blood pounded in her ears, and she gulped in precious air when he finally released her from the kiss.

She felt a huge stab of relief when she felt his hands plucking at the knots about her feet. He swore at the difficulty he had in tugging apart the thin strands of nylon. It took him long seconds, but at last her ankles were free, and she moaned at the rush of blood back to her extremities and the ache of cramped muscles as she was finally able to move them. Unable to help herself, she opened her thighs, wriggled to ease the torment of her trussled limbs. She stretched out her legs, her

27

toes pointing, wiggling with joy of such freedom once more. There were deep red indentations, bracelets of crimson round both her ankles, and he massaged them tenderly, while she whimpered in grateful relief.

All at once, she realised he was not freeing her wrists, and she wept, pleaded with him yet again. He merely laughed. His hands were firm, gentle but irresistible on the insides of her knees as he pushed them widely apart.

"So let's have a look at this treasure our Wayne's been keeping all to himself, the dirty little ponce!" She shivered. She had never felt so mercilessly exposed. His fingers played with her, revealed her moist crevice to full view, pressed at the still tender, swollen outer surfaces of the vulva, while his head dipped forward as though he were breathing in its unique and pungent aroma.

She drew up one foot, rested its heel on the rim of the chair, trying to squeeze her thighs together, but he laughed, took her ankle and moved it gently aside. "Bit late for modesty now, teach, ain't it?"

"Who are you? I'm begging you - let me go. I - "

"Oh I'm sorry. How pig-ignorant of me not to intro-duce myself! My name's Cliffy. I'm Wayne's big brother. Well, half brother, strictly speaking. Same mummy, different daddy. As you migh have guessed from my complexion. Not black as our young-un, but every bit as well endowed. I can assure you." His voice dropped to a syrupy whisper. "And a helluva lot more experienced, teach. You must be the luckiest girl alive. I'll be your New Year's first-fuck, and you won't want any other, believe me!"

"Please!" she implored again, her voice even fainter than his. He moved around behind her and fought with the bonds still holding her to the chair. "Just go, please. I'm not - I

28

don't want - " Her voice died, she wept hopelessly.

He held his fingers up to his nose, and she was wracked with shame. "We know what you want, darling, don't we?" he said.

She groaned aloud, would have fallen if he had not supported her. The agony of moving the cramped muscles of her shoulders and her back was overwhelming. When she rose, she felt the chair's seat sticking to her. It felt as though she had left the skin of her bottom stuck to the raffia. Its pattern was deeply etched in little scarlet bobbles all over her cheeks. Then she realised that, though he had released her from the chair, he had left her wrists still tethered at her back. A fresh feeling of utter helplessness swept over her.

His arm was round her as he steered her out to the kitchen, where he poured the hot water into the two mugs, stirred the coffee vigorously. She had to endure the shame of perching stiffly on the edge of the high stool and having him hold the cup to her lips, giving her little sips of the liquid. Nevertheless, she drank it eagerly, grateful for its revivimg warmth. He dabbed at her chin with the corner of a kitchen cloth when she had finished.

She waggled her bound hands, raising her arms stiffly behind her. "Please?" she tried once more. "The bathroom, I need to go."

He gazed at her in pretended innocence. "Big jobs, is it? Will I have to wipe your bum?"

She began to weep again, sniffling pathetically as she shook her head. "That's all right then," he smiled. "Go ahead. You can manage a piss, can't you?"

Whimpering with degradation, she went through to the bathroom, surprised when he didn't follow her. She sat and urinated, ashamed of the audible hiss of the act, wincing at the stinging soreness.

"Feeling better now, are we? I reckon there's nothing worse than fucking on a full bladder, don't you? Er - by the way, what do I call you, teach? We really ought to be on first name terms, eh?"

"My name's Vera," she muttered, head down, like a sulky child. "People call me Vee."

He hooted derisively. "Vera! Fuck me! What a bloody monicker, eh?"

"Vee!" she answered, staring at him with a spark of hatred. "I told you. Everyone calls me Vee."

"I don't blame 'em. Right! Vee it is then." She screamed as he suddenly shot an arm out, grabbed her and pulled her down. She fell stumbling, face forward, across his knee. "Well, Vee. First things first. You've obviously been a very naughty girl. Or should I say lady? Fucking about with one of your pupils. My poor little bro. How could you, you dirty perv? I think the law would take a very dim view of a teacher shagging her pupils, don't you?"

She began to struggle weakly. She could feel the rub of his clothing on her belly, and her thighs as she squirmed. She felt foolish even answering from this undignified position. "It was him. He was the one - he picked me up - started molesting me - "

"Oh yeah?" His voice was thick with scorn. "That's gonna be the old cry, is it? Rape, your honour. He forced me. Kept me naked and tied up, all over Christmas. That's not the way Wayne tells it, Vee. I think you need a bit of a lesson, teach. Just to show you what's what, eh?"

She knew what was to happen. She had started to kick out, her buttocks dimpled as they clenched in anticipation. Her feet sawed the air, no real threat to his intentions, which were made plain when the first, open handed, cracking blow fell on her reddened behind. SPLAT! After the prolonged torment of sitting glued to that chair, the sharpmess of the fiery sting was almost welcome. Indeed, that primitive part of her which she had always feared sent its spasms of response from deep in her sex, through her writhing belly, out to the very nerve ends of her twisting frame.

He spanked rapidly, the blows falling one after another, until his palm was ringing, and her bottom blazed with the tingle of the chastisement. Her feet made those swift little kicking movements, her belly rubbed against his thighs, she could sense the beat of his excitement through his clothing.

"Please!" she blubbered. "Stop! I - I'll do - oh, please, stuh - stop!"

He did, eventually, and she sobbed abandonedly. He thrust her off his knee and she fell to the floor, squirmed around, clutching at her burning backside, shamed and yet wickedly titillated by the degraded spectacle she presented.

"Get up." She shivered at the new hardness in his command. She felt him kick her, quite hard, on the thigh. Looking up through her tears, she saw him towering menacingly over her. His hand was stretched towards her, and she reached up obediently. He jerked her roughly to her feet, pulled her after him through to the bedroom. He gestured at the tumbled bed. "Your pit's still stinking from the shagging you been doing with Wayne!"

She said nothing, stood there, rubbing at her throbbing behind, snivelling quietly, while he quickly stripped off his clothes. His prick hung, long, but flaccid. He thrust her down on the bed, onto her back, and knelt astride her, over her middriff. He wriggled upward, on his knees, until the penis and its heavy ball bag hung directly over her upturned, tear smeared face.   "Come on, teach. You lot all have the gift of the gab, they reckon. Put it to some use now!"

She raised her head, the tip of her tongue came out, lapped at the pink dome of the prick, tasting the salty emission at the tiny slit, her senses filled with the strange mixture of sourness and talcumed sweetness emanating from the potent genitals. Surrendering herself to the physical sensations which were sending deep spasms of thrill thorughout her, she opened her mouth, poked out her tongue further, and began to lap, with long, slow strokes, at the underside of his balls, and the root of the long column, which was soon stirring, stiffening, to project in promising rigidity before him.

She squirmed up further between his sprawled thighs, raising her head, so that she was on a level with that bobbing prick, and able to encircle its massive dome with her lips. She lapped and sucked at it, tongueing, nibbling, until its mighty beat sent it soaring in a full blooded erection. With difficulty, she succeeded in capturing that helm inside her working mouth, its power filling her to the back of her throat. She swallowed convulsively, began a stabbing, bobbing impalement as far down the beating column as she could.

Dizzily, she wondered if he was going to come in her mouth, crazily found herself wishing he would, even as her heart thudded with fear at the prospect. But all at once his fingers dug cruelly into the hair at her brow and tore her streaming face away from his loins, he swept her thighs apart and plunged his prick to the hilt inside her beating cunt.

CHAPTER FOUR

"Happy New Year, mum. Sorry I - I wasn't in. Earlier. Stayed over at a friend's." Vee recalled the beeping of the phone, seeming to go on forever, while she sat there, tied to that chair, with the muted merriment of the TV burbling away in the background. She had guessed it would be her family. Who else was there to ring her as the old year slipped out? Ruth, her first and former lover? Not likely. She had not heard from her in years. Not since that day in her former life, before Africa, when she had watched her hurry out, head down and body shaking with her weeping and her pain from Keith's thrashing and fucking of her, after he had come back to the flat and caught them in bed together.

Her mother's voice resumed in her ear. "You still sound tired, dear. I hope you're not overdoing it. Sorry if we woke you, but, it is afternoon."

"Yes - no, I mean - it's fine. I - ayeee!" She squealed, gasped at the cold clamminess, and flinched violently at the sudden invasion of her flesh. She stared down at the naked brown figure crouching in front of her. Cliffy was smearing a clinging mess of vivid strawberry jam all over her vulva, and the crease of her thigh, with a knife whose iciness made her shiver. His left hand was dug hard into the cleft of her bottom, holding her so that she could not escape entirely.

"Vee? What's wrong? What is it? Are you all right?"

"Yes, yes!" she panted, struggling monumentally to regain some sort of composure, finally surrendering to Cliffy's ministrations. "Sorry. I just - dropped something. Spilt - my coffee, It's OK."

"I'll put your father on, just to wish you a happy new year."

Her father's voice boomed with his false heartiness.

"And you, daddy. Have you had a nice time? Wish I could have been there." She stifled another squeal, biting hard at her lip. She felt Cliffy's tongue probing deep into the fissure of her labia, licking off the mess he had liberally smeared with her. Her buttock cheeks hollowed deeply. Her loins quivered.

"Oh, you'd have found us very dull, I'm sure. Not a patch on the high life you're living up there," her father laughed, a veiled hint of reproach in his tone, she was sure. Which was quite a laugh, considering that he preferred her to keep her distance. He had never forgiven her for her brief flurry of fame, and the spotlight which had included them in its unwelcome glare, for a time.

She drew a ragged breath, felt herself responding meltingly to Cliff'a vigorous lapping out of her orifice. Her knees felt rubbery, instinctively she pushed her loins forward, thrust her belly to meet his rousing caresses. "Well, it's lovely to hear you, daddy," she breathed. "I'll be in touch. And I'll get down before the end of the month, I promise. Bye." She shakily replaced the receiver, before her father could summon her brother to the phone. Her mind shied away from the enormity of having David's voice in her ear while she stood being lapped out by this insatiable stranger.

With a groan of relief, she folded, let herself go with the mounting excitement, and they tumbled together onto the carpet. The sweet, sticky mess at her loins was compounded with her own juices stirred by his tongueing of her, and when his long, brown prick nuzzled its already familiar path into her throbbing cunt, she was more than ready to welcome the intruder.

"Oh God!" She let her head fall back, exposing the long, working slenderness of her white throat, at which his lips and tongue nibbled now, before moving up to clamp over her open mouth. She could feel, and taste, the sticky sweetness of the jam, mingled exotically with the tang of her own sexual fluids. Her head swam dizzily with tiredness, and with the mounting passion which his slow, rhythmical movements deep inside her were causing

Fleetingly, she wondered if anyone had made love as wildly as this unknown figure, and hazily acknowledged, shamefully, that she had probably thought that about every man she had ever fucked with. Then, blessedly, thought fled, spun away, and she was all screaming sensation, her body jerking, exploding with the force of the consuming power the coupling brought her. They threshed and jerked madly, he came soon after she did, before she was aware of her surroundings again, and they lay, sweating, supine, coiled on the cool hardness of the thin carpet, and she felt their bellies sticking together even as he died and slid oozingly from her stinging vagina.

They were in the bath together, sitting opposite each other, his toes playing, pressing against the cushiony softness of her mons in the midst of the whipped up foam, when they heard a thunderous knocking at the door. They heard a hoarse voice, faint with distance, but nevertheless, clearly distinguishable. "Come on! Open up, you bastard! And you! You fucking slag! Let me in!"

She stared at Cliffy in open mouthed horror. Stunned at her stupidity, she realised she had forgotten entirely about Wayne. Clearly, his brother had not. His handsome face split in a wide grin, while Vee jabbered frantically.

"Shut him up! For God's sake! The neighbours! I - "

Cliffy rose. She stared at the beard of white foam clinging to his long, thin penis, and the tight little scrub of black curls above it. She watched the bubbles sliding over the smooth, shining brown skin as he climbed out. He went out, dripping, and naked while she sat, frozen in her horror, her knees drawn up. She held her breath, strained to listen. She heard the door open, the rumble of voices, the door closing again. Wayne's voice rang out. It sounded painfully adolescent, squeaking in its almost incoherent rage. "What you done to her, you filthy fucking bastard? Where is she? I'll kill you - "

"Hang on, old son! No need to lose your rag. She's had a great time. We're in here. Look who's come to see you, luv. Your old boyfriend. Me little bro!"

She stared up at the two contrasting individuals filling the small room. Wayne's black face was set in a ferocious scowl. His bulk looked even more massive in the thick winter waterproof and jeans. Cliffy's paler, slimmer body still gleamed with wetness. There were odd bubbles of lather still clinging to him. His features still wore that wide grin. He slid round Wayne's glowering form, and stepped back into the foamy water, brushing aside Vee's raised knees to take his place opposite her once more.

"We were just cleaning ourselves up," he said easily. "You know what it's like, eh?" He winked at the scowling figure. "Look. Why don't you make us all a mug of coffee, eh? Go down a treat, that would. You know where everything is, doncha?" Again, he gave that deep chuckle, full of innuendo.

Wayne's lip trembled. His eyes blazed at the crimsoning Vee. "You bloody bitch! You rotten cow!"

"It was you! It's your fault!" she fired back, stung into a response. "You promised! Swore - you wouldn't tell anyone. Talking - bragging about it - about me - to all and sundry."

"Here, wait a mo, darling!" Cliffy interrupted, still with the grin that suggested he was enjoying the whole scene hugely. "I'm not all and sundry, am I? Me and little bro here, we got no secrets. Eh, Wayne? We share everything, don't we?"

"Fuck off!" Wayne spat. His hands clenched into fists, he took a step forward. "I'll smash your fucking head int!"

Vee tensed in alarm, but Cliffy just sat there, not in the least disturbed. Or so it seemed. "Take it easy, will you? She's right, you know. You were shooting your mouth something rotten last night. It's a good job I did get the keys off you and come along here. Apart from the fact that the little lady here was totally knackered being tied up in that chair all night. If I hadn't stepped in, Christ knows what might've happened. You were in no fit state to do anything about it. And she might have had half the toe rags from the Blue Cat lining up to give her a good seeing to. And she wouldn't want that. Would you, darling?" He reached out, with deliberate casualness let his hands play with her soapy breasts. "She's got better taste than that, haven't you?"

Despite his provocative action, his words pricked Wayne's murderous rage like a pin in a balloon. "I was pissed out me mind," Wayne mumbled, his head going down in guilt.

Cliffy clicked his teeth and shook his head in disapproval. "No excuse, old son. She's high class, is this bird of yours. You know that. She's not some tart you hand over to your mates for a gang bang. Eh, darling?" He smiled, leaned even closer, and kissed her slowly, tenderly on her lips. She made no effort to withdraw, though she felt scalded with shame, deeply aware of Wayne standing over them. "You go and get that kettle on," Cliffy resumed. "We'll get out of here before we catch our deaths." Without another word, Wayne turned abruptly away.

Vee made to rise, but Cliffy reached out and caught at her hips. "Not so fast. That kettle's a slow boiler. Not like you, eh?"

"Don't!" she whimpered, her eyes darting towards the still half open door. She could hear the spurt of the tap as Wayne filled the kettle. Cliffy's hand, hidden under the warm water, traced the contours of her vulva, pushed at the slit with which he was already so familiar, and prised the sore lips gently apart. One finger inserted itself in the upper folds of tissue and began to massage gently at the enflamed spot around her clitoris. She felt it throb immediately to renewed life. In spite of herself her buttocks clenched, and slid forward on the slippery surface of the tub, thrusting her belly to meet his caress. Her lifted knees quivered, parted further.

"Please don't!" she whispered pleadingly, but her mouth opened hungrily as his approached and covered it greedily.

He was still playing with her, and she was bending submissively forward, her mouth open, breathing heavily, her hands clutching at the sides of the bath, her nipples pointed when Wayne's head came round the door and he announced aggressively. "Coffee's made." She jerked guiltily, stifled a cry. Cliffy laughed, took his hand away, and Wayne's eyes bugged.

Cliffy rose. She gasped at the sight of his prick, engorged and thrusting stiffly outward, its helm wreathed in foam.

"Will you look at that?" he marvelled, stepping dripping from the tub. "I reckon this teacher of yours could give a corpse a boner, don't you, Wayne?"

When she reached for the towelling robe hanging on the bathroom door, Cliffy caught her wrist. "You must be joking, darling."

In the kitchen, she huddled on the high bar stool, miserably aware of her nudity in front of the two clothed figures, for Cliffy had dressed again.

"We'll have to be going," he said presently, glancing

at his watch. "I haven't been back since last night. Anna will be doing her nut. My friend," he explained, grinning at Vee, who blushed fiercely. "She can be a jealous cow at times, eh, Wayne?" He stood. "Right. Let's be off then."

"I'm not going anywhere," Wayne answered defiantly. "I ain't got no girlfriend to worry about."

"Don't be daft," Cliffy said reasonabaly. He nodded at Vee. "Can't you see the lady's shagged out? Even a goer like her needs a break. Look at those wrists and ankles. See those bruises? You left her tied in that chair half the fucking night, you wicked bastard!" Again the deep chuckle. "Besides, she's had a going over by an expert, remember. She needs to get her strength back, don't you darling? There won't be a good shag left in her till she's had a good night's sleep." He put his hand on Wayne's shoulder, pushing him firmly towards the stairs. "You know it makes sense."

In spite of the brutality of his words, which brought another flood of crimson to her face, Vee felt an enormous relief when Wayne, with no more than a sulky mutter, allowed himself to be led to the door.

"We'll be round about nine o'clock tomorrow night," Cliffy told her. "Be ready with your glad rags on. We're out on the town. Not yours - ours!" The significance of his remark did not register then. She felt a protest leap to her mind, her mouth opened, then closed again. What on earth could she say? How could she prevent them from taking her over like this? Both these men had made love - no, fucked her, her brain painfully corrected her - within the last twenty four hours. She was in their power, and it would take some skill to extricate herself from this sitiation.

Cliffy stepped close, took her in his arms, pulled her tightly into him, so that her naked body made contact with him from knees to straining mouth. His tongue possessed her again, as though to remind her of her subservience. She trembled at the rub of his clothing, her nipples sprang to life again. She was panting heavily when he at last released her. He laughed, generously waved Wayne forwarad.

"Go on!" he urged in invitation.

Wayne hesitated, stared at her, his big black face stamped with pathetic rage. Then he lunged forward, hugged her to him, pressed his lips harshly against hers. She felt her teeth crushed against the softness of her mouth, then his tongue drove in, and her head swam with breathlessness. She staggered, gulping in much needed air when he released her. "Slag!" he hissed, glaring at her before he swung away and thundered down the stairs.

"You'll have to forgive him, Miss," Cliffy laughed. "Kids of today, eh? Where do they learn such language? Dunno what they teach 'em at school these days!"

CHAPTER FIVE

Vee stared at her reflection one last time and applied a dab of perfume in the valley of her breasts. She wondered if she should pay yet another visit to the lavatory. Her insides appeared to have turned to liquid altogether. She felt both sick and empty, in spite of the light meal she had forced down a couple of hours earlier. Her face looked pale and she brushed quickly at her cheeks, adding a touch more colour. Her grey blue eyes gazed vulnerably back at her, the purple shadows making them even larger, giving a hint of the decadence she felt pervading her entire body. But then, she told herself honestly, if anything it added a touch of heightened interest to her features.

It wasn't until the key clicked in the lock that she remembered that Cliffy had kept possession of it. She was standing framed against the light at the top of the stairs, and he grinned up at her. He stayed there.

"Ready, doll? That's excellent. I can't stand a bird that keeps you waiting for hours."

His car was unpretentious, not an old banger but not a gleaming limo either. She had slipped on a heavy coat over her short blue dress, and she pulled it tighter round her as the misty cold of the winter night closed in on her. Wayne was sitting in the back of the car, and did not offer to get out when she appeared. Cliffy held open the front passenger door, and she settled herself, pulling the seat belt across her chest.

"Where are we going?" she asked nervously. "There won't be - I don't want anyone from school to see us."

"Why? Too fucking ashamed to be seen out with your bit of black rough?" Wayne goaded, aand she blushed. She held her silence.

"Take no notice of little bro," Cliffy chuckled. "He's still pissed off about New Year's. Don't you worry, darling. We're going to a club Tottenham way. Members only. I don't think you'll find any of your pupils in there. Bit too grown up for them, eh, Wayne? Don't know if we'll be able to get you in, sunshine!"

"Fuck off!" Waynes snarled. The rest of the lengthy journey was filled with Cliffy's incessant banter. Every now and then, he took his left hand off the wheel and slapped it down on Vee's nylon clad thigh, pushing it up under the silk skirt of her dress. He chortled with approval, glancing at her and raising his eyebrows expressively when his fingers negotiated the top of her stocking. He searched the cool smoothness of her bare thigh until he brushed against the tight little silk of her knickers. She knew he had been seeking for the strap of a suspender, and this was confirmed when a finger slid inside the stocking top and flicked at its elasticity.

"Self support, eh? Better than tights, darling. I can see you've been around a bit." Once again, the colour flooded up from her neck, and she felt more than ever like the whore she had typecast herself as over the past few days.

The Lucky Wheel was certainly exclusive. When Vee got out of the car, and stood shivering while Cliffy parked by the side of the building, she glanced about apprehensively. There was no glittering sign, no sign of life at all. A single bulb, protected in its wire cage, shone bleakly over a blank doorway in a blank brick wall. Cliffy pressed a discreet bell, and Vee saw that there was a tiny spyhole in the door. After an interval, it clicked open. A tough looking man in a white T-shirt which stretched across his muscular chest, and tight black trousers, nodded and led them up a long, narrow staircase, uncarpeted, with bare plaster walls either side off which the light bounced harshly. At the top was another solid door, also with a spyhole, but it opened to their guide's first touch.

A waft of hot air, and the strong smell of alcohol, perfume, smoke and sweat, billowed out to meet them. And a blanket of noise; blaring music and a babel of voices enveloped them. Vee found herself staring down a short, wide staircase into a crowded, dimly lit room of fake and shop-soiled opulence. There was a long bar running the length of one side. Small round tables and chairs took up most of the rest of the space, except for a tiny area next to an equally diminutive, brilliantly lit stage, on which a group was playing and singing, the voices and music distorted by the over amplification. One or two shadowy figures were shuffling in the space left for dancing.

42

At first Vee thought she was the only white person present. It was a while before she noticed others of her hue, mostly heavily made up, flashily tarty girls, though eventually she observed one or two males as well.

"Hi, Cliffy, man! Brought some guests, have you? Sign in, there's a good chap. Cover charge for two, is it?"

Cliffy scribbled in a note book and handed over a twenty pound note. The man who had spoken was short and balding, but his squat frame looked menacingly tough. His wide chest was dazzling in a white shirt, topped off by a thin evening tie. Vee blushed as his eyes travelled with slow and evident pleasure, from top to toe. "Very choice!" he breathed, with a smile that made her cheeks burn.

Cliffy was laughing as usual. "Yeah. This is Vee. A good mate of mine."

"Oh yeah? How good? Does Anna know?" He spoke as if she was not there, or, rather as if she counted for nothing apart from her sexuality. Vee bridled inside, but she hid her anger.

Cliffy tapped the side of his nose with a finger. "You know what they say, Billy boy, a change is as good as a feast, and I am getting my fill my man!" He turned as Wayne gave a growling cough. "And this is my kid brother, Wayne. Having a night out with the big boys. Look after him."

"I can look after myself," Wayne snapped, his face comically youthful in his fury.

Vee's nervousness was growing by the minute as she observed the behaviour of the other customers, especially the girls. Most of them looked like professionals. At least I'm not getting paid for it, she told herself. She saw several curious glances returned in her direction. What's the matter? she thought. Never seen a decent girl before? But she glanced quickly away, and kept her mouth firmly shut.

They found a table near the stage, and Vee was given a glass of cheap champagne. Both Cliffy and Wayne were drinking some foreign beer direct from the bottle. Not quite Cafe de Paris style, Vee thought. It was not long before what Vee thought must be one of the main attractions of the club revealed itself. The band left the stage to raucous cheers which she felt must be mainly of relief. A gaudy inner curtain was whisked aside to reveal a dressing table, with two long mirrors at each side, and a low stool. A slim girl with white blonde hair hanging down to mid-back was sitting there, preening herself before the mirror. She was dressed in a long, glittering evening gown of tawny gold. It left her shoulders bare, and her breasts spilled out of the bodice almost to the nipples.

A black girl appeared, of statuesque proportions, dressed in a maid's outfit so abbreviated it looked skin tight and made the most of her ample figure. A tiny scrap of white lace was fastened in her kinky hair. The flaring skirt of her uniform was so short that at her slightest bending movement, it revealed the equally pristine white of her knickers, scarcely larger than her headgear.

The two went through the exaggerated balletic movements of their mime to the accompaniment of taped guitar music designed to add to the pornographic content of the episode. With slow, caressive gestures and much lingering body contact, the maid stripped her mistress while the audience yelled their encouragement with many obscene suggestions and comments which drew explosive bursts of laughter. Vee, sitting in the dimness, felt her face burning. She glanced furtively about her, feeling all at once a powerful kinship both with the principals on stage and the other women in the audience, a solid pact of femininity against the brute, bulging-eyed, heavy breathing

44

masculinity surrounding her. Then, traitorously, she felt that quiver of damp response at her crotch to the unfolding beauty of the blonde, in spite of the tawdry sexuality of the black and scarlet, lace trimmed basque, the long black ribbons of suspenders leading over milky thighs to the sheer darkness of the stockings and the dagger like five inch heels.

Part of her was not surprised, yet she still gasped with a shocked thrill when the strip-tease continued until the white girl was completely nude. The ministrations of the maid transformed to frank arousal as she turned her mistress-lover on the stool so that she was reclining swooningly, facing the audience, while those dark hands parted her long legs, exposed the shaven mons, and the little dark purse of the vulva, with its crinkled little divide. The audience, practically silent now in collective desire, watched those thin dark fingers with their blood red nails, prise the puckered lips open until the glare of the spotlight revealed the gleaming coral pink of the labial inner surface. Vee's eyes smarted with unshed tears as she felt the quiver of her own sex lips, the growing wetness at her silken crotch.

A red nail disappeared, buried in the upper folds, and the white girl suddenly began threshing, her long legs lifting, jacknifing, her belly thrusting up in what Vee surmised was pantomimed frenzy, before, with an adroit twist she reversed roles and with the skill of a wrestler, flung the coloured girl down underneath her. The pale hands flew speedily about the willing victim, and pulled off the short tunic, the bra and thong beneath, plucked the scrap of white lace from the woolly head. In a slow crescendo of sinuous writhing, the black and white bodies intertwined delightfully, hands stroking, breasts and bellies nuzzling, mouths seeking and lapping, thighs parting, enfolding, scissoring, on and on until Vee fancied she could hear the gasps from all around her, could hardly resist the urge to press the heel of her hand against her own throbbing mound. And she did not imagine the huge sigh when at last the light was cut off and blackness descended.

She had assumed from the name of the club that there must be a casino attached to the premises somewhere, and had looked around in vain for the gambling room. It was not until several strip acts later that the reason for the name The Lucky Wheel became apparent. It was gambling with a difference. Once again those inner curtains parted to display a wheel of giant proportions, more than six feet in diameter, with numbers in red and black, like the markings of a roulette wheel outside its circumference. Vee noted that there were four leather straps set in its surface, whose purpose was soon made clear.

The girl with the long blonde hair appeared again, this time wearing the traditional scanty underwear associated with her trade - bra, briefs, garter belt and nylon stockings, all of which she removed with suitable bumps and grinds, to the accompaniment of a thumping rock band. Naked, she stepped against the wheel and an assistant fastened her outspread wrists and ankles to the straps. She hung there like a white star, every part of her brilliantly highlighted by the glaring spots. The wheel was spun, her pale beauty became a blur as she spun faster, while crowds jostled with the croupiers at the foot of the stage, placing bets on the number at which her golden head would come to rest when the wheel finally ceased.

The game was played at regular intervals throughout the long night, with various girls, all naked, acting as pointer. Vee was secretly shocked at the wads of money Cliffy kept producing from his pockets, both for drinks and for gambling. "Choose a number, darling!" he urged more than once, and, reluctantly, she obeyed him. The noise, the smoke, and eventually the alcohol had a combined effect on her, and she longed for the night to end, though she did not say anything to him. Both Cliffy and Wayne were getting noticeably drunker, but, whereas Cliffy grew even more boisterous, Wayne became more and more gloweringly morose. Soon, his head was nodding on the great column of his neck and he was almost comatose.

Vee felt stale, she could feel the perspiration making her clothes stick to her. In the hip bumping intimacy of the small Ladies, she nervously eyed her neighbours, who were treating her to some hostilely suspicious stares. It made her feel even more uncomfortable, and when she made her way back to their table, she resolved to suggest that they leave. But the evening-suited MC drowned out her hesitant words as he spoke boomingly through the hand mike.

"Now it's amateur time, ladies and gentlemen. Let's have a lovely lady from the audience to bring us luck on the wheel. Who's it gonna be, boys? Which of those luscious lassies is brave enough to take a turn for us?"

There were roars and mock shrieks as menfolk urged on their partners to step up to the stage. Vee felt her wrist seized by the grinning Cliffy. "Here we are! Come on, Vee, get up there and show 'em what you're made of. Here's your lovely lady!" he roared, pulling her to her feet in spite of her struggles.

"Let me go!" she hissed, transfixed with embarrassment, squirming violently now in her effort to escape.

"Don't take any notice of her!" Cliffy puffed, still laughing as he grabbed at her more firmly, hauling her to the foot of the stage. "Come on, girl! Don't tell me you haven't got the guts for it? I thought there was more to you than you made out. Don't tell me we were wrong about you!"

Suddenly, Wayne's sweating face appeared before her,

twisted with emotion. "Yeah! Come on then! What about all that shit you told me about out in that fucking jungle? How you stripped off in front of thousands of those bastards! Where's your guts now, slag?"

The contempt on his face stung her. She had a sudden clear vision of herself stood before him and the others, in class, in her conservative pleated skirt and her thick sweater. Tears poured down her face, but she stared wild eyed at both of them, her head reeling. Who did these swine think they were? They wanted a show? Right! They'd get one!

She turned without a word and all at once it seemed as though a hundred hands were reaching out, laying hold of her. She smelt intimate sweat and perfume as a crowd of eager girls jostled round her. Fingers plucked at the zip at her back, parting her dress, vivid nails scratched at her skin as they unhooked her bra, dragged down the tiny black tanga briefs, laddering the gauzy stockings as they stripped them from her flailing legs. The spotlight blinded her, she felt pinned in its merciless glare which held her every bit as much as the leather restraints they were buckling about her ankles and wrists.

It was as if every one of those hundreds of eyes fixed on her was a hand pressed against her exposed flesh. She was aware of her open thighs, the sandy fleece of her pubis standing out in the harsh light. Then the world exploded in a mad whirl which took her breath even as she screamed. The lights, the heat, the blobs of faces in the dimness beyond, the roar in her ears, melded in a kalaidoscope of craziness which spun her until even thought was impossible. She was lost until the mad whirl slowed and, utterly disorientated she came to a stop, her spreadeagled feet up above her, her head hanging down, strapped helplessly on the wheel for the whole world to see and savour.

CHAPTER SIX

Vee was weeping quietly, unable to stem her tears. She had been crying quietly ever since they had unstrapped her from that disgusting wheel, and the white blonde stripper and her coloured partner had led her away, gently now, to their tiny cubbyhole of a dressing room which stank of the artistes' powder and perfumed sweat. She was shaking uncontrollably, yet their touch as they quickly slipped on her clothing again stirred her, reviving memories of the tender sensuality she had not known since the days of her captivity, with Katya, her co-prisoner, and the fascinating Awina, her African mistress.

She hoped that maybe, even in his drunkenness, Cliffy perceived something of how far she had gone to accept his challenge, for he was ready to leave as soon as she reappeared, still led by her two helpers. Several people called out a raucous farewell, then they were outside in the aching cold which struck through her as though she were still naked. Her belief that he felt a little more sympathetic towards her outraged sensitivity was shattered at Cliffy's first words.

"Get in the back," he said tersely, in a tone that made her obey at once, and without argument. Wayne had already stumbled in ahead of her and was sprawled on the seat. Always the gentleman! she reflected sarcastically. To his young brother, he said, with a callousness which was like a blow to her, "You! You'd better give her one on the way home. You're pissed as a rat again as it is. I'm dropping you off home before I take her back to her place."

"Wo'd you mean? I'm origh", ain't I? I'm the one what found her - "

"Shut your fucking hole! Mum's suspicious enough!

You gotta go back there some time before morning. It's three o'clock now. Besides - " he gave an ugly little laugh - "you probably can't get it up at all, pisshead!"

"Can't I?" Wayne muttered. His fumes filled the back of the car. "Come here!" He grabbed at Vee, who let out a small scream at the roughness of his hold on her.

"Go on, doll!" Cliffy urged, glancing in the rear view mirror with his customary grin. "At least let him try, eh? It won't take long, if he can even find it."

"Fuck off!"

Vee gave another soft whimper. He tore open her winter coat, thrust her shoulders down onto the cold uphol-stery. His hands were at her, clawing up her dress over her knickers, then his rough fingers were tearing at her belly, haul-ing down the scrap of her briefs, and she raised her legs auto-matically, assisting him to drag them clear of her waving feet. As he dragged off the knickers, he displaced her high heels which fell with soft thunks onto the rubber mats. She raised her nylon clad limbs, bending her knees up to her shoulders as he fumbled urgently at his flies to release his prick.

Shuddering, bitterly aware of Cliffy's shape just ahead and above her, and of his amused gaze in the oblong mirror, she wanted only for it to be over. She reached out, felt the startling heat of the long prick and the sliminess of emission at its large helm. It was beating, she seized the thick column and gave it a few strong tugs, up and down its length. It stiffened magically, and she felt its wet head sliding, prodding at her mons, her cold belly, before it homed in on her fissure, driving into her tightness which parted throbbingly to receive it.

Her stockinged feet waved over her head, her toes brushing against the texture of the roof. Orange lights swept and played across the interior, and she wondered if anyone should happen to glance in at the car speeding alongside them, and what they would see. Cliffy's mocking chuckle was like a scourge laid on her. Then thought fragmented at the urgent pounding of Wayne deep within her, and her own elemental response. He bucked frenetically right from the start, eager only to slake his lust, and her own excitement was still soaring when she felt him convulse and spurt inside her. Weeping bitterly, her blood still pounding with want, she swung her legs clear, pushed her dress down over her belly and sat there, slumped as far from him as she could, shuddering at the feel of his come trickling coldly onto her thighs and the back of her crumpled dress. She was still too distraught, too muffled in her misery to take much notice when the car pulled up in a shabby terrace, and Wayne, without a word other than a final mumbled, "Fuck off!" stumbled out into the night.

It was only when she was half way up her own stairs following numbly behind Cliffy, that she realised she was not wearing knickers. She thought of her crumpled garment lying on the floor of his car and opened her mouth to speak. Then wearily she closed it again. What did it matter? She'd only have to strip them off again, right away.

In the living room, he sprawled long legged on the sofa, and yawned. "What about coffee, doll? Black, I think."

"Look. I'm dead beat - "

"You will be if you don't watch your fucking mouth!" He sprang up so quickly as he spoke that she gave a small cry of alarm and shrank from him. But he was still smiling, with that lazy grin of his. "You're not at school now, you know, talking to tossers like our Wayne." He spun her round, pulled down the zipper on her blue dress, and lifted it up off her hips, and over her head. "Wha-hey! Talk about Burma! No knicks, eh? You're so keen!"

51

She was trembling, with nervousness and fatigue, but she made a great effort to summon up her courage. "Listen," she began shakily. "I know you think I'm just a tart. That's how I must seem to you, after all that's happened. But really, I'm not - like this at all. I've been living so quietly - without anyone. Just on my own. No boyfriend - no family. I can't - go on with this. Like I'm - you just using me, like - like - "

"Some slag?" he finished for her. He let his gaze travel slowly, the length of her, and she was conscious of the debauched spectacle she must present, in the lacy black bra and dark stockings. Automatically, her hands folded over the light triangle of her pubis. Her head dropped, she started snivelling once more. He stood in front of her, reached around her and unclipped her bra, drew it off her breasts. He pulled her in close, so that her body was pressed against him, then he kissed her, long and hard, leaving her gulping breathlessly for air. He kept her tight in his arms.

"Don't worry, babe. I know what a class act you are. But even a high class doll like you needs a good seeing to now and then. Eh? With a deep laugh, he spun her round away from him, and slapped her resoundingly on her bare bottom. He gave her a shove towards the kitchen. "Now go and get the coffee. And leave those stockings on. It looks dead sexy."

They were all she wore now. Her face flamed, the tears came chokingly, making it impossible for her to speak. She turned with a huge sob, and moved to obey.

Her revulsion and self-loathing came like a thick bile in her throat. Blinded by tears, she carried out the task of making two cups of coffee, hating her sick subservience, hating even more that unmistakable, muted beat of excitement pulsing between her thighs, in that area still sticky and sore from Wayne's brutal invasion only moments ago.

Cliffy's legs were open wide, his loins thrust forward blatantly on the cushions of the sofa. She could see the large bulge at his crotch, towards which he nodded now, with that insufferable smile.

"I hear you do a superb blow job, doll. You come very highly recommended. I must say, you got a very sexy mouth, Vee. How's about getting it round this lot, then?"

Caught on her private rack of masochistic desire and disgust at her own actions, she knelt at once, and gently eased down the zip of his flies. Slowly she rooted, extracted his long, uncoiling prick, her senses filled with its potent, yeasty aroma. It hung, thick and elongated, yet still only half tumescing, from his clothing. It was hot to her caressive touch, beating, alive. She stroked the thick column, let her fingers and thumbs draw back the collar of foreskin, pushing down to the swell of his balls, then bringing her hand slowly up again, to the exposed, lighter dome, agleam with his fluid. Bending her fair head over it, she pursed her lips, and began to kiss gently, making feather-like contacts as her lips moved from the helm down the pulsing shaft to its base and back again. With finger and thumb delicately holding it at the rim of that bulging head, she let her tongue poke out and flicker in a series of lightning licks all over the satin surface of the helm, taking in the slimy juices liberally oozing from the opening, savouring the taste on her palate. She nipped the tiny slit lightly with her teeth, and was rewarded by his convulsive little squirm, the tightening grasp of his fingers in her hair.

"Jesus, darling!" he breathed, in shuddering appreciation. Perversely, she worked hard to prove the justice of his earlier words, revelling in her skill and its effect on him, remembering how often she had serviced Keith in just this way, and how shatteringly she had brought him to a climax. How proud she had been to do so, Even though it seemed only to add to his contempt for her.

Now, she strained her jaw wide to take his drumming prick inside her mouth, to suck greedily on his manhood, drinking his power, feeling her own crevice streaming wetly, her vagina spasming in urgent sympathy. His fingers tightened on her scalp until it burned with pain, and he moaned aloud.

She lifted her soaking lips and chin briefly clear of him, and gabbled, "Please - don't stop me! Let me do it - let it happen! Please!"

She thrilled at the way his gripping hand suddenly fell away, and his thrusting loins sank back, indicating his surrender to her plea. She worked furiously, her jaws wide, choking as she forced his coluumn to the back of her throat, her cheeks hollowed as she sucked at him again and again. At last his belly rose, heaved against her, and she felt that final, terrifying, thrilling spasm, and the hot, thick jet of his coming filled her. She jerked her mouth clear automatically, so that the semen burst against her lips, ran from her gaping mouth as she choked and retched. But at once, she seized its pumping girth, held it reverentially to her lips again, and let its potent force flood over her mouth, down her chin, onto her throat. She moved as he continued to pump out fluid, pressing the prick now ecstatically between her breasts, on which his seed flowed, until, at last, it died to the last thick gobbets. She raised the shining helm again, the column spent and warm in her grip, and lapped at his glans until she had cleansed its surface of the last trace of emission.

She slumped exhausted between his slack knees, sitting on the floor, her mind flayed with the portrait of degeneration she showed, in those tawdry, laddered nylons, her face and her upper body redolent with his come. Her thundering blood gradually subsided, her breathing finally steadied. Neither of them moved for a long time. At last she felt his hand on her tousled head again, but this time it was gentle, caressing her like a favoured pet.

"Good God, Vee! You are something fucking else!"

For once, that cocky, masculine superiority was gone entirely, and she felt a great surge of pride and pleasure at her success. "Am I as good as you'd heard?" she asked, with tremulous boldness, looking up at him, not minding for the moment the fluid she could feel already crusting and drying on her face, her neck, between her breasts.

"A thousand times better, doll. At least!"

In spite of her exhaustion, she forced herself to take a bath. He was already snoring in her bed, and she crawled in beside him, her brain in a fever at what the eventful night had brought. She thought of herself spinning naked, sprawled out, in front of that whole roomful of people, wondered if anyone there had known who she was. Despairingly, she face the realisation that soon, inevitably, this weird double existence she had begun over the past ten days or so was going to end in disaster. Someone must find out, most probably through Wayne. In spite of his aggressively manly frame - and she was racked with shame to think how excitingly he had roused and satisfied her before his older brother had come along - his adolescent attitude would undoubtedly lead to a catastrophe.

Like a blow to the gut, she reminded herself that the new term was only three days away. That was the moment she was truly dreading. Returning to school, to the school marm persona she had adopted and whose cover she had so comprehensively blown with Wayne and his brother. And returning to having to walk into that class room and see Wayne there, with all his class mates. Sickly, she told herself that she wouldn't have the courage to do it.

She woke to find Cliffy hanging over her, nudging her thighs apart with his knees. He was into her and rutting painfully before she was fully conscious, and discharged and out of her before she had time to register her own mounting Excitement.

"Sorry, love, gotta dash." He was dragging on his clothes. She looked blearily at the bedside digital clock. 7.38. "Got a bit of business to take care of. Away. Won't see you today, doll. Mebbe tomorrow. Be good." He turned back from the doorway. "Don't get up," he grinned. "I know you older birds need your beauty sleep. Keep it warm for me. Ta-ra."

She heard the outer door slam. My key, she thought. He's still got my key. A sudden wave of anger made her fingers curl, her body tense under the bedclothes. She was his slave! Just as she had been in the rebel camp. She lay there, remembering the feel of General Mavumbi's whale like frame battering on top of her. Then she recalled those shivering dawns when she had to prepare Awina's washing water, lay out her clothes, bring her tea. And those last days, after they had become lovers. The cocooned warmth of that narrow iron bed, their intertwined bodies. Her anger ebbed, a slow hunger stole over her, she found herself stroking at her belly, her vulva. She was shocked at the responsive throb, and at the sticky mess of the residue of Cliffy's use of her seeping from her distended lips.

She flung the blankets off her, and hobbled stiffly over to the bathroom. As she sat on the toilet, her despair and her overwhelming foolishness at the mess she had allowed her life to slide into made her want to scream as loudly as she could. The next minute, she was moving hurriedly back to the bedroom, flinging things into her blue holdall, with desperate haste. An hour later, dressed weightily for the outside chill, bag in hand, she took a last glance around the flat. What would happen in three days' time, she had no idea. But for the moment she was running away. Back to mummy and daddy! her inner voice sneered. Yes, and to hell with Wayne Grainger, and his big brother, and all the dirty voyeurs who had watched her spinning naked on the lucky wheel.

She emerged from her front door like a criminal, and all the way through the crowded street which would take her to the underground station, en route for Waterloo, she prayed that she would meet no one who would know her. Like a snivelling kid, she mocked at herself. But she felt a great sense of escape. And she told herself that when she got back, she would tell Cliffy - and Wayne, if she had to - that her brief aberration was over. She simply would not see him any more, would take charge of her life again, and withdraw into the defensive shell she had so carefully constructed around herself. She began to feel better as the train pulled away from the great terminus - she was even able to convince herself that that was how things would really be.

CHAPTER SEVEN

Vee was shaking. She felt physically sick when she put the key in the lock of her front door. The January night was mild, but a clinging drizzle fell, and she could feel the black, gritty dust underfoot. She had left it as late as she could before leaving her parents' home, even though tomorrow was the start of term and she had made no preparations whatsoever for it. She had even phoned in from Hampshire to explain that she would not be able to attend the staff meeting, which had taken place that afternoon, because of illness. She could imagine how disgruntled the Head, Mr Addison, would be, and how bitingly unpleasant to her the following morning. He was an icicle of a man, balding, neat, with Himmler glasses and personality to match. He bullied his staff wickedly, to make up for the discipline he could not instill in his unruly pupils.

But, looming larger than the dread she had of facing all that in a few hours, was the fear of what she would find waiting for her on the other side of this shabby door. In vain, she had tried to tell herself all through the journey back to the capital that she was ridiculous to feel this fear, as though somehow she belonged to the weird Cliffy, or even Wayne. All right. She had been stupid, not for the first time, driven by her sexual neds, and got herself involved in some kinky and extremely foolish goings on. But they didn't own her. What was she scared of? That they would expose her, destroy the anonymity she had so carefully built up over the past months? And if they did? She could always run again, disappear, as she had before. There was even a kind of desperate appeal about it, particularly at this moment, as she thought of all the ennui, the daily grind of struggling on in a job for which she was not cut out and in which she performed so poorly.

The stairs were in blackness, no light showing from her flat above, no sound. When she got to the top and switched on the light, she stood in the doorway and let out a mew of dismay. The living room was a shambles of empty bottles, cans, and glasses, cartons filled with the pungent remains of takeaway Indian food, the carpet puddled with spilt liquor, peppered with ground butts and sprinkled ash. The bedroom was little better, while the bed itself was in a riot of disorder, the sheets and blankets flung back, trailing the floor, and covered in stains she had absolutely no desire to investigate too closely. All her things had been rifled, flung about in abandon. Her knicker drawer was open, its contents scattered like confetti round the room. There was more of the same in the kitchen, the sink piled high with what looked like every pot and dish she owned.

Grimly, she stripped off to bra and pants. The place was far from cold, for whoever had partied had left the central heating burning merrily away at full blast. For an instant, she almost wished that Cliffy or his brother would show up. She was in a mood to let them see that she was not the total sex toy and doormat they obviously had her marked down as. She worked hard, determined to remove every trace of this vandalisation. It took her nearly three hours. It was after midnight when she stood at last, arms akimbo, in the middle of the floor and pronounced herself satisfied.

The thunderbolt, the first of many, fell heavily on her within minutes of walking through the entrance of the already run down brick and glass block built in the Seventies which was Hague Road Comprehensive School. She had spent a largely sleepless night, not only hollow gutted with thoughts of the morrow, but half expecting to hear the latch click and to find Cliffy's grin appearing round her bedroom door at any moment. Then, during the walk and busride to school, she had anticipated Wayne's louring bulk leaping out in ambush, even though she had set off at an unusually early hour, to help avoid that contingency.

Now, his thin lipped smile one of pure malice, Mr Addison's eyes gleamed behind his rimless spectacles as he informed her that she had been given Form 5C as her class.

"After all, you'll be seeing them six times a week for English, and the double period for Social Awareness. No one knows them better than you do. I know you're quite close to

59

them already, aren't you?" She could not help the colour that flooded up hotly from her neck, and her toes curled inside her sensible shoes as she stammered an inadequate reply.

She hid in the back row on the platform at Assembly, refused to look out at the sea of faces, the majority of complexions far darker than her own, let the excited buzz of voices roll over her, while the fingers of her sweating hands twisted together. The bell for the start of lessons drilled like an electric current through her. An interminable two hours stretched ahead, for, until break, a Form Period was designated to get the administration over with before the timetable came into operation again.

He was there, four square, solid, right in the front, at the centre, and she had an almost irresistable urge to turn and flee, to run out into the open air and keep on running. Twin spots of crimson glowed like badly applied rouge on her cheeks at the rowdy cheer that went up from twenty four throats when she took her place at the teacher's table.

"I've moved down here, Miss," Wayne rumbled, his eyes piercing her with their challenge. "Soon as I heard you was our form teacher, I moved down here, to be near, like."

"Were," she muttered faintly, not able to meet his direct stare. "Not was. Were."

"Are, I reckon," he answered, with an infuriating grin. "Reckon we're stuck with each other, eh, Miss? And I for one couldn't be more delighted. Real lady you are, Miss." He turned round to his grinning audience. "Ain't that right?" There was a chorus of agreement. "Yes, a real high class lady. Maybe you can teach these slags here how to go on proper like. Teach 'em how to behave like decent totty, know what I mean?" There was a shrill collective squeal of protest from the girls, who were almost equal in number to the boys. The obscenities which flew from their painted lips were as pungently vigorous as any their male counterparts might have come up with.

In the midst of this, Vee stood helplessly. What little fight there might have been drained from her in those first few seconds. Her lips slightly parted, she gazed at Wayne, meeting his eyes now, with a look of naked appeal, and surrender, which made his triumphant grin all the wider. It was he, really, who took charge, stemming the chaos which followed, and which was noisy even by Hague Road's glaring Standards.

"Come on now!" he roared, making comparisons with her old sergeant comrade even more apt. "Let's have a bit of hush! A bit of respect, you tossers! Show Miss you know how to behave."

"Good old Pee-Pee!" someone called out, and got another cheer.

"You can pack that in an' all!" Wayne growled, a warning finger pointed at the offender. "The name's Miss Wainright." She had of course assumed her maiden name from the moment of her arrival back in England. "Vee to her friends. Ain't that right, Miss?" His knowing grin made Vee long to sink through the floor in her mortification. The rest of the class roared their appreciation of his familiar insolence. But it was true that he kept them in check, his efforts only serving to add to her feeling of helplessness under his malicious power. At Break, he hung back, dismissing the others with a blatant disregard for her nominal authority which brought the fierce blushes back to her face. As they filed out, there were many leering winks and nods and exclamations of surprise at her surrender to his flagrant cheek.

When they were alone, he said, "You don't have to worry, doll. I'll keep 'em in line. As long as you play along with me."

61

She swallowed, bit back the angry retort which sprang to mind, deciding that she must use her weakness as her only weapon. It wasn't difficult for she was close to tears. "It's no good," she murmured huskily, her eyes moistening as she gazed at him. "I can't - I mean, I've got no control at all. They'll soon see - put two and two together... "

"I've told you. I'll keep them right. Keep them off your back. But you'll have to play fair. And you know well enough what I mean - don't you, Vee?"

"Don't call me that!" she answered quickly. "Not here. That's what I mean. We can't go on - "

"That's up to you, I reckon. Bit late to start getting uppety now." He gave a hard, ugly laugh. "I'm not the only one after you. Cliffy's dead pissed off with you doin' a runner like that. You shouldn't've done it, taking off like that. Not without saying nothing. He'll have your guts for garters."

"You - you don't own me! Either of you!" Her heart thudded, she could hardly force the words out. She made a great effort to pull her tattered dignity together.
"Now get out of my way. I warn you - I'm not putting up with your rudeness in front of the others. I don't care how much you think you can threaten me!" She moved round him, out into the corridor. Her legs were shaking, she had to stop herself from breaking into a run as she headed for the brief refuge of the staff room.

When she returned to the scene of her private torment for afternoon registration, she saw a crowd gathered in front of the board behind her desk. There was a volley of snorts and sniggers as they broke up and scuffled to their seats. She saw a piece of black cloth hanging from the board, secured by a safety pin. She peered closely, took in the diminutive size, the silk material, the band of lace, before recognition and shame flooded her, and she snatched the tiny pair of knickers down and thrust them out of sight in the drawer.

"Oh! They yours, are they, Miss?" Wayne aped innocence. "I found 'em lying around on the floor. I wondered whose they were."

She stood there, fighting to hold back the choking tears, while the storm of cruel laughter beat all round her. "That's not funny!" she gasped.

"I didn't mean nothing, Miss, honest! It's just I knew they couldn't be anyone else's here." He glanced round at the grinning faces of the girls behind him. "I mean, none of these slags wear knickers. Too much trouble dropping 'em every time they have a shag, see?"

Her mouth opened and closed, no words came out. With another gasp, she turned on her heel and fled. "Don't worry, Miss," he called out easily to her disappearing back. "I'll fill in the register and take it back to the office."

At the end of the afternoon school, she settled in the staff room, afraid that he would be waiting for her at the gate. Wretchedly, she tried to put her mind to some work, and failed miserably. She kept telling herself she mustn't give way like this. She must resolve the situation which had got so bizarrely out of hand. Gradually, the room emptied. Mr Addison put his head round the door, grunted when he saw her sitting at the long central table, nodded sourly. Was that his sign of approbation? she wondered sarcastically. It was nearly six, a sleety rain rattling against the pitch black windows, when Mr Curtiss, a plump, middle aged Afro-Caribbean, his tight curls dusted with iron grey, came in and banged about pointedly with a broom and duster. As chief caretaker he wielded far more power than most of the staff, Vee gathered her things together and threw on her outdoor coat.

There was no sign of Wayne in the freezing night. Now, all she had to worry about was his older brother she reflected grimly, letting herself into the silent, pleasingly spotless flat. She vowed she would arrange to have the locks changed the following day. Or why not simply demand her key back - and tell Cliffy that he had no further rights over her? The thought made her stomach churn with terror, even while she despised herself for her cowardice.

She tried to eat, then to settle to work, failing on both counts. It was almost a relief when she heard the sound which had made her jangled nerves shriek, and she stood to face the intruder she had been expecting. She gaped at the figure which appeared at the top of the stairs. A tall, good looking coloured girl stood there, pushing back the hood on her bulky waterproof scattering droplets onto the carpet. She held up the door key, shook it at Vee.

"I borrowed this off Cliffy," the girl announced. "I'm Anna. I thought you and me had better have a little chat, babe. OK?"

She advanced into the room, unzipped and slipped off her coat. She looked even better, the white sweater moulding the shape of her superb breasts, while the denim jeans hugged the splendid curve of the hips, thighs and bottom in equally appealing revelation. Fashionable, glossy black boots with four inch heels gave extra height, thus enhancing the attractive spectacle she presented.

Vee was still gawping, her mouth opening and shutting without forming any coherent sentence. "I'm sorry - I don't - you've no right - "

"Fuck off, slag! Don't give me no bullshit, all right? I know Cliffy's been shagging you, so don't try to talk your way out of it! I just want you to know how I feel about it, right?"

"Look!" Vee, scarlet faced, strove to summon her dignity. "I don't know who on earth you think you are, but you've got no right - "

"I'm Cliffy's bird, that's who I am, sugar. Let me make it clear to you." She moved forward, and Vee cried out in alarm. Automatically, she raised her arms, tried to ward off the attack she could see plainly coming. Next second, her feeble defence was swept aside, one brown hand fastened in her hair and yanked her painfully round, while the other delivered a thunderous slap to the side of her face that made her teeth rattle and her vision lose itself in a red mist of agony. She felt herself lifted bodily off her feet, then she crashed down on the floor and the breath was driven from her by the weight of the body which sat unceremoniously on her midriff. The hand still clutching her scalp hauled her head up and down, thumping it dizzyingly on the carpet. Vee tried dazedly to ward off the rapid, open handed slaps which descended on her face, but her efforts met with only limited success.

Her heels hammered on the floor, and she yelped at each stinging blow. The fusillade ceased, and the fingers dug into her hair were withdrawn, only to seize on the hem of her sweater asnd tug it up over her head. The crushing weight about her middle eased too as Anna raised herself to her knees and hauled the sweater clear of Vee's waving arms. Vee was too stunned and demoralised at the onslaught to put up any fight while her aggressor stripped her with rapid, brutal efficiency. Hauled this way and that, the thick skirt followed the sweater, and was tossed aside.

Vee sprawled, cowering, arms across her chest, in the thick winter body and the black woollen tights. Anna paused briefly, with hoots of derisive laughter.

"Jesus Christ! You're a fucking schoolmarm all right!

Aren't you a sexy old cow?" she mocked, before she resumed her task. The fingers seized on the waistband of the tights, dragged them down over thighs and knees, and off the kicking feet.

Only the white body shaper remained. Vee lay sobbing helplessly while the fingers ripped at the pop studs nestling beneath her crotch, and this last cover was torn up over her head and shoulders. She made a belated attempt to escape, scrabbling up, but a strong arm encircled her neck, another her waist, and flung her face down on the couch. A knee dug into her back, trapping her in the lumpy upholstery. The next second, a fierce burn of pain rippled over her upturned bottom and she threshed wildly. Even as she screamed, another loud splat heralded the descent of another fiery blow, as the avenging girl knelt astride her pale body and belaboured her squirming behind with one of Vee's discarded slippers until both cheeks were vividly crimsoned and throbbing with abominable pain.

The steady throb told the sobbing victim that the assault was over. But not for long. Once more, the hand fastened in Vee's blonde hair and hauled her savagely upright. Anna ran her through to the bedroom and flung her headlong on top of the covers. Vee lay there, shivering and weeping while Anna turned and rummaged with swift success in her drawers. Only later did Vee deduce that the coloured girl's familiarity with the layout meant that she had been one of those who had partied here in Vee's absence.

She made no effort to resist while Anna tethered her by her wrists and ankles to the four corners of the bed, using the tights she grabbed from the drawer to do so. She tensed, held her breath, too frightened to scream, when Anna's wickedly curling hand covered her mons, and stroked at the dewy fissure of the vulva. "You like black cock, yes?" Anna hissed, with one last caress of the curve of flesh. "Then don't go away, you stinky slag. I got a real treat for you."

She went out. Vee sobbed wretchedly. She heard the feet passing rapidly downstairs and the front door slamming. The sound brought little comfort to her racing, terrified mind.

CHAPTER EIGHT

The fury of Vee's sobbing gradually waned, and her mind returned to more cohesive thought. She was vividly aware of the throb of her bottom, as each shuffling contact with the covers beneath her reminded her of the drubbing she had received. With the consciousness of pain, however, came other less clear emotions and sensations, in response to her treatment at the hands of the lovely coloured girl. She recalled other episodes - the fiery cut of Awina's swagger stick as she brought it whistlingly down across Vee's quivering behind, the thrashing she had endured when Keith had used his belt on her, blistering not only her buttocks but also the backs of her thighs, and her writhing back itself, in his final display of rage at the confirmation of her infidelity.

Like some secret, hidden, underwater plant buried in the depths, she felt the slow, uncoiling physical response to such chastisements spreading from within, from the beating funnel of desire at her centre, the cleft whose fleshy lips spasmed now with the fatal electric pulse of hunger. The tights cut into her ankles which moved of their own accord, trying to draw together; to close the gaping thighs whose helpless openness in such lewd invitation reinforced the sensations stealing through her. Their muscles bunched, she flexed them, as though to draw further quivers of arousal from their very helplessness to shelter her beating sex.

Her mind began its wickedly titillating games. Like

some avid voyeur she visualised her body, tied and stretched out. Her mind's eye began to rove lasciviously down across the taut mounds of her breasts, her concave stomach, and the oval shadow of her navel. Then as her treacherous pulse quickened, she visualised the abundant wiry growth of fair curls cresting her pubic mound, which tapered down to the cleft between her wide spread legs. She saw the long pout of the labial divide curling away to meet the swelling flesh of her buttocks. With growing, fearful excitement she visualised it all laid out for inspection - and invasion. She couldn't forget the significance of the vengeful Anna's parting words.

Vee let a soft whimper escape from her lips as she lay, twisting gently in the silence of the brightly lit room, staked out like a sacrifice - to what? she wondered, in an ecstasy of fear and physical desire that made her strain automatically in a vain attempt to alleviate something of the fierce need by touching herself.

She had no idea how long she lay there in that strange state, before her heart leapt at the sound of approaching footsteps and voices.

She stared helplessly at the men who entered, she was facing a roomful of strangers. Anna was there, her face smiling with a triumph which showed nothing of mercy in its slow appraisal. And three men, none of whom she knew, all of whom were staring at her naked frame with looks that told all too plainly what their thoughts were.

"There she is, boys," Anna said hoarsely. "She's all yours. And don't worry about those ropes. She just loves it, don't you, Vee, honey? The rougher the better. How's your ass, honey? Did I sting it enough for you? Maybe I'll give you a little more later, if you're a good girl. OK, guys, I'll leave you to it. And don't be shy, huh? She can take anything you care to give her and come up screaming for more! Go to it!"

She went out, and closed the door behind her, leaving all three men standing there, still gazing down on the pinioned figure. Vee was whimpering quietly. "Please!" she whispered tragically. "Let me go. I don't - she tied me - "

"Shut it, white slag!" The tallest of the men, who were all coloured, began tearing off his clothes in haste. It was hard to say what age he was, except that he was not old. His complexion was as black as Wayne's, his face long, with a prominent lantern jaw, and covered with fine wrinkles. His body was long and thin, too, his bones showing under the opaque darkness of the skin.

The other two followed suit, and Vee's cries rose in intensity, fear gripping her throat. She gave up her attempts to plead with them not to touch her. "Don't hurt me!" she begged now, humbly. "Just don't hurt me."

Perhaps in instinctive reaction to her frightened pleading, and her tears, the first man lowered himself almost gingerly onto her supine frame. Her skin felt scorched by his touch. His big hands held her by the sides of her head, the fingers spanning out over her neck, into the hair at the temples, holding her face still while his thin lips descended, sealing off her terrified cries, trapping them within her throat. She felt the relentless pressure of his teeth through their combined lips, and she opened her mouth, self preservation dictating her compliance. His tongue filled her, and, in all the spinning shock of her fear, and her outrage, this nameless stranger's kiss sent the blood coursing wildly through her veins.

At the same instant, she felt the hot column of his penis trapped between their bellies. It squirmed like an animal, she felt its giant dome slide through the small fleece of her pubis, felt it smearing its wet trail over her throbbing flesh. The bonds burnt at her wrists as she strove to move, to take his prick and steer it safely into her receptive sheath. He reared up, lifting his chest from hers, his back curving like a rearing snake, and he seized his prick, steered it to her cleft, jabbed at the labial divide. Her knees lifted, again in automatic response to his touch, and her belly, too, seeking to accommodate his invasion of her. The bonds held her and chafed at her twisting ankles.

She gasped with the pain of his entry. It burnt into her because of her tethered limbs, which she could not lift about his pumping hips. It hurt mightily, but also, weirdly, gave her a heightened physical sensation, the angle at which he drove into her bringing unusual friction against the uppermost peaks of her vulva, thus increasing the spasming thrill of the area around her clitoris. It was so intense she shivered, juddered under him, biting savagely at her bottom lip in an excess of feeling. But soon the pain overrode everything, and she sobbed at the cruel burning, like a poker driven through her narrow orifice, so that she was glad when she felt the spurt of his discharge inside her.

Only now, when he withdrew messily from her, did she recall the two companions who had been spectators of all that had taken place. They, too, were naked. They stood side by side, one quite short, and plump, with a round, tight little belly. A golden brown colour and roundness which in other circumstances she might have found quaintly attractive, curving sharply as it did to a neat little triangle of black curls, and a puckered, jutting spout of a prick, already lifting in anticipation of pleasures to come.

The last fellow was a more muscular type, the muscles swelling out on his arms and his thighs, their shape erotically stimulating in the formation of the little paps on his chest, centred with the dark purple of his tiny, pointed nipples and their areolae. The heavy rib cage fell away to the potent narrowness of loins and belly. From the scrub of his pubis jutted a prick of impressive proportions in a state of engorged rigidity which drew her helpless eyes, in spite of her pain and shock.

Yet, most physically attractive of the trio as he undoubtedly was, he was clearly considered the most junior in status, for now it was the fat bellied individual who swung himself for another fiery impalement but was startled when it did not come. He was kneeling and she saw that he was not erect yet. That spout of a prick curved in semi-tumescence, short and squat, hanging like Damocles' sword over the livid gash of her vulva. With no trace of embarrassment, he held it in his fingers, masturbating himself vigorously. The dark head, shining with his emission, revealed itself through his fingers and jerked its narrow eye at her.

"The best is worth waiting for!" he wheezed, with rising mirth, His teeth flashed. She caught the glint of a gold filling in his grin. "Why don't you climb aboard, Dwight?" he chuckled, nodding at Vee's head, his hand moving rapidly all the while. "Keep yourself on the boil, so's you're ready when duty calls!"

Again, Vee experienced that strange blend of both pain and pleasure at the stout man's plunging invasion of her, though this time, her labial cleft was already well lubricated by the coupling which had gone before, so the stabbing thrust into her vagina was accomplished with less difficulty. And there were other potent distractions to capture her attention.

The athletically built fellow moved to the top of the bed and carefully swung his legs over the blonde head, straddling Vee's face, which stared up from between his thighs in transfixed terror. The sight which filled her vision was his great, jutting cock, enormous when seen from her lowly perspective.

71

At the base of its shaft was the fecund swell of testicles, which soon settled down across the bridge of her nose, neatly parting so that one warm, heavy ball rested in each of her eye sockets. The unknown Dwight let out a hiss of pure rapture at the feathery caress of eyelashes on the satin, sensitive skin with which they came into flickering contact. She felt the divide of his buttocks, which had rested snugly on the top of her head, clench and lift. She saw, through vision hazily distorted through proximity, the upsurge of his already rampant prick. She was seized by a mad longing to reach up, to take its pulsing length in her grasp and pull it down to her eager mouth.

As though divining something of her crazy thought, Dwight placed his fingers over the column and pressed it down on the pale face under him. Vee felt its hot, throbbing hardness like a vizor down her nose and chin. Unable to prevent herself, she strained her neck muscle to raise herself, and her tongue came out to lap greedily at the underside of that magnificent weapon. He assisted her, flexing it in his fingers, and continuing to push it down against her now gaping and straining mouth, the long pink curve of her tongue.

Distractedly, she felt the penis now occupying her pulsating sheath discharge in its final consummation, and she let out a deep, low gut cry, not of fulfilment, but of elemental hunger for the phallus so throbbingly erectile over her upturned features. As pot-belly left her and the athletic Dwight swung round, fiercely ready to take his place, Vee arched her breasts up to him, her soaking face suffused with longing. "Untie me, please!" she murmured, her eyes holding him. "Just my legs. I want - to hold you."

He turned, scrabbled furiously, dragging at the tights, cursing his clumsiness. It was a while before he could release both her ankles. Her thighs were already moving, undulating in a need which she was powerless to deny. They came up about his lean waist and driving hips, as his length sank to the hilt in her streaming, clamorous cunt.

She was soaring from the very first lunge of him inside her. Her belly slammed up into his, her feet crossed at his back, her heels hammered on his pumping frame. She started to come, her head thrashed with the force of her orgasm, she speared herself on him, battered herself against his splendid frame, howling and sobbing, lost in the private apocalypse, clenching, squeezing, yielding, swept away on the headlong rush of ultimate sensation, until she was lost entirely even to the potent force of the body so thoroughly in occupation. It was a timeless pinnacle, so that when she at last slid down to consciousness once more, she was genuinely shocked, dazed at the stabbing ordeal of the sweating body over and in her, the crushing weight of him pinning her to the bed. She clung on, shaken, all agonising pain now, until he jerked mightily, flung back his streaming face and yelped like a dog at the surge which jetted deep within her.

Pain again, of a different, steadier kind now, as she realised he had gone, she was alone, racked on her own bed, defiled by three perfect strangers who had taken her, whose mingled fluids seeped from her, whose combined sweat dewed her quivering, flayed flesh, every inch of which ached, stung, throbbed, screamed with their utter possession of her. Her legs were sprawled, spread as wide as they had been when they were tied. She made no effort to close them, was not capable of doing so, even though part of the pain which filled her was the awful knowledge of how she must look, gutted thus and displayed in all her shame.

The voices swan through the mist of her torment and her misery. "Bloody good screw, eh?" "Best fuck I've had since

Christmas!" And Anna's voice, containing its own little lash to flay her suffering with one final, refined agony. "Well worth fifty quid, eh, boys?"

Each? Collectively? Vee's spinning brain wondered. Could they have really paid a hundred and fifty pounds for her? How long had they spent fucking her? Half an hour? An hour? Two? She had no clue, but, as she lay shivering, muscles knotted with the physical agony she was enduring, she hugged to her the awesome knowledge that she was, finally, a genuine whore, and a pricey one at that. Part of her warring self argued that that was nonsense. She was a victim, pure and simple; helpless. A victim who that bitch of an Anna had beaten, stripped and tied down. And she, Anna, was therefore as guilty of her rape as the three men who had just used her and paid for her. It was the part of her whose rationalisation she was so fmailiar with. She had been striving to believe its sophistry through most of her adolescent and adult life.

Her musings were interrupted by Anna's coarse tone. Through the film of her tears, Vee stared up at the shapely frame towering threateningly over her. Anna smiled.

"Feeling better now? They reckoned you was the best grind they'd had this year." She gave a raucous laugh. "Mind you, it is only the second week in January, eh?" She held up a bundle of notes. "Still, they were happy to fork out half a century for you, the stupid tow rags!" She held out a note, let it flutter down onto Vee's belly, and laughed raucously again. "There you go, sugar. Why not treat yourself to some decent fucking knickers or something? Instead of those fucking granny's liberty bodice things you had on. Jesus! I can't believe Cliffy could bring himself to give you a poke!"

Then the pretty face took on a ferocious scowl at the mention of his name. She leaned forward, and Vee tensed yet again, gasping with fear. "But you'd better make sure he don't do you no more, girl, or I'll spoil what little looks you might think you got, you scrawny cow. Understand, darling?" The dark fingers, with their glinting pale nails, settled like spiders on Vee's heaving breasts. Slowly they curled, dug in harder and harder until the slight mounds were twisted out of shape, and Vee could feel the cruel pressure against her ribs. Anna twisted the soft flesh in her grip until the thin shoulders bucked and Vee gave a shrill scream at the wicked pain. When Anna finally released them, the pale flesh was scarred with a series of thin red lines, running up to the quivering nipples, the stigmata of her suffering. The shoulders hunched and twisted even more violently, for Vee's wrists were still secured to the bed. Her knees were drawn up, as though striving to ease the pain by their movement.

Then she whimpered, stiffened, and remained quiveringly still, as a hand fell on her uplifted thigh, pulled it away from its companion. Then the hand slid upward, to the sticky, crusted mons, the fingers trailed throught he stiffened little tufts of pubic hair, to the swollen sex lips beneath. She shivered at the light, blatantly sexual caress which stroked the length of the curving vulva. The dark face, its full lips pursed in a parody of amorous tenderness, hovered within inches of her own. "Just one more thing, darling. Cliffy doesn't actually know I borrowed these keys, all right? Best if you don't say anything about our little visit, eh?"

Too terrified to answer, Vee gazed up, hypnotised, until those fingers moved, gave a quick, knowledgeable wriggle, and for the fourth time in that eventful evening, Vee felt her most intimate flesh invaded by another.

"Yes, yes!" she babbled, the tears spilling again from her. "I swear it! I won't say a word, I promise! Please - "

The fingers moved, withdrew so swiftly Vee could feel their impress on her smarting labia after they had left.

"Please what?" Anna gurgled mockingly. "Ain't you had enough yet, girl? You want me to do you an' all, you sex mad dike, you!"

CHAPTER NINE

"Who wrote this - filth?" Vee felt a wave of heat sweep right through her, then an icy coldness. She felt flayed, stripped, every nerve end nakedly exposed to their merciless, glittering stares. Tears danced, blinding her vision. She turned, rubbed With the felt duster until the crudely printed message across the board was a meaningless swirl of faint, cloudy white. "PEE-PEE SUCKS BLACK COCK. FROM ONE WHO KNOWS." It blazed, branded irremovably in her tortured mind.

There was absolute silence. She could feel their eyes fastened on her. Her legs melted, she wondered almost detachedly if she were about to faint. She moved mechanically to her chair, behind the table, and sat. She winced as she did so, the sharp pain in her buttocks bringing her to full consciousness.

"What's wrong, Miss?" Wayne's voice, full of false, dripping concern, smote at her. "Feeling a bit rough? Not that time of the month, is it?"

There were several gasps, even from his hardened audience, and one or two uncertain titters, mainly from the girls. She closed her eyes and felt the tears on her lashes detach themselves and roll slowly down her cheeks. She didn't move, made no effort to hide them, or wipe them away. She wondered if there was anything that could really shock her any more. The throbbing in her behind nudged her back to the reality of it all. She could picture the thin, dark, parallel striped across the rounds of her buttocks, overlaying the earlier, less distinct bruising from the thrashing Anna had delivered with her slipper.

Cliffy had used a bamboo cane, searching around her flat until he came across the bundle of canes she had bought for her indoor plants.

"This'll do nicely," he had said, in that chirpy tone he habitually used. He had come the day after the episode of Anna and the three strangers. After another day of raw nerved torment at school. She was slumped apathetically on the sofa, still in her 'schoolmarmy' outfit of thick skirt, sweater, black tights, sighing with relief at being in the fragile haven of the flat once more, when the front door had opened, proving just how unreliable a sanctum her bolthole had become.

He was brisk and friendly, made it sound as though the whole thing was nothing more than a joke, even though she knew, as soon as she saw him that it would be anything but that.

"You shouldn't have done it, doll," he tut-tutted. "Taking off like that, without a word. Oh, I hope you don't mind, by the way, but I brought a few mates round. We had a bit of a shindig, like. Shame you weren't here. I wanted you to meet them."

Including Anna? she wondered waspishly, but she said nothing. Not even, at first, when he turned up her skirt, and pulled her tights and her cotton panties down. He whistled softly when he saw her bruised bottom. The red patches on both cheeks were just beginning to turn an autumnal variety of hues from wine dark to old ivory.

'Who did this? Young Wayne? The little bastard! I'll

77

do him good and proper. He should've asked me, the cheeky sod! He was out of order."

He made her complete her undressing then, standing reluctantly in front of him, while he sprawled on the sofa like a client at the Lucky Wheel. She kept her arms folded pathetically over her breasts after she had slipped the cups of her bra from them, but he reached up good naturedly and moved her wrists away. He gave another exclamation of surprise at the sight of the still vivid claw marks symmetrically marring both breasts.

"What the fuck?"

She started to cry and he took her on his knee, held her gently, like a child, stroking and kissing her, like a real lover, which only made her grief worse, so that she sobbed heartbrokenly, clinging tightly to him all the while. Eventually, between gulps and sobs, and convulsive sighs, the true story came out, even to the point where the men had paid out for her services.

Vee sobbed wearily, "She made me promise not to tuh - tell you. She'll kuh - kill me, if _ "

"No way, babe!" He assured her confidently. "Don't you worry your pretty little bonce. I'll look after you." His gentleness made it all the more startling when, after further more explicitly amorous cuddles and kisses on the sofa, he slapped her thigh and said briskly. "However, that don't excuse your pissing off, do it, darling? You got anything like a cane or something? Being a teacher, and all that?" He chuckled happily.

Somehow, a few minutes later, she found herself bending over the back of the sofa, her bottom raised, playing the schoolgirl in their own private SM scenario. There was nothing of pretence though in the whistling force with which the

78

cane came down. It struck a line of fire bitingly into her backside, and there was no pretence in her shriek and farcical capering dance of agony which she performed, until his ungentle hand seized in her hair and forced her down again over the sofa back. She even managed to stay down for the rest of the blows, convinced by his assurance that there would be more if she didn't, though her hips jerked and her legs twisted madly at each flaring stroke. But even as she writhed and sobbed at each crack of the cane across her bottom, she was aware of that treacherous heat in her vulva. That heat which was ignited so inevitably whenever she was put helplessly to use or abuse. She lost count of how many strokes Cliffy delivered, but there were certainly more than six, she had begged him to stop although she had known that would only make him cane her harder. And he had.

And now, here, she thought, as the tears trickled and the dull ache in her rear continued, came the public nightmare to match the private one. And yet... that old, inner voice of conscience mocked her, drew her attention to the other area of soreness adjacent to her striped and throbbing bottom, the smaller cleft where a storm of a different kind had been raised, and magically calmed, by the very individual who had wielded the cane on her so painfully. And what were you screaming then, at the height of the storm? Her inner voice pursued. "Don't stop, oh, please, don't stop!" it mimicked in her whirling mind.

Wayne's deep voice was like another rod, flaying her sensitivity. "No good sitting there bawling! Wasn't me what wrote it you know."

She opened her eyes, gazed tragically at the swimming faces before her. "Don't make a noise," she murmured, in a beaten voice."Wayne. Please. Tell them to be quiet, will you?" She saw his lips stretch in a smile, and shivered. It was

79

like an illicit caress. She recalled his hand sneaking up her leg, over the thick tights, in that steamy cafe. Less than three weeks? It was a world, a lifetime away. She sat numbly, longing only for escape, making no further effort to communicate with them in any way, while they chatted, moved around, settled in laughing, noisy groups, and virtually ignored her for the next eighty minutes.

"That Wayne's a bastard. You don' wanna put up with it, Miss. Tell the Head or something." Vee was startled by the breathy gentle tones. She had not heard the girl come into the blessedly silent room. She had decided she could not face the so-called normality of the staff room, with its plaints and banter, and sat on in the deserted form room. She stared at the young face, with its dramatic eye make-up and vivid slash of lipstick. She had always thought Melanie Thomas attractive, in a precious, pre-
Raphaelite way, with her thin features and figure, her child-like, almost elfin beauty. Vee thought her attractiveness was not generally appreciated by her contemporaries, especially not by the boys, who were more into the Pamela Anderson, big boobed image of female beauty.

She had a great deal of sympathy for Melanie, picturing her, with her flowing, curling brown hair down past her shoulders, and her huge, limpid brown eyes, her pale, delicate features, in a long, trailing gown, her feet bare, in some Victorian painted scape, of long grass and trailing vines; a grey ruined abbey in the background. She felt privately sorry for all the half dozen white girls in the class. Outnumbered, they were always guarded, watchful, an edge of veiled fear in their attitude towards their more exuberant class mates, who, in the main, treated them with an amused contempt. There were, significantly, Vee felt, no white boys at all in 5C.

Now, the unlooked for warmth and sympathy in the quiet voice almost brought the stinging tears back again. Vee shook her head helplessly. "It's - difficult."

Melanie's face pinked, the brown eyes moved away from Vee's gaze. "He says some terrible things about you, Miss. Real bad. It's disgisting. He shouldn't be allowed to get away with it. It isn't right."

On impulse, Vee reached out, took hold of the slim white hand. It was meant to be a fleeting acknowledgement of the girl's kindness, and Vee was startled when the hand clasp was fiercely reciprocated. Their fingers wove together, stayed Intertwined.

"He makes me sick!" Melanie said vehemently. Vee was even more surprised at the sob which caught in the girl's throat. "Course, nobody believes - what he says. But I hate it - to hear him saying such filthy things - about you, Miss! You wouldn't credit - not you! You're - you're so decent. Nice, like. I wanted you to - to know - how I felt - "

To Vee's amazement, the face crumpled, and suddenly Melanie dissolved into tears. Vee found herself standing, cradling the dark head into her, felt the tears from the girl's cheek brush against her own, felt the thin form trembling, felt its delicate warmth laid against hers. Her arms moved of their own accord and came round the thin shoulders to hug her close. Her mouth nuzzled at the long strands of hair, the dainty ear, the sweet, clean, feminine smell setting Vee's senses reeling, her pulse racing. My God, no! Not now! her mind screamed its warning at her. You've got enough on your plate, you fool! More than enough. But these alarm bells were useless against the surging throb of desire the contact with the weeping girl aroused. All at once that side of her nature which had been

81

suppressed for so long, since that last tearful embrace in the cold dawn of the rebel camp, in Awina's arms, and the farewell kiss with Katya, the Danish girl, in the hushed quiet of the hospital in Makamba, blossomed again. Irresistibly, even in the midst of her uncertainty and misery, Vee felt that leap of joy and thankfulness at this precious moment which had come so unexpectedly.

Melanie had withdrawn, the tears now pouring down her tragic features. "I'm suh - sorry, Miss. I had to speak - say - I've always felt - you were special. To me - since you first come - I thought - you were so lovely, and so gentle. Oh, Miss!"

Vee's arms opened again, took her in, their breasts touched, she held the shaking figure tighter than ever, then her lips descended, planted themselves on that fragrant, slender neck, where the fine angle of the jaw met its exquisite, slim roundness, and she felt the girl shudder in her arms. Then the mouths met, open, seeking, and gloriously finding, the bliss that transfixed them both, before they sprang guiltily apart, with an echoing whimper of both joy and dismay at what they had discovered, and unleashed.

Vee studied the beautiful young face opposite with rapturous wonder. Melanie wore only light make-up, and her unadorned youthfulness touched Vee so deeply she felt her throat clog with emotion. She reached over the small table, crowded with the tea things, and they held hands, kept hold.

"You look gorgeous," she murmured, her eyes showing the feeling behind the words.

Melanie blushed prettily, the long, dark lashes flickered modestly. She was clearly thrilled with Vee's admiration.

"Yes. Well, you have to make the effort at school. They expect it. I expect you thought I was a right little tart, all

82

that stuff plastered all over me. But you have to. You can't be yourself. You know?"

Vee nodded compassionately. "I know. It's like me - I'm nor really the dowdy schoolmarm I made myself out to be. Miss Pee-Pee." She smiled ruefully, and felt her hand squeezed adoringly.

"You were never dowdy. Not you. You were - beautiful!"

The words came out in a gush of enthusiasm, and it was Vee's turn to pink with pleasure. Again, she felt that beat of excitement, of desire, deep inside. She drew the thin hand closer, studied it, the colour staying in her features as she went on Hesitantly.

"We have to be careful. No," she said hastily as she felt Melanie's instinctive withdrawal, clinging tightly tot he captive hand. "I didn't mean - well, you and me. I want to - see you." She was sure the girl understood what lay unspoken behind her words. "It isn't that. I want - I find you very attractive. I want - to be with you."

Now the pressure was returned. Melanie leaned forward, her expression made her emotion plain.

"I'm glad. I'm not ashamed. Of how I feel - about you. I know it's for real. I haven't - I've never felt that way - with boys. I mean."

Vee simply nodded. "What I meant - I've got myself into a very difficult situation," she resumed carefully. She saw the dawning look of hurt on Melanie's face, and again rushed on. "No, there's no one else. Don't worry. No one like you - but..." She drew a deep breath. "This business with Wayne Grainger. What he's been saying," Melanie was staring at her, wide eyed, her lips slightly parted. Vee felt the quaver in her voice, the mounting colour, the tears that threatened. "It's partly

83

true. I did get involved. Over the holiday. It's crazy - it was with his older brother, too." She stopped. Sickly, she realised that she could never in a million years explain it to this lovely young girl sitting so close to her. How could she? She couldn't explain it to herself.

But Melanie spoke, her face drawn into a fierce scowl. "Oh no! That scum Cliffy? He's worse. He's evil!" The dark head bent and her voice, too, shook with emotion. "He found out - about me - and this girl. Emma Houghton. You won't know her. She left last year. She's older - anyway, we had a thing. You know?" She glanced up. The huge eyes glistened with tears as she gazed appealingly at Vee, who nodded. "Just kids, but we really felt - " She shook her head, ploughed on in the same breathless, small voice. "I dunno who told him. Whether it was Wayne or not. Wayne had already been sniffing round - trying to - you know. Anyway, Cliffy started chatting us up, gave us a lift one day, then said he was going to tell our folks. Maybe even the pigs - he said I might get taken away, put in care. I was only just sisxteen, see - I hadn't a clue. He threatened us both. Unless - " suddenly a sob rose, choked off her words. Vee passed a tissue over and waited and waited until Melanie composed herself again.

"There was this party - he made us go. And then, he - he made us do things - with each other. While they all sat around, watching." Her face crumpled once more. She fought against the tide of grief. "Then, him - and his mates - they made us do it with them. Kept us all night." She shook her head, clutched the soaking tissue to her. "We couldn't stop him," she whispered hopelessly. "We had to do what he said. It went on - for weeks, like. Before he eventually got sick of us."

Vee blinked back the tears in her own eyes. "Oh, my dear. I know exactly how it is. It's the same sort of thing. He -

he's got me in a similar situation. He treats me - like his property. That's how Wayne..." She let her words trail off, while inside her conscience blasted her. Not being quite honest yet, are we, Vee, old girl? What about the launderette? Wayne's hands up your tights? And his black cock well and truly up you? Before the wicked Cliffy came along, I think, yes?

Vee continued. "That's why I couldn't take you home. Back to the flat. He just - turns up, any time. Uses me - " She blushed, shook her head determinedly. "That's why we had to meet here." She nodded at the busy cafe. "But there's a way we can meet. Not at my place - "

Melanie's gaze was fixed on her in dismay. "Not at mine," she murmured. "No chance. There's always someone around. Me dad, or -"

"No. Of course not. Somewhere where no one knows us. Our own secret place." She paused. "I've booked a room." She could feel herself blushing, like some stupid virgin. "For the night. In a guest house. Over in Richmond." She gazed at the tearful face in tense anticipation. "Do you mind?"

For answer, Melanie looked at her with an expression which made Vee throb with a blazing desire for her. "I can't wait. When is it? I'll be like a cat on hot bricks till then." She giggled, her nose wrinkled in an impish grin as she added softly. "My knicks are already wet and it's not with wanting to go to the bog, neither!"

CHAPTER TEN

Vee glanced round the anonymously confortable room, trying to imagine what it would be like when Melanie Thomas would be sharing it with her. The twin beds were separated by a brightly floral rug. Which one would they use? Vee wondered, and blushed at the thought. She remembered the single beds out in East Africa, which the expatriate couples always pushed together. She knew she wouldn't have the nerve to do that here. But then lovers could manage on a single bed. It could even be more fun that way.

She had spent last night, Friday, here alone, not that she had slept much. She had been far too excited, and tense. It had been so hard for her to carry out her vow that she would not pleasure herself at all. In fact, she had failed, for she had been unable to keep from caressing herself in the shower. Then as she lay naked in bed, her hands slid down her thighs, then up to cup her tingling breasts. She exerted every ounce of will power to prevent them from alighting on the pulsing centre of her sexual hunger. Failing again, she had kicked back the blankets and, her knees drawn up wide, opening herself in lewd invitation, her fingers traced the puckered folds of her labia, pushed at the fleshy mound, squeezed and teased until she could feel herself oily with the secretions she had brought forth.

But at least she had managed, somehow, not to continue after a while. Her whole body thrumming with urgent desire she had forced herself to stop. She had even got up and pulled on her dressing gown, binding it tightly around her, sat in the easy chair and struggled unsuccessfully to read the novel she had brought with her to Richmond. She cursed the necessity that had brought her here to spend the solitary night at the guest house. But she was determined that she would not submit herself to Cliffy's demands.

"I have to go home this weekend," she had told him nervously. "It's a family thing. I can't get out of it. I'll be leaving straight after school tomorrow. I won't be back till late Sunday." Her toes curled with her impotent rage at her feebleness in not standing up to him. She had not even had the courage to change the locks, or to ask for her key back. That was why she daren't risk staying at the flat on Friday night, just in case he turned up for another drunken orgy with his friends.

So she had booked in here for two nights. "My cousin will be joining me tomorrow." she told the proprietress. "That's why I need a double room. She'll be staying the one night."

And now it was almost here. Her stomach felt hollow, jittery, yet it was a different kind of tension. One that thrilled her, not with fear, just the concern that it would all go as she so fervently wished.

When Melanie got off the train Vee hurried forward, moved by the blossoming happiness she saw in the youthful face which turned so eagerly towards her. Their lips brushed together. Ingenuously, Melanie slipped her arm around Vee's waist as they left the station, and Vee did the same. "God, you look so lovely!" Vee whispered, the fair and dark heads touching as they leaned intimately in towards each other. She said hesitantly, "I don't know - do you want to go somewhere to eat? We can - "

"Let's go straight back to the room. If that's OK?"

"That's perfect!"

The nervous tension gripped them for a moment, once they stood there, in their rented privacy. They were both blushing. Melanie looked even younger than her seventeen years, and Vee was almost painfully reminded of Katya and how the young Danish girl had been so shy and reluctant when they had first made love. Though she was not by nature inclined to take the initiative, now Vee gave a nervous laugh, and stepped forward.

"Oh hell! Don't let's be shy. Come here, my angel!"

She advanced on Melanie, and began to pluck at her clothing.

87

"Let me!" she said quickly, when Melanie's hands moved to assist her. "I'll do it. All." She eased the sweater up over the dark head, and off the slender arms. Melanie's skin was a milky, almost translucent white. She was fashionably thin, with that waif like quality which most young girls would envy. The bone structure stood out, there were deep hollows at her shoulders. She was wearing a white cotton vest, or camisole, with thin straps. There was no bra beneath, and Vee could see the slight shape of her breasts, even smaller than her own, and the small circle of the nipples showing faintly through the material. When Vee unhooked the flaring mini skirt and let it fall about Melanie's feet, she saw a pair of cotton briefs which matched the top. She was also wearing those thick woollen stockings much favoured by the senior girls for winter, which ended at mid thigh, and which the wearer seemed constantly to be hitching up, thus giving an opportunity for all who were there to see and appreciate the wearer's legs.

"They're so immodest!" Vee had exclaimed, many times, playing her Miss Pee-Pee role to the full, to the hooting delight of her audience.

Melanie blushed now, her hands fluttering indecisively over the area of her crotch.

"I know you don't like them," she gushed indicating the dark brown stockings, "but they're warm."

"You'd look good in a bin liner, darling!" Vee said, already bending, lifting up a foot to remove the short, pointed and highly poilished ankle boot, then its companion. She put them aside, picked up and folded the skirt, laid it on the chair with the sweater and other outdoor things. "But you're not cold in here, are you?" Gently, she drew the stockings off. She stood. "You want to keep your undies on?"

Melanie's face was crimson. "Why don't you get

comfy, too?" she murmured breathily. "It's not fair me being - like this."

"OK. Why not? Though I don't want to shatter your illusions straightaway." Vee forced a laugh. Melanie made no offer to undress her. Am I the butch? Vee wondered wryly, but quickly she stripped off her blouse and skirt, shoes and tights. She had decided against her body shaper, and had put on one of her 'special' sets of underwear, a lacy wisp of a bra in deep blue, the cups formed of net which allowed her nipples to be on misty view, and thong briefs of matching colour, again with a net panel in the diminutive crotch through which her pubic hair peeked saucily. It left her buttocks bare, for the thin strap nestled deep in the cleft, out of sight.

Melanie giggled, made an appropriate noise of approval. "Sexy! Dead sexy! If they could see you now!" They both paused, Melanie suffering agonies of embarrassment at the crassness of her remark.

But Vee laughed. She turned, presenting her behind to Melanie, and touched it lightly. She had meant to keep her tone light, but failed. "Sorry about the marks." She touched the dark bars of Cliffy's beating. The bruises of Anna's punishment with the slipper had all but vanished, but the weals inflicted by the bamboo were still very apparent, though no longer painful. "A present from Master Cliffy. I think it really turned him on. Caning a teacher."

Oddly, this painful evidence, and the mention of that dreaded name, seemed to release them from any initial embarrassment at this tryst. With a compassionate cry, Melanie came forward, then they were in each other's arms, their bodies strained together along their length, while their mouths were glued in a kiss that brought all the passion they had been suppressing exploding to the surface. They were suddenly lying on one of the beds, still clamped together, crying, gasping, and kissing, tears of hunger and happiness mingling. Hands were feverishly plucking at the dainty scraps of clothing still covering them, fingers deftly unhooking, sliding down straps, tugging at elastic. Melanie's top was gone, then the cotton briefs, and Vee buried her face dizzily in the fragrance of the thin white thighs, the startling black bush of pubic curls, and the tangy treasures of the tight fissure at its base.

Her tongue licked eagerly at the little, pointed nipples, and the blue veined sweetness of the mounds which they crested. Then down the sweep of the midriff, the exquisite little puckered dish of the navel, the quivering belly. Her fingers stroked the triangle of those glossy, springy curls, until, reverently, Vee's lips worshipfully centred on the tight pout and divide of the sex lips. Melanie had surrendered. Her own ministrations had ceased. She lay back, knees jutting, falling slackly apart, her hands bent up beside her tossing head, her eyes closed, lost in the urgent world of running need and ecstacy which Vee's loving was creating.

The labia opened to Vee's gentle pressure. The inner surfaces, their colour shading from pink to a deep coral, shining with the juices Vee had conjured up, and the saliva which came from her own greedily lapping tongue and passionate kisses, revealed themselves more, peeled open like a ripe and luscious fruit. The narrow hips, the white belly were lifting now, Melanie was whimpering, emitting short cries as the desire grew to a sweetly unbearable pitch. Vee felt her hair grasped convulsively, the whole slim form arched and convulsed, the heels drumming on the counterpane. "It's huh - happening!" Melanie howled, torn by the orgasm bursting upon and through her. With the instinctive knowledge which could only come from one of her sex, Vee knew exactly when to cease her actions, and lift her face from that fount of bliss. She lay, gasping, her lips sore and puffed, lying there between the slackly spread thighs while the sobbing girl came slowly out of the storm of pleasure Vee's loving had caused.

There was a touch of genuine reluctance about Vee's weak protests when, minutes later, roles were reversed, and it was she who lay spreadeagled, the raven black hair spilling generously over her thighs and belly, as Melanie in turn made love to her, and with results equally shattering. The winter daylight faded, the twilight deepened until the room was dimly shadowed, and still the naked figures lay inseparably locked, drugged with the surfeit of their passion, which was only to be truly savoured now in their post-climactic intimacy, and love.

Now that the relentless physical urgency had been, for the moment, sated, they could revel in the tenderness they shared with every caressive touch, each gentle kiss. They talked eagerly, greedy to absorb everything about the other that they could cram into their consciousness. Vee found herself once more confessing the truth of her past life , while melanie's dark eyes rounded with wonder.

"I remember that!" she gasped. "You were - were the one? Hostage in that African place?"

Vee nodded. "With another girl. Katya Burnsen. We became - very close." The pause, and the shy, apologetic expression as she uttered Katya's name, told their own story.

"You and her?" Melanie gestured now at their entwined nakedness. "Like - you know?"

Vee nodded.

"Was that the first time?"

Vee smiled, shook her head. "God, no. I was still at school. There was another girl. In my class. She - " Vee's colour intensified all at once. And here I am, she reflected uncomfortably, still sleeping with schoolgirls. "We were seventeen," she went on slowly. "Your age."

"Old enough to know what you're doing," Melanie offered strongly. "I knew ages ago. I think I always have," she added, with a touch of defiance.

It was even more difficult to go on, but Vee somehow found the courage. "I'm not - just lesbian. I mean, obviously, part of me - maybe the strongest part - is. But - I like sex with men. Sometimes. A lot of the time," she confessed, almost whispering.

Melanie frowned. "Sure. It can be all right. As long as they don't force you," she ended darkly.

Vee said nothing, her mind shying away from the area of shadowed uncertainty the remark opened up.

"We'd better go and get some food," Vee suggested, presently, though both were reluctant to leave the curtained and lamplit cosiness of their temporary home. As they crowded together in the narrow shower stall, hunger was forgotten in the reawakened hunger of another kind, so that, after lathering each other heavily with the scented body foam, they stumbled, still dripping, shedding damp towels on the way, and fell across the crumpled bed again. Their thighs wrapped round each other, their hands and tongues and lips working to whip up the fury of loving that seemed as though it could never be satiated, until it was, and they lay yet again, in a coma of glutted happiness. Then finally, Vee slapped at Melanie's pale little bottom and leapt to her feet.

"Come on. No shower. Get some clothes on, otherwise we'll never get out of here alive."

They found a place, brought back fried chicken and chips to the room, shed their clothes as rapidly as they could, and sat lewdly cross legged and on display while they ate ravenously with their fingers, stopping to feed each other titbits and wipe greasy fingers gigglingly on sensitive parts of each other's anatomy.

Some time in the long night, they settled down, still embracing, to sleep. Vee, her nose buried in the long waves of scented hair, felt her eyes moisten, the lump in her throat causing her to swallow hard before she could speak.

"God, this is wonderful, Melanie. You don't know - it's so marvellous, to feel all this again. It's been - shit, I'm trying to say thank you. And I love you."

Melanie turned into her, their breasts and bellies rubbing snugly. "I can maybe stop fantasising about you now. If you knew - all the nights I've dreamed about this. About making it with you. I love you too."

They woke before dawn, swivelled round so that heads lay between gladly parted thighs, and they made love simultaneously, with slow, langorous pleasure until their desires grew too urgent. It was Melanie who yielded first, and lay back, spread herself beneath Vee's crouching form, offering herself as willing victim. The grey morning was filtering through the curtains before she recovered sufficiently to take the active part and bring Vee to the same helpless climactic state as she herself had enjoyed.

They had to vacate the room by ten o'clocl. It was a kind of delicious, self inflicted torture to spend the rest of the day wandering together, fully clothed but seeing each other's naked body, stealing surreptitious caresses in restaurants, passionate kisses in briefly hidden corners. They took the risk of travelling back into London together, Melanie's head resting on Vee's shoulder, hands firmly clasped, ignoring the briefly curious glances or smirks from some of their fellow travellers.

At the tube station, they kissed open mouthed, strained together, in a last desperate declaration of their new found love, whispered its magic formula to one another. "I mean it," Melanie breathed, her brown eyes moist with her emotion.

Vee nodded. "Me, too. We'll work something out. So we can be together when we want. I promise."

Her head was spinning as she walked home through the cold night. How complicated could her life get? she asked herself, both miserable and deeply stirred by the two days she had spent with Melanie. Why couldn't she have found her, instead of Wayne, when she was at her most defenceless? Why couldn't it have been Melanie in the launderette? And why, oh why, had all these months sped past, without either of them getting it together? But you have now! her heart surged, and she was filled with grateful happiness.

Cliffy was waiting for her, shoes off, feet up on her sofa, TV blaring, a drink by his hand. It felt as if something had sucked her insides out. She stood there, blinking in the living room brightness. She tried to summon up anger, courage, to tell him to go to hell. Suddenly, she felt as if her brain was paralysed, she could scarcely form a sentence. "Look, you shouldn't just - come here. It's my place. My home. You've - "

"Where've you been?" For all the dazzling smile, the question was like one of his cuts to her behind.

The sinking feeling increased. "Wha - what do you mean? I told you - I had to go home."

"Bollocks! I rang your place. You haven't been anywhere near. Your mum told me."

"My - my - " She stared at him helplessly, pinned there by his glittering snake smile.

He nodded carelessly towards the phone. "I got the number from your pad. Nice body your mum. Sounds just like

you. Ever so posh. Now then, doll. Kit off, quick as you like."
He snatched up the cane which lay beside him, and she flinched
as he brought it whictling down to thud into the cushions. "You
and me had better have a very serious chat, slag!"

CHAPTER ELEVEN

Snivelling pathetically, Vee obeyed his order to undress, pulling off the heavy sweater and the skirt, slipping down the tights
and fumbling out of them. Lolling at ease on the sofa, Cliffy
whistled when he saw the blue underwear.

"Fuck me! Must've been someone real special to get
you into this gear. And out of it, I bet, eh?" His good natured
chortle did not alleviate the icy dread she could feel spreading
through her.

"Please," she blubbered. "You've no right - why can't
you leave me alone? I don't want you - "

"I bet you don't, doll!" he grinned, still with no sign
of losing his temper. "Not with what you got lined up. Now
come here, and let's have a proper look at you." To her chagrin,
he pulled her in close, holding her trapped between his knees
while he carefully inspected her, starting with her head, turning her this way and that, while she blushed and trembled - and
waited breathless with guilt. "Ah-ha! What's this, darling? Is
this a fucking love bite or is it not? Turn round" He unhooked
her bra, slipped it from her breasts.

"It's probably one of yours - from you," Vee murmured wretchedly, and he Laughed.

"No way, slag. That's fresh as this morning's dew, is
that." His fingers had seized the elastic of the tiny knickers and
he edged them off her hips, down her thighs, so that her geni-

tals were exposed. He gave another bark of triumph.

"For fuck's sake! Look at that!" His finger jabbed at the dark bruise, high on her inner thigh, just below the crease of the belly, made by Melanie's eager attentions during their hectic weekend. Vee's head sank onto her chest, her shoulders began to heave as she sobbed piteously.

"Please, let me go!" she whispered. "I can't go on like this. You don't own me."

The tiny blue knickers were clinging in a crumpled frill above her knees. Cliffy's fingers pulled at them, stretching them away from her body, and exposing the narrow little band of the crotch. He bent forward until she could feel the tight curls of his head brushing against her skin.

"Just look at that, doll. Covered in come, ain't they?" He moved, and she shuddered as his nose grazed against her pubic hair. He drew in an exaggeratedly deep breath. "You can smell it a mile off, darling. Like Billingsgate of a Monday morning! You been well and truly shafted, my little slag, and no use denying it." His fingers moved, prised gently at the labia, opened her, the pressure of his knees tightening about her legs as she tried to draw away from his frank inspection. She could feel him holding her open, then his fingers slid inside her, exploring, and she winced.

"Raw as a poufter's arsehole, and twice as sore, I betcha!"

He leaned back, pushed the knickers down her calves, and obediently she stepped out of them. He pulled her down heavily beside him on the cushions. "Now, sweetheart," he said pleasantly. "Just tell me who's been fucking my girl. You don't have no secrets from me, remember."

She tried to pull away from him. His hand was like iron on her wrist.

"You've no right," she muttered faintly, hopelessly. "Just let me go. And get out of my flat."

He laughed as though she had cracked a good joke. "Come on. You know better than that, doll. You're in rebel hands again, babe." She glanced up sharply, her eyes wide, and he nodded. "I know all about you, Mrs Green. I been doing a spot of research. Digging up some old news. I'd never have known - if you hadn't gone shooting your mouth off to our Wayne." he chuckled again, shook his head in disbelief. "Jesus! You must've been desperate for a shag, though! To go picking up your own fucking school kids! Anyway, game's up now, Vee. We know all about you. And I mean all! So you see - I'll tell you when I'm going. And when I'm coming, too!" He gave a lewd parody of a wink. "If you know what I mean!"

He stood briskly, pulled her to her feet. "Right. It's late. We better get some kip. You got work in the morning, don't forget. Now then. Who's been slipping you a length? As if you haven't been getting enough lately, you dirty little bitch!" he added admiringly.

"Get off me!" she cried, suddenly allowing all her frustration at her helplessness to buirst through. She sobbed in anguish. "Let me go! Get out! Now! I'll go to the police!" She was putting up a genuine resistance now, turning and twisting her arm in vain effort to break free.

He held her easily, despite her struggles. "I do believe you love it, don't you, you kinky tart? So be it, my love! Anything to oblige!" As he finished, he grabbed her and hauled her round behind the settee, thrust her face down over its high back. She felt the edge cut into her belly, her screams were muffled as he thrust her head down among the cushions. "That's it, doll! Keep yelling like that. You'll have the police here in no time. Is that what you really want? That should make the News of the Screws, eh? Teacher's secret love nest. Seducing her own pupils to have sex with her! They'll do their nut. Specially when they find out who you are. The famous Mrs Green, who's been shagged by a whole fucking rebel army, and as if that wasn't enough, half the white folks out in - wherever it was - according to your ex-husband, anyway!"

The violence of her sobbing doubled as the resistance ebbed from her at the brutality of his words. She hung limply over the back of the sofa, her bottom raised, the rounds dimpling as she clenched them instinctively in anticipation of the pain she knew was swiftly coming. Before he struck, Cliffy seized her by the hair and pulled her head up again.

"Here!" he commanded. "Just in case your shrieks of fucking ecstasy get too loud." He screwed her knickers up into a tiny ball and thrust them into her mouth, which opened blindly until the nylon and lace was wadded to the back of her throat, in a makeshift but reasonably efficient gag.

It was as well, otherwise she might well have roused the neighbours, or a passer-by, with her full blooded screams, which were muffled by the soaking scrap of cloth wedged in her mouth. He struck even harder than before. The springy bamboo cut deep, setting the little rounds aquiver, carving a deep groove of fire, a blazing crimson bar branded on the pale flesh. He held her down, his left hand spread at the back of her neck, and her body jerked, her legs kicked out. She writhed like an out of control marionette. He struck again quickly, the dreadful whistle through the air preceding the line of rippling agony, and the whole area of her behind blazed. She could feel the thick vomit in her throat, her world was a swirling mist of red torment, the blows descending without interval, it seemed, and without end, until she thought the flesh must be in ribbons, the skin burst in a brilliant splash of scarlet blood. And to her horror the extent to which she was being forced to suffer, the very ferocity of the caning itself was making her juices flow. Deep down below the fires of pain raging through her, was a deeper burning, ignited by her own helplessness in the face of Cliffy's cruelty.

Only dimly did she come to understand that the flogging had ceased. The burning was steady, the abused flesh throbbing in an undefined generality of pain. She couldn't move, apart from the violent involuntary trembling. She hung there, head down, the livid weals darkening, rising now above the surface of the surrounding skin, in long, hard blisters, purple with filling blood. Later, when she was able to register such things, she was genuinely amazed that the skin had not been broken, for it felt as though it had been flayed from all over her bottom.

When she did finally move, it led to yet more searing pain which spread throughout her body. It would scarcely have been possible without Cliffy's assistance. He supported her as she hobbled, doubled like an old crone, to the bedroom, where he laid her face down across the bed. He brought some cold cream and gently covered the scorched buttocks with a generous layer until they shone in the lamplight, though even his feather-light touches made her hiss and whimper with renewed suffering. Then he wrapped ice from the fridge in a towel and laid it carefully over the abused area.

Slowly, the anguished weeping diminished. He sat by her side, his hand tenderly resting on her bare shoulder.

"Now, as I was saying, Vee." His voice was as gentle and friendly as his touch. "Who is this super prick you've been seeing on the QT? Where were you this weekend?"

Her voice was a croaky whisper. "I can't tell you."

He chuckled quietly. "Oh but you can, doll. And you

will. Now - I can take you back out there and thrash your arse all over again. Only I might put a bit of real muscle in it this time. I know you like having your backside whipped, but there must be a limit even for you! Then of course, there's the fact that we know all about you. And like I said, the papers, the telly, the whole fucking lot, would be very interested to hear about your latest little escapade. I'm still working on that, as a matter of fact. There's a fortune to be made if we play our cards right. But I'm prepared to let it ride for the moment. I'm prepared to let you ride - you know I'm not the jealous type. I let Wayne get his end away, didn't I? And I didn't even object to you going on the game and letting those three toe-rags shaft you. Egged on by Anna, I know," he conceded generously." But I got to know who's in the fucking saddle, baby. That's only reasonable, ain't it? Surely you can see that?"

She felt as though she were going crazy. Her mind was whirling. What could she say? Was it really impossible to escape from him? Her behind was throbbing abominably, every muscle ached, her head was pounding. She just wanted to be left alone, to wallow in her misery. The weekend of gentle loving with Melanie was a world away, and seemed no more than some wonderful erotic dream. Cliffy had effortlessly brought her face to face with that darker side of herself. The side that needed to be a victim. She knew he would torture her, perhaps literally, until he got the truth from her. And she really could not endure another caning, despite, or maybe because of, the forbidden pleasure it would stir up in her. And anyway, what was the point of not telling? Why suffer any more than she already had? He had even telephoned her mother.

What on earth had he said? What would her mother think?

"It wasn't anybody," she croaked spiritlessly now. Her

face was turned away from him. A tear gathered in the corner of her eye, trembled, then ran down the side of her nose, dripped onto the pillow, already wet with her grief and confusion. "At least - not a man. It was a girl."

Once again, she had succeeded in surprising him. She heard his long whistle of amazement, his deep laugh, felt the incredulous shake of his head.

"Fuck me, Vee! You're a right goer, incha? You're fucking bi on top of everything else! Who is she, this dike of yours?"

All at once, Vee sensed the danger, knew how perilous the situation was, recalling what Melanie had told her about her acquaintance with Cliffy and his hold over her. "It doesn't matter," she whispered faintly. "Just a girl. Nobody - you don't know her. I - "

She cried out as he suddenly plucked the sopping towel off her bottom. In a trice, he was kneeling, his knees pushing at the insides of her thighs, holding them wide apart, exposing the cleft of her buttocks and the divide of her vulva beneath. It was this sensitive flesh which was brutally invaded by this thrusting hand, the fingers burrowing deep into the crack, between the raised weals. His left hand bore down on her arching back, presssing her down into the yielding mattress, pinning her there while his right hand delved. The fingers sought and found the slippery groove of her vaginal entrance, at the point nearest the anus, whose secret, puckered little bud his thumb searched for, and located. The nail pressed against its tightness, penetrated, gained a fractional entrance, thrust on burningly, then fingers and thumb closed, nipping the narrow little bridge of flesh separating the two apertures.

Vee screamed at the refined agony his mercilessly squeezing grip caused. "Oh God! No! she blubbered. "Please!

Don't! Don't! It was a guh - girl from school. Melanie Thomas! Oh please! Stuh - stop!"

He stopped at once, the hand withdrew, and her whole body jerked in the storm of sobbing that tore through her.

"You are a fucking case, Vee!" he said very softly, his tone one of hushed admiration. "You certainly know how to pick 'em. So now you're knocking off the fucking girls as well as the lads, eh? I tell you, you'll end up doing time, my girl, I swear you will!"

She groaned as he carefully turned her onto her back. She lifted her knees, pressed down on her heels, keeping her behind clear of the covers. He tucked her thighs under his arms, raising her belly, and only now she saw that he had discarded his clothing below the waist. His prick, long and hard, reared its predatory head in expectation. She whispered abjectly, "Please don't - don't tell anyone. Don't do anything - to Melanie. She's just a kid."

"Want her all for yourself do you, you dirty old school teacher?" He let his prick nuzzle at the entrance to her sex and, despite her agony, she felt a responsive thrill at the touch. Slowly, he pushed into her, and her belly came up to meet his thrust. "Don't you worry your pretty head about her," he grunted, moving into the rhythm of fucking. "She knows what it's all about, does our Melanie. You got enough to think about, ain't you, teach?"

Vee gazed up at him through her tears. He held her thighs high up, tucked under his armpits, thus keeping her throbbing buttocks clear of the bed. The dark little scrub of his pubis nestled against her own sandy fleece. She saw the muscles of his stomach standing out at his controlled movements, she felt the long, pistoning glide of his prick in her narrow passage, her blood stirred at the quickening spasm inside her. She experienced a kind of helpless disgust at her own body which did nothing to halt the mounting tide of excitement. Far from it. Soon she was wriggling, her feet kicking in the air, her hips twisting to maximise the feel of his invasive lunges. Oh God, it was going to happen - it was happening, oh God! She flung back her head, let out a rising wail which slowly died, her body shaking with the intensity of her orgasm. As the overwhelming power of the climax ebbed, and she returned to aching sawareness once more, the deep, knowing triumph of his laugh was a scourge every bit as painful as the deep scars which were raised on her quivering behind.

CHAPTER TWELVE

"I've injured my back," Vee murmured. Her face was chalk white, her expression strained. She felt their eyes fixed on her. Very slowly, she lowered herself onto her chair, wincing at the pain which shot through her as her bottom made contact with the seat.

"Good weekend, was it?" Wayne guffawed, from his place in the front of the class. "You wanna take it easy, Miss. You can have too much of a good thing, you know. What sort of a state's your boyfriend in? Is he knackered an' all?"

"Why don't you shut your filthy trap?"

Everyone turned and gaped at the violent outburst. Melanie Thomas was standing, her face, as pale as Vee's, twisted in fury. "Leave her alone, you dirty scumbag!"

"Please, Melanie! Don't - " Vee whispered helplessly, her gaze seeking hers in desperate appeal. "Leave it! It's all right. Don't - "

"What have they done to you? You don't have to put up with it! Why don't you tell them?" The rest of the class were

103

staring in astonishment, not least Wayne. Then a slow grin of dawning comprehension lit his broad features, and Vee groaned inwardly with despair. She had long since given up even trying to stand up to him in this public arena, and her stomach felt hollow with new fear at what this outburst would lead to.

"Sit down, Melanie," she whispered. But she knew it was too late.

She left the class in uproar, walked stiffly along to the office. "I shouldn't have come in this morning," she told the secretary. "I've done something to my back. I'm in agony. I'll have to go to the doctor."

The Head came out, glared at her with unconcealed annoyance. "It's most inconvenient. You really should have given us some warning. You must have known."

Vee was just too beaten and weary to argue. Not for the first time the thought occurred that she would be happy never to see this place again, as she hobbled throught the entrance and lowered herself gingerly into the passenger seat of the secretary's car, who was to run her home.

"I couldn't sit in the surgery," Vee told her. "I'll have to call and get someone to come out to me. No matter how long it takes."

"Don't forget to send a sick note in if it's more than three days," the secretary called out when Vee extracted herself awkwardly from the car. Don't bother to help, Vee thought, standing while the car drove off, but she felt a huge relief. All she wanted was to get inside her front door, even though she knew how poorly her flat served her as a refuge these days.

Groaning with pain and relief, she stripped from the waist down as soon as she was inside. She had laid a pad smeared thickly with antiseptic cream inside her knickers - a pair of high waisted panties in thick cotton, with a sprigged pattern. Not quite the traditional flannel bloomers. but a far cry from the soggy little screwed up ball she had found down the cushions of the settee after Cliffy had finally departed the previous night, and much more in keeping with the persona of the prissy schoolmarm, which she felt she had been stripped of for ever.

As she stood before her dressing table, glancing over her shoulder to examine the dark bars across her bottom, which shone with the cream she had used, she experienced a stab of guilt at the realisation that only now had her thoughts returned to Melanie. What had happened to the girl in the furore that must undoubtedly have followed her outburst and from which Vee had fled with typical cowardice? Bitterly, she reminded herself that it was not only Wayne she had to worry about, unpleasant as he could, and would, be. It was Cliffy of whom Vee was much more afraid - and Melanie must be, too, for she had already had cruel first hand experience of how malevolent he could be.

He had been dismissive last night when Vee had sobbingly pleaded for him not do anything to the youngster. "It wasn't her fault," she had pleaded, in an effort to save her, and to ease her own conscience for the craven way in which she had told him about the affair. Affair? she tormented herself. Is that what it was? One night together - the first time she had allowed herself to slip - to rekindle that side of her nature which, in the past, had brought her so much hectic and tender pleasure - and such pain. And this is what happenmed when she did give way to her impulse.

She lay down on her stomach on the bed, the tears coming yet again, not only for herself but for the lovely young girl whom she had only just found. Their love doomed before it had really begun. But then other feelings intruded as she recalled all too vividly the passions they had shared. She found her hands stealing down her belly, her inner thighs, stroking the throbbing centre of her desire. Responsively, her bottom clenched at her touched, and the pain reminded her, too, of the unfortunate results of their tryst. Unable to stop herself, she leaned over and reached inside her drawer for the smooth white plastic instrument discreetly hidden under her other things. Deeply ashamed, she nevertheless held it to the base of her belly, shivering at the purring contact, moving the rounded tip over the sensitive area of her mound, the creases of thighs and belly, before inevitably homing in on the dampening divide which parted eagerly to welcome its intrusive nuzzling.

She teased her flesh with sweet torture, until, excitement overcoming and fusing with the throbbing pain in her behind, she rolled onto her back, opened her thighs wide, bent her knees, and slid the humming shaft of plastic deep into her clinging passage. She whimpered, cried out softly at the final throes, the climax spreading shudderingly through her, while her fertile imagination ran through the hectic consummation of loving with the pale, slim form she had discovered only two days ago.

She fell deeply asleep, woke hours later, sprawled in abandon, her jumper round her waist, the rest of her bare, the vibrator dropped between her slack thighs.

There followed a now familiar period of hollow gutted, sick waiting, wondering who would be the first to penetrate her fragile protection. Wayne, or Cliffy? She half hoped, half dreaded, it might be Melanie, but she knew the flat would not be a safe place for them to meet. In any case, Melanie did not know its location. She ran a bath, lay in brief relaxation before clambering out. Bitterly, she reminded herself she had no need for modesty, for the only people who had called here recently were those from whom she had no secrets, least of all those of her unclothed body. But then, after she had tried to eat and lounged on the sofa with the television flickering away, she got up and pulled her black silk robe around her, in a petty gesture of defiance.

Once more there was almost a perverse sense of relief when she heard the click of the key in the lock. But when her heart fluttered with alarm, her stomach somersaulted with shock, at the sight of the newcomers trooping up her stairs. Most of all, she was transfixed by the spectacle of Melanie, dark head down and sniiffling already with tears. Cliffy was beside her, holding her above the elbow, grinning with his glittering shark's smile, as usual. Behind him was Wayne, and then - and Vee felt the colour sweep up to her features - came two men, one complete stranger, the other whom she recognised at once as the athletic individual who had been the third in line when she had been used as a prostitute at Anna's instigation.

"Coupla mates of mine," Cliffy said easily. "Dave and Dwight." His beaming smile widened. "Oh, I forgot, You met Dwight already, aint you? Cost him fifty sovs to say hello to you. Ain't that right?" Dwight looked nearly as unconfortable as she did, but Cliffy chuckled. "And you also know this young lady, don't you? Say hello to Miss, Mel." For answer, the girl burst into a loud sobbing.

Vee stood aghast. Melanie was wearing a short outer coat, of shining black PVC, which Cliffy undid, like a fond parent with a child. When he drew if off her shoulders, he revealed an even shorter black dress, a mini with bootlace shoulder straps. It came only to the tops of her thighs, leaving her legs, clad in sheer dark tights, fully on show. Her shoes were flimsy, open toed evening sandals, with ankle straps and spiked heels four inches high. She looked dressed for a night on the town, clubbing. Her hair hung, brushed straight and gleaming, down past her shoulders, her youthful face carefully and dramatically made up.

"Well, teach," Cliffy said, in tones of mock reproach, "ain't you gonna greet your little dike friend here? After she's gone to all this trouble to pretty herself up for you! Don't you think she's fucking gorgeous? Don't tell me you've gone off her already now that you've got into her knicks?"

"You bloody bastard!" Vee burst out passionately.

At the same time, Melanie cried out, the tears shining on her face. "Why'd you tell him, Vee? Why'd you let him know about us?"

Wayne gave a bark of contempt. "You were a bit fucking obvious yourself, this morning, you daft cow!" He sneered at Melanie.

"Let's be fair," Cliffy continued in his reasonable voice. "She did need a bit of persuading, didn't you, doll? Show her."

Vee gasped as he moved to her, then, fully aware of the uselessness of any attempt at resistance, she wilted, stood limply while he spun her round, tugged at the belt of her robe and thrust it from her. He moved her by the shoulders, presenting her scarred backside to the assembled company, and smiled at Melanie's little whimper of Distress.

"Naughty girlie, your teach," he chuckled, directing his remark at Melanie, who was staring at the weals standing out on Vee's flesh. "Hope you've got more sense. Mind you," he shook his head in amusement, "I think our Vee was only having me on. I've never known a girl what likes to have her arse tanned more than teach, here." He turned to the others. "Sit yourselves down. lads. Make yourself at home. Wayne, son - you know where everything is." He winked at the two other men. "And I mean everything! Get some drinks, there's a good lad. Whisky - and there's some cans in the fridge. Unless this randy little cow's drunk 'em all!"

Both girls were standing silently, their minds locked in the fear of what was to happen to them. Vee scarcely registered the fact of her nudity, or of the men's lingering study of her. When the drinks had been handed round, including two glasses of neat whisky for Melanie and Vee, both of whom made no demur, but sipped and shuddered obediently, Cliffy stood in the centre of the floor, like an MC.

"Well, girls, we're here to celebrate your new - er, engagement, is it? It came as a bit of a shock to us, though, as I said, nothing should surprise us where Vee's concerned. Needless to say, we're delighted for you, ain't we, Wayne? And we know you won't mind giving us a treat, and putting on a bit of a show for us. Us lads are always keen to learn more about how you lezzies work. Who does what to who, eh?" He chuckled. "I've even brought along a present for you two that'll blow your minds. And everything else, unless I'm much mistaken! So." He rubbed his hands briskly. "You seem ready for action, Vee, my love. Why not give Mel a hand to get her kit off? And we can get on with the exhibish."

Vee stared at him in horror. Melanie's face flooded with colour. "You fucking pervs!" she wept. "You lay off me. I'm going home. Don't no one touch me.!"

"Vee!" Cliffy protested in tomes of mild reproach. "You shouldn't oughter let her talk like that, doll. Not with you being a teacher. Can't you teach her some manners as well as how to screw around with you?" Vee flinched as he suddenly slapped her on her tender bottom. "Or d'you think I should give her a bit of what you enjoy so much? Tickle her arse a little with the old bamboo, eh? Might be good for a laugh. What you reckon?"

Melanie's eyes were huge, her face a picture of dismay. Vee stepped forward. Suddenly, she felt the swift flow of fatalism of secret, quivering thrill as she yielded fully to her own helplessness to do anything but obey.

"Don't give them the satisfaction, darling," she said quietly. Her arms came up, slipped round the trembling form. "You know what they're like. You told me - they made you do things - before. They want to see us loving. OK. Let them."

She ignored the raucous cheer as she pulled Melanie close, until their tear filled eyes held one anothers', their faces only inches apart. 'Don't be scared,' Vee whispered. "I won't let them hurt you." She saw the glossy lips, felt her own moving towards them. They met, kissed with slow but clinging passion, while the men roared their lewd approval. Vee's hands moved gently to Melanie's back, drew down the zipper, eased the dress up, over the long, flowing hair. She unsnapped the lacy black bra, knelt and rolled the tights and tiny thong briefs down together in a wrinkled band, over the narrow hips, the thighs, the pale legs. Finally, she slipped off the high heels and drew the last of the garments over the delicate feet, with their darkly vivid toe nails.

The noise of the four onlookers had subsided now, caught as they were in the sensuality of the scene before them. The two naked figures, the tenderness with which they moved, touched, finally stood and embraced again, bodies meshed together in a frank display of their love. Vee's lips moved against Melanie's ear as she whispered. "Forget them, my love. Forget all about them," and they kissed again, slowly, consumingly, until their frames trembled against each other with the hunger they had so quickly aroused. They sank, locked together, onto the worn carpet, their intertwined limbs and bodies an enchanting vision of feminine loving.

Later, Vee told herself desolately, she should have known that a mind as inventively evil as Cliffy's would never allow them to seize such happiness out of their adversity. No sooner were they stretched out on the floor than he leapt forward with a cry of good humoured restraint.

"Oy! Steady on, you randy sods! Whoa there! You ain't seen what I got for you. I told you I had a present. I can see how much you like to go at it, and I know you both like it all ways up. So I'm here to make your day. Your dreams come true. What is it you two both like more than anything, apart from diddling with one another's dicky didohs? What you both wish the other one had when you're busy muffing each other? That's right. A big black juicy cock to shove up those greedy little twats, right? Well, tonight your dreams have come true, girls. Hey presto, your wish is granted!"

He turned with a magician's flourish, and a sniggering Wayne passed him a bag, into which he delved. Vee stared in round eyed astonishment at the object he came out with. About eighteen inches long, it was made of flexible latex, in glittering ebony black. On each end was an identical phallus, of breathtakingly realistic appearance, down to the massive helm, complete with tiny aperture at its helm, then the lower rim, which led to the thick column, knotted and roped with swollen veins. Only the very centre of the column was smooth and unadorned. The only feature which was perhaps lacking in authenticity was its dimensions, for the thickness, as well as the length, of these twin dildoes, was awesome.

The girls were too stunned to cry out, or put up any kind of fight. As though caught in some erotic dream, or private fantasy, they felt themselves being grabbed and crudely positioned, their thighs apart, while the tips of their facsimiles were introduced to their tense but throbbing vulvas. From the bag, Cliffy also produced a jar of vaseline.

"You sort out your little class mate," he nodded at Wayne," and I'll deal with teach here. Not that either of them really needs greasing, I'll bet." Vee shuddered as she felt his invasive fingers applying a coat of the greasy material of her labial area. then another to the massive knob end of the phallus, which glistened even more in the lamplight. Wayne was carrying out the same task on the sobbing Melanie. The ends of the latex instrument were once more brought into contact with living flesh, and the simultaneous penetration managed with comparative ease, despite the thickness of the intruder. Inch by remorseless inch, their black hands spreading over the pale rounds of the girls' clenching buttocks, their tormentors eased the skewered loins closer together.

Involuntarily, the weeping girls reached out, clung to one another in an effort to slow down and ease the burning invasion as the implement stretched their vaginal sheaths, so that they appeared to be, and indeed were, embracing each other. The undulating bellies, one blackly capped, the other pubis of sandy paleness, came closer and closer, until, fully impaled, only a few inches of black rubber obscenely spanned their quivering bodies. Like wrestlers they stood, thighs spread, arms locked, heads together, their mouths now touching once more, in desperate need to impart the closeness which this two way sword of imitation flesh parodied so sickly. However, when their vaginal sheaths had been stretched to full capacity, still a few inches of space separated their straining bellies. Vee could feel the entrance of her funnel gripping the mighty girth of this substitute penis, while the end of the massive glans pressed against the very neck of her cervix. The black umbilicus both held them and emphasised their cruel separation, and the audience grunted with delight at the girls' increasingly frantic gyrations. These were considerably enhanced when Cliffy and Wayne stationed themselves one behind each of the naked figures, and, using two of the bamboo canes as instruments, struck with playful but painful force at the clenching buttocks. Impaled on their dual link, both girls writhed and blubbered, their upper bodies and arms still clinging helplessly to one another, their lower limbs jerking in the wicked parody of loving for the endless minutes it took for their tormentors to grow tired of the spectacle and their sport.

They could not free themselves. Both Cliffy and Wayne had to ease the victims from the dildo on which they were embedded, and whose withdrawal elicited fresh yelps of agony. They folded to the floor, their hands clutching their abused, throbbing vulvas, their thighs squeezing in a vain attempt to alleviate their suffering. But they were not left for long.

"I know what you two slags are thinking," Cliffy said mercilessly, over the sound of their whimpers. "You can't beat the real thing. And we'd hate for you to go away disappointed, wouldn't we, fellers?" He prodded Vee with a foot. "You can't complain, doll. You been getting plenty lately, and I should know. And Wayne, here, not to mention our friend, Dwight! But from what I hear, poor little Mel here has been going short of the old dark meat injections. Don't you worry, darling," he crooned at the terrified girl, "we're gonna rectify that situation right now. Let's you and me make ourselves comfortable, eh, Vee? I know you'll love this little show. And I know you won't begrudge your little friend getting what you could never give her, however clever you are!"

"Oh, please, no, Cliffy! Please! I beg you!" Vee sobbed, as he hauled her up and across his knee on the settee. Hopelessly, she struggled, kicking out, twisting in his arms, her struggles only adding to his enjoyment.

"Better quieten her down a shade," he advised easily, as Melanie began to scream piercingly. Wayne slapped her viciously across her thigh, then he, and the other two, pinned her down on her back. They forced her discarded knickers into her mouth, holding her by the hair to keep her head still, then tied them in place with her tights. All at once, her desperate writhings ceased, and she lay moaning softly through the gag, while all three of her persecutors stood over her and quickly shrugged down the clothing from their rampant pricks.

CHAPTER THIRTEEN

The drilling clangour of the front door bell brought Vee to immediate, heart thumping consciousness. She scarcely recognised it for it seemed so long since it had been used. Now that Cliffy had taken her over, the people who came into her home and her life did so with a full and careless possessiveness over which she had no control. Automatically, she glanced now to her side in the tumbled sheets, before recalling that he had left her in the early morning, just as the first grey winter light was seeping into the room. With wicked clarity, the bizzare events of the previous night flashed through her brain. The vision of Melanie's thin, pathetic white limbs, raised around the dark bodies potently covering her, and how the movements had changed in character, from those hopeless kickings of protest, when Dave had quickly spent himself and ceded his place to Dwight. The writhing legs had ceased their frenzied sawing in the air. The long muscles had stood out on the pale thighs as they squeezed now in involuntary surrender and acceptance of the lithe frame pumping away on top of her. The narrow, dainty feet had come to rest on the backs of those bulging calf muscles, white erotically on black, the smothered pale hips moving now in perfect rhythm with the lunging thrusts. The nature of her cries had been transformed, too, muffled through the make-shift gag, growing in rapidity, rising to a crecendo of shrill wails of excitement.

Vee watched, transfixed, fascinated, her mind hardly registering her own body's running excitement at the arousal which Cliffy's fingers, sunk deep into the folds of her soaking vulva were drawing from her. She saw those round little heels begin a wild drumming on the driving, dark limbs, the long, black hair, spread like seaweed on the carpet, threshed and the soldered frames jerked and spasmed in what looked like a si-multaneous explosion of release.

When Dwight finally withdrew, after lying in heavy deadness on her for what seemed like an endless interval, Melanie's dark eyes stared up unfocused. Until, brilliant with tears, they encountered Vee's intense gaze, and the same, help-less, crimsoning acknowledgement of shame and guilt suf-fused both their faces before both glanced away, unable to bear this mirror to their tumbling thoughts.

"Here! Clean yourself up, you slimy toe rag! I'm not going in there!" Wayne's brutal words fell like blows on the spreadeagled form. He thrust a towel at Melanie's loins. Sob-bing bitterly, she made a half hearted effort to comply, and Vee cringed with shame for her. "Anyways, you're too shagged out to be any use now! You had plenty to say this morning, cow! Put your mouth to better use now! Make a change from muff diving old teach's twat, eh?"

The others roared their approval as he grabbed Melanie by her streaming hair and hauled her up from the floor. He ripped the soaking tights and knickers from her face as he did so, and she let out a piercing scream which cut off abruptly as he struck her a solid, open handed blow across the side of her head. Now, both his great hands were planted firmly in her hair. He fell back into an arm chair, and dragged her down to press her face into his naked loins. His mushroom coloured prick, swollen and half erect, bent and stabbed its massive glans into her contorted features. He twisted her neck viciously, and with a gasping sob of defeat, she bent forward, a shudder passing through her kneeling frame, and opened her lips to take in the rearing prick.

When, long minutes later, she fell, retching and choking, back onto the carpet, her face and neck coated in a mixture of Wayne's semen and her own sweat and saliva, Cliffy suddenly pushed Vee aside, withdrawing his fingers so swiftly from her throbbing and opened vulva that she bit her lip in instinctive frustration.

"Sorry, doll," he grinned at her, already shrugging off his jeans and the miniscule red briefs he wore beneath. "For old times' sake, you know. Just so she won't feel left out or nuthin'!"

Courteously, he pushed the towel at the weeping figure's face, hidden in her hands as she knelt shivering on the floor. Then, with an appreciative leer at his grinning audience, he knelt upright behind her bent form, steered her slender hips to his own loins, from which his penis jutted in long, brown potency, and drove it, with a slow, remorseless glide, between the tight little buttocks and into the puffed and slippery entrance to her vagina hidden beneath. Powerless to stop her own tingling desire, Vee lay back, ignored, on the sofa and breathlessly watched the sinuous beauty of their combined and contrasting flesh, while Cliffy slowly and expertly fucked the sobbing young girl, drawing from her a helpless, jerking whimpering climax before he dimpled and stiffened in the final lunges of his own release.

The girls did not even exchange looks, much less embrace, when Melanie, after being made to take a shower, dressed and left, in the company of Dave and Dwight. She kept her head down, while Vee, sitting naked on the settee still, looked on in a leaden despair. With old fashioned politeness, Cliffy held the shiny coat, and Melanie obediently turned, slipped her arms into it.

"That was real nicem Mel. We must di it again some time. Soon." She did not register the threat in his words.

"I ain't fucking going yet!" Wayne growled aggressively, glaring at his brother. "I ain't even had my end away."

"And whose fault is that then?" Cliffy replied, with tolerant humour. He clucked like a patient adult with a fractious child. "Oh, go on then. You can shag Vee. But don't take all night! Go on! Take her in the bedroom if you want. I'm just gonna make a few calls. And keep the fucking noise down, if you'll pardon the expression!"

Vee would have liked to be able to claim, if only to herself, that she had felt nothing, at Wayne's fierce rutting, but, painful though it was to admit it, she was dangerously close to orgasm when he finally ejaculated. His fingers had been dug hard into her ravaged buttocks and she had had to bite her lip to prevent the painful pleasure from tipping her over the edge. The tattered remnant of pride with which she comforted herself that she hadn't let herself come, seemed even more pitiful on later reflection.

Besides, the situation was rectified, shatteringly, several times during the long night that followed, spent in her bed with Cliffy, who, to her chagrin after the nightmare sequence of events which had unfurled in the living room, behaved with

117

all the easy gentleness of a familiar lover. This unnerved her even more. After he had gone, she had fallen into a deep, dreamless sleep of exhaustion, which she saw now, with a bleary glance at the bedside clock as a second piercing series of rings at the bell erupted, had lasted more than six hours, for it was now mid afternoon.

Half puzzled, half alarmed, she grabbed at the silk robe and tied it as she made her way down the long, freezing staircase. Her jaw dropped, and she put a hand to her wildly dishevelled hair. Mr Addison, spectacles glinting accusingly, nose wrinkled as though he could already detect the aroma of fetid sexuality emanating from her, stood forbiddingly on her doorstep.

"I'm sorry," she gabbled, almost incoherently. "I was asleep. Pills - the doctor - I rang to say I wouldn't be in. I think I might manage tomorrow - I haven't got a sick note - "

She felt a chill premonition of disaster catch at her, in keeping with the biting cold which was penetrating through the thin silk. She turned, gestured him in, blushed as the narrowness of the lobby made them brush together briefly as he sidled past her. She clutched at the lapels of the robe over her breast as though he might have glanced indecorously at her cleavage. "Come on up," she croaked. All at once, the idea that there might, indeed be some lingering reek of the sexual abandon which had taken place a few hours earlier seemed all too plausible. She found herself staring over his shoulder, wildly searching for telltale stains, discarded underwear, instruments of chastisement.

She was shaking so much she feared her legs would fail to support her. She sank weakly onto the edge of the sofa, grabbed at the hem of her robe as a pale knee appeared, and a brief expanse of the flesh above it. Even her bare feet, the painted toes squirming on the carpet, shrieked her immorality at him. The silence, too, screamed, as he sat stiffly when she waved him to a chair, but continued to say nothing, his eyes glinting like diamonds behind his glasses. She noted that his carefully groomed features betrayed only by their colour a hint of emotion, for they were a dull red, from collar upwards, instead of the pallid deadness of their normal hue.

"There have been some very serious allegations made. Of gross misconduct. I felt I must come myself to inform you. You are suspended until further notice. Until we can look properly into the matter. It is most serious."

She gave a small cry, her knickle came up to her mouth, she gnawed at it. For several seconds, she could not get her breath, then she felt the hot, rising tide of compounded guilt spread through her entire body until it shouted out her wickedness.

"What charges?" she whispered faintly.

He stood, looked fixedly over her head, as though he were too embarrassed - or too disgusted? - to meet her trapped gaze.

"Sexual misconduct. With a pupil. Pupils," he ammended, the final consonant hissing like a snake. "It came to light through a complaint, from the parents of a girl in your form. Melanie Thomas." Now his eyes were on her, glittering menacingly, seeking out, and finding, Vee was certain, her guilt. "She was absent this morning. Her parents came to see me. They accused a fellow pupil - a boy - of sexually assulting her last night. Wayne Grainger." Again, he paused, and Vee's head dropped. She began to cry, quietly, the tears splashing down, her hands, twisting in her lap.

"I have questioned Grainger," the hateful voice resumed impersonally," and the others in the class," he added significantly. "He alleges that you and he - that you have had a sexual relationship with him, since before Christmas. Also that last weekend, you spent a night in a boarding house, with Melanie Thomas. I have just come from the Thomas's home. I talked to Melanie. She was very distressed, but - she confirmed Wayne's statement. She said that he assaulted her in revenge - for you and her..."

As his voice tailed away, Vee gave a despairing, shuddering groan, and collapsed sideways, her head buried in the musty cushion, her body racked with heaving sobs, while the glittering eyes behind the spectacles fastened on the spectacle of her white limbs, exposed now to the upper thighs as the gown parted. The sound of her anguished weeping filled the flat for a long minute before he cleared his throat noisily.

"Naturally, these accusations must be investigated fully. You will be given every opportunity to - er - to deny, to refute them. But you must realise that I cannot allow you back into school until - the matter has been cleared up. I will have to put it before the govenors. You will need legal representation. Perhaps your union?..."

Again he waited, and watched the sobbing figure. "I don't know what other proceedings might arise - outside the education department. If the police would be involved. Or you may wish to bring a civil action yourself. Slander. The charges are very serious. Though both students involved are over sixteen, I understand - "

"No!" Vee raised her head. The tears shone on her face, she glared wildly at him. The gown hung open, he could see the pale round of one small breast, but she seemed totally unaware of the spectacle she offered. "I just wuh - want to be left alone!" She flung herself face down again, and drew up her feet onto the sofa. The Head studied the curve of her flanks,

120

the shape of her slimness, under the shining silk. She was naked beneath that flimsy cover. The redness at his neck and face deepened.

Mr Addison had difficulty in speaking. His collar was tightening around his throat, which he cleared again, noisily.

"I've told no one yet!" he said hoarsely. "Not even the parents know the full story. There might be one possible way -
"

He thought she had not heard, or registered his words, for she continued to sob, for several seconds, before she stirred. The tragic face lifted, she turned to him. His face blazed as he saw the beginnings of recognition, of understanding, glimmer on her countenance.

"You could resign," he managed, his throat like sandpaper. "At once, on medical grounds - anything. We might avoid a scandal. The girl's parents seem reluctant to make a fuss." Now his eyes were on hers, and they carried an oddly similar message to her, as though he, too, was like her, somehow a victim in these circumstances which had enmeshed them. "I also learnt something else," he went on, still with difficulty. "About your - background. You were not truthful - about your past. Your unfortunate experience, out in Africa."

"Wayne!" she said bitterly, the one word clearly confessional of her involvement in this sordid affair. Not that she had any real thought of denying it. That fatal fatalism which was so strong a part of her nature, the masochistic acceptance of fortune or misfortune which was so integral a part of her convoluted personality, had already taken over. As this inescapable fact weighed down on her, she felt inmediately a kind of weird relief. Suddenly, with equal clarity, she saw the path ahead.

Wearily, she sat up, made an effort to master the sobbing grief, wiping at her wet cheeks, then holding the edges of her robe together, her knees and feet primly aligned. "I did behave extremely foolishly," she whispered, her head down, but now almost mockingly admiring her own subservience. "I've been very lonely. Going through a bad time, alone in London these past months. Not that I can offer any excuses for my - my indiscretion." She looked up at him now in naked appeal. "I'll do whatever you want. Anything! To avoid any publicity - I couldn't bear it again. The hounding - I'll resign. Disappear. Whatever you want."

Suddenly, she dropped melodramatically to her knees, like a penitent in a medieval pageant, and reached up, clinging to his suited hips. From his position towering over her, he could see the twin shape of her unfettered breasts as the silk billowed gently free of them. And she could sense rather than see the throbbing heat of his loins as a scalding sensation overtook his outward coldness. She was crying again softly, her fair head bent, her brow brushing against the front of his dark trousers. "I mean it. I'll do absolutely anything. Anything you want me to. Just help me. Please!"

He bent, his hands under her arms, pulling at her, and she stood. Part of her wanted to burst out laughing at the transformation. His face looked boiled, a sheen of sweat lay on his upper lip, which was twitching violently. His eyes darted, trapped now, behind those square little spectacles. "You've been a bad girl. A very bad girl," he whispered, his thick voice conjuring images of nostril flared old men in dim porno cinemas, wanking furtively into their Daily Telegraphs.

"Yes, I know," she quavered, blushing, glancing up at him, with her head still lowered, like some precocious Lolita. "But I can be good for you. If you'll help me. You can do what you want to me. I deserve to be punished, don't I?"

She saw the leaping spark in his features, knew a way out had been found - for Now.

"Yes," he breathed. "I'll punish you. And we'll keep our secret. Yes?"

She pulled at the sash of her gown, and it fell open. His glittering eyes swept greedily over her body before he pushed it off her shoulders. He pulled her by the arm towards the half open door of the bedroom. She felt a quick stab of shame at the tumbled disorder of the stained sheets, another at his exclamation of surprise on seeing the still evident scars of Cliffy's caning on her bottom. But then he sat and pulled her over his knee, she felt the rub of his clothing on her belly and her kicking thighs, and she gave herself up to yet another bout of punishment. At first she cried out at the stinging, fiery throb of his slaps, her feet sawed the air at his rapid spanking. It revived the heat of the weals left by the caning, and her wriggling under the fleshy smacks which echoed round the room as his hand made hard contact with her juddering globes melded her pain and excitement. She was a victim again, and soon his spanking wasn't enough. She needed more.

"Harder!" She heard herself yell. "I need punishing more!"

He paused for a second and then began to spank more slowly, but more deliberately. Each blow was now a solid burst of satisfying pain that sent shivers of illicit pleasure through Vee as he swung his full weight into each smack.
When at last her bottom and flooding sex were an indistinguishable blaze of mingled sensations he thrust her onto her back and eagerly peeled off his clothes. Her pulsing, slippery sex was more than ready to receive the stabbing possession of his prick ramming home into her tightness.

123

CHAPTER FOURTEEN

Vee ran the shower as hot as she could bear it, as though the sting of the water would scourge her pink flesh to take away the stink of corruption that metaphorically clung to her. As she had expected, Addison's squat little cock had hardly burrowed its way into her before she felt the gummy discharge of juice and it spilt precipitately out of her again. It was a wonder he hadn't come while he had had her over his knee, she shuddered. After the thrashings she had experienced, his spanking had scarcely made her behind tingle, though he seemed to be mightily roused by it. But once she had asked for more he had unleashed a reasonable force, she grudgingly admitted to herself.

He had dressed quickly, trying to keep his back to her, to conceal that diminutive prick.

"I'll do my best," he told her, unable to meet her gaze now, anxious only to escape. "Let's hope we can keep it under wraps. You write your letter of resignation, let me have it by post. I'll give you a ring. We can discuss it - when we meet."

Shit! she had thought. Now, he, too, believed he owned her. Would want to get his shifty oats whenever he felt like it. With a wicked sense of grim pleasure, she let the tears flow once more, as he stood awkwardky ready to depart. She came close to him. She was still naked, his come was still secretly oozing from her sex lips, and he just stopped himself from backing visibly away from her.

"It isn't just Wayne," she wept, her solemn gaze on him. "It's his older brother. He - found out. Now he comes and goes as he pleases. He's taken my door key. He - he uses me - whenever he wants. Takes me to terible clubs, brings his friends,

124

to - to do what they want. I'm scared. I'm sure he's some kind of criminal. I daren't refuse him - "

Cruelly, she wanted to laugh at his bug eyed stare of horror. That might make him think twice about coming sniffing back for more! He practically left at a run, stammering out a hasty goodbye. She was glad to see him go. His furtive kind of shameful rutting, the way he had needed to be told to punish her harder, was almost worse than the brutal possession of her body Cliffy had assumed. However, her outburst to the Head had not been completely insincere.

The way Cliffy had taken her over was indeed frighteneing. Now that the whole thing had burst in all their faces, she must extract herself from the scene altogether. And she had a strong feeling that, even now, he would not let her go that easily.

But go she must, and as quickly as possible. Things were far too dangerous. It was only a matter of time before the media got onto her, scented another juicy reason to blazon her name and those infamous pictures of her all over their pages once more.

She cursed the necessity for flight, yet part of her welcomed it, despite the drama that had caused it. She had had enough of this grotty place, those nightmare kids, she told herself. A painful stab of guilt came when she thought of Melanie's sweet body, lying open in willing surrender to her. And a thrill of erotic desire, too. But sadly she recalled that final exchange of looks after the girl had been fucked by those men. And, more significantly, the looks that had not been exchanged as the girl had left, her dark head down, between those two hulking shapes who had used her so casually. That special, exclusively tender intimacy which was so essential an ingredient of her lesbian liasons had been brutally shattered, right there on

125

the floor of her own living room, and by the man who had taken such complete control of her life. It could never be revived. In fact, there would only be increased misery for both of them if they tried to continue their relationship. It had been killed off before it had really begun. Even more reason, she told herself, to get away from this evil figure who thought he owned her. Just as others in her life had thought.

Choking tears came as she dressed, began to pack the things she would take with her in her cases. There were the East African labels still stuck to her luggage. And she felt the scars were still visible on her, too, for she was discarded baggage, thrown aside by the one man whom she had truly belonged to. And would still, in any capacity, even that of spurned slave, if only he would have her. She knew Keith, her ex-husband, continued to build a glittering career out in Makamba. Pathetically, she had vowed that she would not touch a penny of the money he had settled on her, even though David and the rest of her family, as well as the family solicitor, had urged her not to refuse it. The lump sum of twenty thousand pounds, and the monthly payments of a thousand pounds, had gone into an investment account, were still untouched. There must be in excess of thirty thousand in there, not counting any interest accrued on the capital.

Well, she acknowledged bitterly, now the last of her pathetic tatters of dignity were about to crumble, for she would have to use at least some of it to support herself in starting a new life. She had saved very little of her teaching salary over the past months. As an unqualified trainee it had not been much to start with, just sufficient to supply her modest needs in her anonymous new existence. In spite of her tears, there was a little butterfly flutter of excitement at the thought of a new life, another opening. But where? What? The thought was daunting. And she had to escape from the very real clutches of this one first.

"Hi. Thanks for coming. I had to talk to someone. There was absolutely no one else I could turn to. Certainly not mum or dad!" She laughed bitterly and shook her head. She gazed at her brother, David, across the impersonal luxury of the five star hotel room. Through the sound proofed windows she watched a Jumbo lift off from the runway into the formless grey of the winter day.

"Why here?" David gestured around him, then sprawled into the deep arm chair, nursing the drink he had helped himself to from the room's well stocked mini-bar.

"I had to get away as fast as possible. They were onto me. Some newshound thing. Sensational stuff. You know. Vee Green hides away in London. Just an ordinary school teacher."

"You should've stood up to them," he asserted strongly. "You have rights. Invasion of privacy, all that."

She shook her head. "No. It was - I was fed up any-way. I was the world's lousiest teacher. And those kids. Ugh!" She gave an exaggerated shudder, and blushed, hating herself for her lies, thinking of Melanie's delicate beauty, even of Wayne's hulking, erotic manhood. Stirred by the thought, she sneaked another look at her brother, recognised how like her own his features were. Her sex gave that secret spasm, she felt the tight moistness of her crotch at the emotion which could still catch her off guard whenever she came face to face with him. Or thought about him in too much detail.

Once more, she remembered that eventful day, the confortable family home, their parents away for the weekend, the knowledge gripping the two of them with irresistible at-

127

traction. But David had - what? she had often wondered privately since. Succumbed? Or not succumbed - whatever, he had shunned that deep, unstated attraction between them, fled the spectre of incest by introducing a surrogate lover, to take his place and to take her virginity.

She had desperately tried to show him, to tempt him, her head spinning with the unaccustomed amount of alcohol, yet using it as an excuse for her lewd behaviour. Flinging herself against him, letting him feel her slight breasts mashing against him, longing for ther feel of his throbbing loins touching hers, her wet mouth open, offering herself just as those beating, hidden lips in her dampening knickers were clamouring for him to claim her. Instead, he had practically pushed her into the arms of his so-called best chum, practically stripped her for him, turned down the sheets in her pristine bedroom for him, before he fled and left the chum to have his wicked way - a way Vee herself was too clamorously eager for by now to deny him. Though, with shameful tears afterwards, she acknowledged that any male animal would have done, and during the hectic deed she had shut her eyes and fantasised her brother's form cleaving so furiously to her.

She had upbraided him furiously afterwards, screaming at him like some demented fishwife, her face transformed in her anguish. "You went off - and left me - your precious mate fucked me! Yes, he screwed me, thanks to you, bastard!" And she had crashed her door in his face, lay sobbing heartbrokenly on her bed, longed Through the endless night for him to come and tap on her door. But she heard her parents' car returning, the mumble of his voice, greeting, chatting, pretending. And she lay on, lost, desolate in her isolation, the soreness between her legs a scourge to remind her of what she had never had.

Would never, it seemed. They never referred again directly to that momentous day, even though the chum, elevated to first official 'boyfriend', had sex with her several times after that. Vee took a perverse pleasure in seeing how David's friendship with him withered almost immediately. She extracted her own cruel revenge, making sure David caught far too many glimpses of her naked or semi naked, wandering carelessly to and from the bathroom, hiding silently in there behind an unlocked door, until he walked in, and she stood there, unclothed, merely smiling coolly, making no effort to hide herself, saying wickedly, "Why don't you knock, you dirty sod?"

He had left home at eighteen, gone to marine college and she had blamed herself, seeing his move as an attempt to flee her 'fatal attraction', half penitent, half thrilled by the idea. And although her mother had eventually told her that they were both children of failed first marriages, when they had been very young, and only brought up as brother and sister, she had been disappointed instead of relieved. A dark part of her had relished the torment of being subject to a forbidden desire. They had seen very little of each other since then, he had certainly helped her after the crisis in her life which had brought her, hurt and crushed, back to England. He had been married while she was abroad, and now he had a child.

His wife, Margaret, had sensed something from the first. She was distant and had a sort of false girlie bonhomie. At least that was how Vee intuitively felt.

She could sense David's hidden anger and unease at being dragged into the intimacy of her life again. Her own resentment simmered at this knowledge.

"I'm sorry," she announced tightly now. The wide bed, with its cream satin cover, screamed its own sexual message at them. "I shouldn't have bothered you. You're a married

129

man. You've got your troubles - "

"What do you mean?" He fired back, so quickly, and with such a sharp, suspicious glance, that her instincts were roused. Oh-ho. All not well with la belle Marguerite? she surmised cattily, then felt ashamed.

"Nothing. It's just - I shouldn't have expected you to come running, bro. It isn't fair - "

"Where on earth did you pick up that disgusting expression?" he asked, with a strained smile.

She blushed deeply, mentally squirming as she recalled Cliffy's frequent use of the term. "Seriously. I am sorry. I - " she shrugged, swallowed hard. All at once the tears, entirely genuine, came springing up, choking her. "God, I'm so useless, aren't I?" she stammered, angry with herself.

"Hey. Come on! You've been through a hell of a lot. And come through it, too. We're proud of you. I know I am. You've stood on your own feet, you've coped tremendously well."

His words, meant to encourage, startled her with their warmth, and tipped the emotional scales even further. She began to cry, then to sob, unable to stop, until her whole body shook with her grief.

"Come on, Vee. Don't - please. I hate to see you - please, sweet, don't!"

Sweet? She looked up in wonder, her eyes swimming with tears, her face shining with them, and all at once he was up, crushing her to him, and his mouth swooped, that mouth whose shape she knew so well, and it was over hers, crushing it, sealing it, in a passionate kiss. Their lips were parted, they gnawed and worried at each other, their tongues drove in, twisted, and the forbidden desires of a lifetime flowed like electricity through every fibre of their joined bodies as they strained together.

"Jesus, Vee! I'm sorry!" He was almost sobbing, too. He groaned, crushed her to him, until she fought for breath. Still clinging desperately to one another, they fell across the bottom of the wide bed. "Oh God! Oh God!" he murmured, over and over, his mouth now frantically devouring her wet face, burying itself in her fragrant neck, sending darts of exquisite excitement tingling throught her. "We mustn't. Christ! It's - we can't - "

Her fingers plucked at his shirt buttons, popping them open, feeling the warmth of his smooth chest beneath. His hands had delved madly, thrusting up under her sweater, running over the nylon cups of her bra. She struggled to sit up, catching her breath, tugging wildly at the sweater, dragging it over her head.

"I've wanted you to make love to me since I was a kid!" she panted. "Just forget everything. Except this!" She wriggled, knelt up, unzipped the thick skirt, struggled out of it, then pushed down the nylon tights. She wore pale grey satin knickers, with their wide trimming of lace at the high, cut away legs. "Undress me," she whispered, her voice thick with siren desire.

His fingers shook, but he was not clumsy as he unsnapped her bra, lifted the cups reverently from their breasts, bent and nuzzled his warm face in their sweet softness, took the tiny, budding nipples into his mouth, suckled then until she moaned and arched her body up to him. Now! she gasped. "I - I've waited too long. Do it to me, now!"

He was kneeling, shedding his clothes as quickly as he could. Finally, he was naked, she saw his penis standing out rigidly from the luxuriant growth of dark hair, so different from her own. Which he now bared, as, gently still, he slipped down

131

the silk knickers, with their telltale, spreading stain of her dampness and eased them over her feet. She caught hold of his prick, felt its mighty throb, shivered with the ecstasy of it, heard his gasp. Then he was up, his knees pushed at the insides of her thighs which parted at once. Her hand drew him to her, and he slid home, burying himself to the hilt in her encompassing, throbbing wetness. And they sighed, their mouths fastened as eagerly as their joined bellies as they moved in the rhythm of the coupling which neither had known, and both had dreamed of, for so long.

CHAPTER FIFTEEN

Vee woke, shivering, her body goosebumped slightly, in spite of the room's central heating. She was lying on top of the ruffled covers still, they had not made it under the blankets, even after the hectic splendour of their loving. Then she saw David's wonderfully expressive eyes, fixed on her nakedness, as though he wished to brand indelibly on his memory every part of her. His hand lay gently on the curve of her hip. She felt its warmth. She smiled shyly, moved to nestle into him, and his arms enfolded her, their legs entwined, and she pressed herself gratefully against him. "We should get under the clothes," she murmured.

"I wanted to look at you."

The tears came stinging to her eyes at his tenderness. She swallowed hard. How long was it since she had shared such a precious feeling with a man? Had she ever? Painfully, she examined her relationship with Keith. Their first days of intimacy, before and in the early days of their marriage, seemed blurred with the mistiness of long ago. She had loved hin, fiercely, completely. And he had loved her, too. But love, for him, had always been inextricably mingled with possession. He loved her because she was his. And, for all his fearsome intelligence, he had not been able to take the idea of anyone else laying any kind of claim to her. Someone else's lips on hers, someone else's prick in her vagina, someone else's image in her mind, no matter how briefly, were things he could never stand. She was sullied, could no longer belong to him, not exclusively, the way he had wanted. It made it no less painful that she could so fully understand his primitive feeling. And even, despairingly, endorse it.

But this - this love - yes, that's what it was, she told herself resolutely - this love for her brother, and, more marvellously, his for her, which had burst upon them so shockingly, so brilliantly, after all this time. It was different. Different from anything. More delicate, more precious than anything she could have imagined.

"I want you," she murmured, reaching under his arms, pulling him strongly over onto her as she rolled on her back, drew up and opened her knees. She saw the rising blush, that vulnerable look steal into his eyes. "I love you." she said intensely, holding him in her gaze. "I've wanted you as long as I can remember. I wanted you for my first lover. My only lover."

An expression of pain gripped him. She saw the line of his jawbone tighten until it quivered. But she felt the responsive leap of his penis, it flamed to her touch when she seized it, the potent sex force throbbing rigidly through it, and she guided it to her already peeling, urgently slippery vulva, quivering with fulfilled joy as its length slid deep into her spasming passage. Their pelvic bones clashed, and they strained to one another, lost in the bliss of their coupling. Until the rhythm of the loving carried them inexorably up the long, long slope of passion to the tumultuous crest, and the outward, downward plunge to the ultimate release whose power dazzled them, and from which they returned alowly, awed by the experience.

They shared the wide, sunken bath tub, sitting opposite each other in a welter of foam, flesh intimately touching, caressing, under the warmly hugging water. "What happened? Who gave you a hiding? He nodded, at the fading but still visible marks of Cliffy's strokes, concealed now beneath the lather.

She blushed, felt the cold frisson of returning reality nudge at their capsuled happiness. The world outside was inescapably there. She hated herself for her lies.

"That's part of it. Why I had to run. Someone I got mixed up with. Who found out about me. And extracted payment. Too much. I had to get away."

He gazed at her with an abstracted, troubled look, but said nothing. She felt uncomfortable, wished that he had erupted in righteous anger on her behalf, or in the simple rage of jealousy. His silence told her that he knew, or suspected, far more of her complex personality than she would have wanted him to. "That's why I think I'll have to get right away," she continued. "He won't give up so easily. He'll think there's money to be made somewhere."

That at least was something David must give her credit for, she thought. She could have made a small or maybe a considerable fortune by going to the papers, or the TV companies, riding on her temporary fame, or notoriety, when she was released from Mavumbi's rebel stronghold. In fact, she had exerted a great deal of energy and ingenuity avoiding them, until they had, as David himself had predicted, swiftly forgotten her.

"We'd better get something to eat." His eyes flickered

away from hers, as he added, "I'll give Margaret a ring later. Let her know..." His voice faded, and there was a catch in hers as she tried to answer casually.

"You have to go back today, I suppose. I wish - anyway, you know how much I appreciate you coming so quickly - when I needed you - "

He stood. The bubbles clung thickly about his belly, clustered around his pubis, the hanging tube of his penis. "Let me rinse you off," she murmured thickly. She was still sitting, his prick was on a level with her eyes as she reached forward, gently swept at the clinging foam with her hands. She held his heavy, warm testicles in her cupped palm, the fingers of her other hand stroked the column of his prick, which stirred, its helm peeping from the collar of foreskin. He gasped, his hips jerking, and she looked up quickly at him, her expression one of defiant challenge. "I love you!" she said again, almost aggressively. She pushed her face forward, rubbed the satiny glans across her brow, then fitted the planes of her cheek bone, the delicate hollow of her eye to it, holding it so that it traced the contours of her worshipping face. It throbbed mightily, reared up, she felt it thickening, stiffening, and she seized it boldly, circled it below the helm in her fingers, and slid them firmly down the pulsing shaft. She let her lips form an O, which closed over the red tip. Her tongue came out, lapped at it, tasted the salty issue from its tiny slit. She stretched her mouth wide and took it in fully, her cheeks hollowing as she sucked deeply, drawing him into her warm, wet, working throat, and he groaned, his hands gripping her thin shoulders, thrusting his belly into her face. She felt the column of flesh slide easily back and forth, now touching the back of her throat, now hovering at the very threshold of her eager lips. She reached between his legs to grasp his buttocks and pulled him to her. He groaned again and she began to move her head urgently back and forth, hungry to taste his spend. Suddenly his hands clenched in her hair and she felt his prick swell and begin to pump. She rode the jerks of his rigid shaft as it jetted his warm sperm against the back of her throat, spurt after spurt splashing out as she swallowed again and again. Vee felt an almost climactic pleasure kindle between her legs as at long last she tasted David as he took his pleasure in her humbly offered mouth.

"Do you have to book a separate room?" she asked, when, after they had eaten a late and leisurely lunch, they approached the reception desk in the busy foyer.

"I think we'd better. I'm not sure we act like husband and wife." He flushed, but met her gaze. "And it's strange how we even look alike in some ways." he said.

"I know. It feels like..... I feel so close. Even though you are my big bro." She squeezed his arm against her side as she spoke, a frisson of delight running through her at the thought of how close to forbidden this liaison was. "Thanks for staying with me. It'll be such a waste, paying for a single room. I won't let you anywhere near your own bed, I promise."

"I don't know why you couldn't have checked out last night. And come straight down here," Margaret said, the thick curtain of her dark honey hair flicking across her face, indicating her agitation. "Such a waste, forking out for two rooms like that." She stood, turned away, and Vee studied the trim figure, responding to the alluring curve of her buttocks, and the way her flanks filled the tight denim of the jeans which clung to them. She thought of her own almost flat behind, envied her the feminine fullness. It was the same with her bosom. The twin mounds of her breasts thrust ripely against the checked shirt, their firm roundness looking entirely natural under the thick material. She had rounded out quite considerably since the birth of Stephen fifteen months ago, to her advantage, Vee conceded honestly, though Margaret regularly bewailed her fuller figure with mock dismay.

Just now, though, all Vee could pick up on were the clearly disturbed vibes which she was giving off, and which in turn gave Vee a deep and discomfiting concern. Impossible as the concept seemed, Vee could not dispel that inner voice of warning which whispered constantly. "She knows."

"Well, I'd already booked in for the night. It just seemed easier. And I needed some time, to think. Get things straight."

"And you couldn't do that here? It had to be at some airport hotel?" Margaret flushed, looking embarrassed herself at the vehemence with which her comment had come out.

"Look, I'm sorry. If you think I shouldn't have bothered David - and you..."

"No, it's not that. Of course not," Margaret returned, too quickly. The awkwardness hung there in the air between them. Vee wished desperately that David were still present. There was a guilt about the inordinate haste of his escape after they had arrived at the modest comfort of the new semi just before lunch. "Got to check in at work. Don't know when I'll be back." The quick peck on the cheek for his wife, the instinctive start towards Vee, who had already turned her head before he swung away, with a clumsy gesture of a wave.

It was Margaret who had suggested she should come down to stay at their place for "a few days". After yet more passionate love making, Vee had lain with David while he talked, painfully at first, then with increasing ease and candour - after all, they were lovers now - about this unhappy marital situation. "I suppose it's a common enough tale, but poor wee Stevie has made a hell of a difference to our life. She's sullen, resentful, and yet makes him the be-all and end-all of her existence. She's hell to live with most of the time. Resents everything about me. The fact that I go out to work - she seems to think it's all part of a plot to get away from her - and Stevie. She's not interested at all in - in sex." Shame caught at him, he gestured at their naked bodies. "That's not - I mean I'm not saying - that's not why - "

She grabbed at him, rolled violently on top of him, searching for his mouth, stopping his tortured protest. "Look, for God's sake! There's nothing wrong with wanting sex. Or feeling starved of it, is there? I haven't - haven't been loved, like this for - for years," she continued bravely, thrusting aside her own cloudy thoughts on the issue. "You haven't gone out and jumped on the nearest female, have you? And I haven't flung myself at the first rampant prick I've seen. And even if we had - so what? Oh, why the hell do we make sex such a complicated bloody thing?" But they had made love again, almost all night. He had slid down, spread her legs wide, dipped his head to her musky loins, and used his mouth and tongue and fingers on her, and in her, until she was one writhing mass of rapturous sensation, and frantically grasped at him, hauled him up onto her heaving frame, felt his penis drive home into her to complete an almost unbearable degree of physical happiness whose mounting intensity dissolved thought altogether.

"It might be as well if you did come down, just for a day or two," he had told her. She had sensed a kind of unspoken plea there, and had agreed, even though she had felt uncomfortable at the thought of facing Margaret, with the knowledge that She and David were now lovers. Infidelity and almost incest! She could imagine how colossal a barrier that was for David to surmount. Now, facing the crackling tension in this bright room, Vee knew just how much of a mistake it had been for her to come here in these circumstances. Neither she nor David were efficient liars, even though she had been living a kind of lie ever since her return to England. And given Margaret's heightened perception, and her hostility, it seemed now doubly a mistake.

"I never realised - you and David were that close," Margaret said now, that same brittle tautness underlying the apparent lightness of her tone. "He never - you know - gave that impression. It was a shock - when you sent for him - "

"I didn't send for him!" Vee answered, her face flaming. "It was - I - I've got no one - no one else I can turn to. No friends - and mum and dad!' She tossed her head, rolled her eyes expressively towards the ceiling.

"You know, they've been devastated." Margaret's voice clanged with accusation. "What happened to you. Worried almost out of their minds when you were being held hostage. Then afterwards - when all that other stuff came out, about you - and Keith. Those terrible pictures of you!"

Vee knew of course that she was referring, not to the pictures of her and Katya in the rebel camp, but to the nude drawings of her which the libidinous old Greek, George Kyriakos, had made, months before her capture, and which her ex-lover, Gerrard, had subsequently released to the press, along with all the salacious details of their clandestine affair, in a bitter vengeance against Keith which had proved all too successful in that it had damaged their shaky marriage irreparably.

"Why on earth did you - allow all that to happen?" Margaret's voice rang with indignation, flaying Vee's sensitive conscience, which had suffered enough already with her self flagellation. "It broke their hearts. They nearly died of shame! And then - all those horrid reporters. Hanging about outside the house, ringing up all hours of the day and night! Spying the whole time, talking to friends, neighbours! Have you any idea how terrible it was for them - for all of us?"

Her voice had risen to a shrill torment. Vee sprang up from the deep settee, her face alive with her emotion. "It wasn't any picnic for me, either!" she cried. "And now they're after me again. All set to ruin my life for a second time!"

"Seems to me you did a good denough job yourself. Why should you come running, expecting people to jump to it whenever you think you need them?"

All the ugliness of her dislike, of their mutual antagonism bristled, and they faced each other like spitting cats, faces blazing. "Maybe it's not only a one way thing!" Vee retorted, unable to stop her furious thoughts from expression. "Maybe it isn't only me who needs David. Matbe it's the other way around, too. Perhaps he's the one who needs help, and a bit of understanding. And love! When he doesn't get it from the place he has a right to expect it - from his own home - and wife!"

She was panting, regretting the words even as they left her mouth. She saw Margaret recoil, as though struck, the naked hate making her face momentarily ugly.

"What would you know - about love? You cheap slut! All the disgusting things you've done!" Her voice caught on a sob, then she rushed on, her words tumbling wildly forth. "There's even something sick about the way you latch onto David! That simpering, sexy, false little girlie voice! 'Oh, please, David - can you come - I need you.'" She cruelly mimicked the breathless childishness. "You sound like a tart. Like you're coming on - to him for God's sake!"

The import of her words held them, so that they

seemed frozen, like a still photograph for one awful instant. Vee was trembling violently, she felt hysteria rising like a bubble all about her. With amazement, she heard herself laugh, and say, in a voice of admirable and contrasting calmness. "And you know what? It works every time. You should try it. Then he might get what he needs from home and not look for it elsewhere, in places where he shouldn't!"

She walked out, leaving Margaret standing open mouthed and as speechless as though she had been struck an unexpected blow.

CHAPTER SIXTEEN

Vee stared at her suitcase standing in the middle of the rug in the neat guest room. She was glad she had not started to unpack. She would phone for a taxi, take the next train back up to London, to the lonely anonymity of one of the large airport hotels. But she had scarcely time to frame the thought before the door crashed open behind her, as she knew it would. Margaret, her face transformed into a snarl of fury, screamed at her. "Just what the hell do you mean by that? You're telling me David's having an affair? Is that it?

"Look, Margaret," Vee began, her tone conciliatory, her heart thudding with fear at the rashness of her outburst. "I didn't - "

"You filthy bitch! You're saying he confided in you! And you couldn't wait to blab it out, of course! To let me know - "

"I shouldn't have said anything" Vee tried to keep her tone calm, in order to stem the rising hysteria in her sister-in-law's voice. She made to edge past her, towards the door. "I'll

141

just phone for a taxi, if I may. I shouldn't have come in the first place. I knew it wasn't a good idea - "

Margaret clutched at her arm, spun her round forcibly. "Hold on! You think you can say something like that - that my husband's unfaithful to me - and then just walk out? I want to know everything! All he's been telling you!"

Vee struggled free, shook her off. "Let me go!" she half sobbed. "Just forget it, will you? I was just shooting my mouth off! It's not - "

"No, you bitch! There's something going on. I could tell, straight away - the pair of you - skulking about something! I demand to know! Tell me!"

Vee cried out as the spitting figure leapt at her, one hooked hand clawing at her hair, knocking her off balance, sending her sprawling back across the bed. The breath was driven from her as Margaret straddled her, pinning her down. Vee's elegantly heeled shoes flew off as her feet kicked helplessly. She sobbed as she tried to throw off the pinning weight. Margaret's talon like fingers seized on her wwrists, bent them by her head, held them down.

"Guh - get off! Let me go!" Vee wept impotently, still struggling. Her skirt had ridden up, revealing her nylon covered limbs almost to the tops of her thighs. Then she squealed in genuine fear as Margaret's right hand moved swiftly and delivered a cracking, open palmed blow across Vee's cheek which left an angry scarlet brand. "Ow! Oh! How duh - dare you! Please, don't - "

More ringing blows followed in quick succession, until Vee's head swam, her vision blurred.

"It was a lie!" she screamed. "I swear it - I only said it to hurt you! It's not true!" She was blubbering now, her struggles had ceased, she slumped under her attacker. She froze in renewed alarm as those punishing hands hauled up her sweater, fastened on the rounds of her breasts, hidden in the dainty cups of her bra.

"Oh no! Please!" she begged, feeling the remorseless fingers tighten, dig into the yielding flesh. They tore at the stiffened nylon, flipped the flimsy cover up and off. Vee felt the cool air on her exposed body, the nipples hardening, peaking, felt the displaced bra pressing uncomfortably against the upper swell of her chest. She cried out again at the biting pain as those fingers clawed now at the breasts themselves, twisting cruelly.

"Ow - uh - oh!" Vee sobbed. "I lied to you - I wanted to hurt you. He told me - you were having problems - your private - with the sex! That's all!" She gave one more agonised scream as Margaret wrenched at the softness in her grasp before letting go. She was still kneeling astride Vee's midriff.

"You spiteful, wicked bitch! I've always thought you were a right little cow! But I never realised how vindictive you were. You've cocked up your own life so completely you can't bear to see anybody else happy. Is that it? You even want to wreck your own brother's life for him!"

Vee's hands were folded protectively over her throbbing breasts, and now she yelped again as Margaret struck her over the side of her head.

"No, that isn't true!" she stammered, through her tears. "It was just - when you started on at me - having a go at me - I just hit back, that's all." She flinched, expecting another blow, yet unable to keep herself from adding, with cowering truculence. "Anyway, he isn't, is he? Happy! That wasn't a lie, was it? Or are you going to deny it? You and him - "

"And what's that got to do with you, eh?" She leaned menacingly close, and Vee whimpered, her hands coming up

143

to ward off another blow. "What would you know about it? Or care?"

"I'm very fond - " she felt herself blushing, the guilt spreeading like a stain through her conscience at what she and David had done. "I do care - about him - a lot. I want him to be happy - "

"Oh yeah!" Margaret sneered. "And you think I don't? You think - "

Vee was shocked at the sudden crumpling dissipation of Margaret's rage, the way her spirit seemed to fold up. A racking sob tore through the supple frame, and she suddenly flung herself sideways, toppling off her opponent, falling onto the bed beside Vee. She hid her face in her arms. Her whole body shook with her grief, her sobs coming from deep within her.

Vee sat up slowly, staring down at her in appalled silence. In spite of the vicious attack, from which her face was still redly marked and stinging, Vee was startled by the wave of compassion which swept over her for the wretched girl who, in her despair, seemed to have forgotten her altogether. She had difficulty in making out her words at first, so storm tossed by her pouring sorrow, jerking out harshly between each volcanic sob.

"I cuh - can't huh - help it! I've tried - I've been - tuh - told the doctor. But I - can't even talk about it with David. I don't know why - it's - like I clam up - ever since Stuh - Stevie - I don't want it at all - it disgusts me. But we never talk - I can see how - it's hurting him - but still - "

She gave a loud wail of despair so utter that Vee found herself shuddering, her eyes filling with sympathy. Automatically , she reached out to enfold the hunched shape in her embrace. The trembling shoulders stiffened at her first touch, then

144

they wilted, Vee felt as well as saw the resistance ebb from them, and all at once she was fitting her own frame spoon shaped along the curve of the heaving back, the flanks, the bent limbs. Her lips nuzzled gently at the wild tangles of the honey coloured hair, she kissed the fragrant, vulnerable neck.

Sobbing abandonedly, Margaret swivelled round. Her face was swamped with grief, tears pouring over its surface, its beauty blurred, dissolved in this cataract of despond. And Vee's lips were covering it, her tongue licking at the tears, her own mouth fastening on lips pulled back, childlike in hurt and loneliness. Margaret's arms came up, they clung desperately together, their bodies seeking contact until they lay full length, straining to one another, limbs locked, mouths glued. Their embrace, their kiss, was rawly sexual, yet seemed the most natural thing in the world to both of them then.

"My darling, I'm so sorry," Vee crooned. All at once, she was filled with a sense of noble resolve. She had been vouchsafed this opportunity to make amends for what she had done with David, and, in the innermost recesses of her thoughts, she had to force herself to acknowledge that, while she might have been able to live with it and to go on breaking the taboo society had placed on their love, for David it would have been an impossible burden. That it had happened, for one glorious night and day, must content her. And perhaps, now, through her, the poor girl weeping in her arms might be brought back to a recognition of the physical needs and desires which were vital for everyone.

"You're so beautiful," she whispered, and realised, from her own unfolding, dampening response, how sincere her admiration, and her arousal, were. At first, Margaret lay there, still shaken by her weeping, as though unaware of Vee's movements. Meanwhile, Vee's fingers were plucking at the belt and the zip of the jeans, unbuttoning the shirt, pulling its folds from the tight waistband, tugging at the tight denim, trying to ease the jeans down over the firm curve of hips and thighs.

And now, the face, puffed and agleam with her fit of crying, was suffused with colour, and with confusion. 'What - what - are you doing?"

"I've always envied you - your looks, your figure. Because - I've always fancied you! I'd never dare say it - but - "

In spite of her deep embarrassment, Margaret was making no real effort to prevent Vee's busy hands. In fact, she even moved, ashamed as she was, to assist her, and Vee fought the clinging jeans down off her legs, stripping her of her boots before she pulled them free of her feet. The shirt was easier to manage, and soon Margaret was lying in the white bra and briefs. Not for long, though she gasped and did make a belated and token move to stop Vee, which Vee ignored. Vee's excitement was throbbingly intense, as she peeled away the cover from the splendid breasts. The nipples, much larger and of a richer, deeper hue than her own, were already erect, their swelling surface tinily pitted, as lusciously tempting as a ripe fruit which Vee's mouth longed to taste - and did so, even as her fingers eased down the cotton briefs, exposing the thick, dark bush of pubic hair. Over the swelling, tangily rousing sex the cotton slid though Margaret wept quietly for shame, and for the whirling sensations speeding through her dizzy mind. There was no uncertainty about the message her racing blood and throbbing body was sending. Her body bent and arched with its urgency, and her hands clasped the fair head to her bosom, pressing Vee's working face into her resilient flesh in an ecstasy of excitement.

Helplessly, she moved like a lifesized doll when Vee rolled her onto her back, and, taking hold of both ankles, opened her legs wide. The long, dark divide of her vulva pouted with promise, flowered to Vee's light caresses until it opened, gleaming, slippery with the juices of desperate need, to which were added the fluids From her ardent lover as Vee's tongue and lips worked busily, tasting the unique nectar for which she craved. Margaret's hands clutched spasmodically in Vee's hair, though whether to restrain her or to hold her there at that melting nub of her fierce desire was not clear, even to herself.

Vee knew the female body, had loved many times like this, knew the degree of hunger in that beating, opened crevice, each hidden fold and exposed, screaming nerve, and she used all her instinctive knowledge to make the loving as perfect as it could be. At the vital moment, she withdrew, so that Margaret uttered a sharp, forlorn cry at her desertion, but, after a hasty groping in her bag, Vee returned, to crouch once more between those sprawled and supplicant limbs.

There was a soft click, a gentle purr, and Margaret's body convulsed, her dark capped belly leapt upward at the exquisite invasion of the smooth, humming object which Vee slowly and skilfully inserted until it occupied the wildly beating passage of her vagina. It glided smoothly back and forth, Vee extracted it until only the bullet nosed tip stirred the sensitive tissue around the entrance. She slid it in deep again, one last time, until it all but disappeared and Vee's nails rested on the scarlet, puckered rim of the surrendered sex. Margaret's frame locked, her thigh muscles bunched, her heels scrabbled and feet drummed on the counterpane. The orgasm's brilliance burst on her, tore like a whirlwind through her, setting every nerve end alight, ebbed, flickered, and blossomed yet again. She jerked, and jerked, her features clenched, the cries torn from her seizing throat, until she collapsed, shuddering, consumed and utterly lost to its elemental force. Vee held her to her, their mouths glued once more, her own bodily needs blazing so intensely that she, too, spasmed and sobbed in the excess of emotion that took ageless moments to fade from her shaking body.

"Listen, I've booked you in at the Metropole. Now you go and have a great time. We'll be fine here. Honestly, I know I'm no good with kids but Kirsty here'll take care of things." Vee could hardly bear the looks they cast at her, each with its secret message to teart at her heartstrings. Margaret's gaze seemed to her so naked in its proclamation of the love they had so shockingly and wonderfully discovered together that she almost blanched in fear that the others must see its plainness. And David - such a blend of emotions in the look he gave her. Pain, still, and shock at what had happened between them. And dazed gratitude at the transformation wrought in his wife. Did he suspect anything of the truth which lay behind it? Even though she blushed at the thought, Vee could not really claim to be surprised. Things happened so swiftly, things that were still virtually unable to be referred to, however close they had become.

And what a tangled, webbed complexity enfolded all three of them now! Yesterday, when he had at last returned, the girls had been safely locked behind the bathroom door, still shaken and undoubtedly stirred by their new role as lovers. Margaret's transparent rapture was sure to give them away, Vee thought, terrified and delighted at the same instant with her unlooked for success. "I never knew - never dreamt!" Margaret kept repeating, in the same shocked whisper, shaking her head in disbelief. "Me! A lesbian!" Then collapsing, giggling like an overgrown schoolkid until Vee could not help but join her.

"You're not really," Vee argued, far from convinced by her own sophistry. "It's just - you see, you do need sex. Want it still. We all do. You've got to work at it. Promise me - David loves you, I know he does."

It was her idea to send them off for a night, to let them recapture the sexual attraction they had clearly shared. She had insisted on paying for the hotel, trying not to let her vivid imagination relat the scene, driving from her mind the potent recall of just such a night she had so recently shared with David.

Uncharacteristically, she had taken feverish charge, made rapid plans, coerced them into agreement - it was a measure of the unreality of the whole situation that she was able to do so, for, habitually, she drifted through her life feeling completely helpless and at the whim of anyone and anything which came into her sphere. And that everything seemed to cooperate with her plans was another sign that this was somehow meant to be, she thought. The friendly girl from down the road, Kirsty Somebody, had readily agreed to help out with Stephen, David had raised no objection about taking further time from work, had not even argued seriously about Vee's footing the bill for their trip.

It was a relief to see them go. She knew she must make herself scarce on the morrow. But where? To what? And then, to add to her already strong feeling of Fate's wheel turning, that very night, as she sat in comfortable lethargy watching the nine o'clock news, she found herself staring at a face so vividly etched upon her memory that she felt her flesh stirring with a fluttering response which snatched the breath from her body and left her giddy with hotly flowing desire.

"Today, the trade delegation from Makamba met the Minister for..." Her blood hammered, the words faded from her consciousness as she stared at the group clustered on the steps of the government building. And there, at the back, breathtakingly elegant in a high collared coat whose contours could not disguise her svelte figure, elegantly beautiful and smiling, those magnificent dark eyes looking right at her and into her, stood Awina, her one time captor, mistress and lover. Vee leaned forward and almost rose in the strength of the need to go to her, to answer the call of her heart.

CHAPTER SEVENTEEN

Vee spent a further two lonely days and nights back in the solitary luxury of a hotel, plucking up the courage to translate into action her deeply felt urge to contact Awina once more. There were plenty of arguments to summon against it. The beautiful African would probably be just as reluctant to have her past brought into focus as Vee had been. Now she was a rising star in her country's diplomatic corps, a high flier. Just as Mavumbi was no longer a self styled general of rebel forces, but ranked third in the overall command of Makumba's armed forces, confidant and right hand man of the president against whom he had waged bitter war only eighteen months ago. So she delayed, until, the next morning she was leafing through one of the tabloids when she found herself staring at her own naked image - not, thank God, the infamous drawing of her sprawled in that chair in George Kyriakos's shack, but the bog eyed photo of her standing next to Katya, in the rebel camp, with the startled young Edward, their guard, which the news man, Frank Tully, had taken, and which had been circulated around the world. The article accompanying the picture leapt at her from the page.

"Mrs Vee Green, former hostage of Makumba rebels, whose captivity, and the later revelations about her exotic expatriate life style, brought her worlwide publicity little more than a year ago, has once more emerged from obscurity. Masquerading as a school teacher, under her maiden name of Wainwright, Vee is now at the centre of a possible scandal involving some of her students, with whom she had a relationship extending far beyond the classroom.

"Mr Clive Addison, Headteacher of Hague Road Comprehensive School. the inner city establishment where Vee has been giving of her unique services, was understandably tight lipped about the incident, and could only tell us that "the matter is being carefully looked into." Ms Wainwright, meanwhile, is suspended on full pay. Also understandably, we have been unable to trace her for comment. Another bizzare twist is that one reliable informant told us that someone so like the attractive 26 year old as to be 'her double' was recently performing as a stripper in a private club somewhere in Tottenham.

"Could it be that the pretty divorcee had been trying to augment her meagre salary as a teacher with some extra-curricular activity? Readers will no doubt recall that, though in the picture above Vee's pose 'au naturel' was not by choice, subsequent event proved that she was by no means averse to being seen as nature intended."

When the storm of weeping had subsided, Vee snatched up the receiver. "I'd like the number of the Makumba Embassy, please/"

"My God! My little stick insect! Is it really you?" Vee moved quickly into the open arms of Awina, who had hastened round from behind the large desk to greet her. Vee's neatly groomed, fair head rested on the curves of the high bosom, and she shook with the force of her tears as Awina cradled her, her lips touching the hair as she whispered soothing endearments.

"Oh, God! I'm so sorry!" Vee dabbed and blew, using the supply of tissues Awina handed across to her when they finally broke the embrace and Vee was sitting shakily opposite her. "I can't believe it, either," she smiled dewily. The figure across from her was as lovely as she remembered. She had filled out a little, the breasts, the curve of the hips were fuller. Or perhaps they were simply being displayed to more advantage, in the elegant, dark striped suit of tailored jacket and sheath skirt which clung to her outline. Maybe, too, Vee speculated, titillated by the thought, Awinas's underwear was more fashionably flattering than the simple cotton bikini pants Vee used to lay out for her alongside the military uniform.

Vee stammered out her story. "Everything seems to be going wrong again. The papers - " She was surprised at first at Awina's sympathetic nod, indicating that she already knew about the latest unwelcome publicity, but then she realised that the still young independent state of Makamba kept a close eye on any world events reflecting on its own image internationally - "I needed to get away. Then I saw you on television the other night." She blushed prettily, lowered her glance. "I felt I had to see you again," she murmured, her voice thick with threatening tears yet again.

"Would you like your old job back?" Awina asked, that deep gurgle of laughter Vee knew so well much in evidence, and she glanced up quickly. "As my maid," Awina continued, grinning. "I miss you, you know. My little stick insect." The warmth in her words made Vee blush again, this time with pleasure, as though Awina had caressed her. "Listen," she said,

152

her old brisk efficiency showing through. "I've got a busy schedule just now. We've got some apartments. Mayfair,' she added, her teeth flashing in a wide smile. "No more bush huts and long drops in the jungle, eh? Where are you staying? I'll send a car for you at six. Have your things ready. You can move in with me. We must get those press bastards off your back." She came close again, and gently lifted Vee from her seat, her arm firmly round her wiast.

"I've missed you - a lot," Vee whispered, at the door. "There's been many a time - and none more than now - when I've wished I was back in those huts. Your prisoner."

"That can be arranged," Awina breathed, her puckered lips swooping to alight on Vee's proffered mouth, in a kiss of slow promising passion.

Vee knelt worshipfully, her head dizzy with the sight, and with the musky perfume, of the brown belly, the little, tight scrub of curls covering the swelling mound, the exotic redness of the long divide beneath, which was opening up and yielding its juicy treasures, to her loving ministrations.

"You white witch!" Awina groaned, her legs lifting, the feet waving in the air, her fingers clutching Vee's head to her loins. "For God's sake - do it! Don't stop! I can't - a-a-rgh!" The belly jerked upward, buffeted against Vee's sore mouth as she buried her face in the running cleft, and Awina's supple body arched. The orgasm sent her shuddering into a lost ecstasy, its waves possessing her, her body writhing until she subsided in sobbing exhaustion. Her own vagina spasming, her vulva seeping her own lubricious arousal, Vee lay gasping, blissfully, her cheek resting on the trembling, dark thigh.

They were sharing a bath when a startled Vee heard the rasp of a key in the lock, then footsteps and a cheery masculine voice calling out in English. She smothered a cry of alarm, hurriedly folding her arms over her soapy breasts as a head cane round the door.

"Hi, Victor." Awina said casually. "This is Vee. Remember? Mrs Green - our guest a while back!"

He advanced, grinning hugely, his hand held out in formal politeness. At a loss, Vee stared up, accepted his hand, shook it, then quickly covered her breast again. He was tall, and extremely thin, his complexion the velvet black of the northern tribes of which Awina was a member. He had the strong lantern jaw of his ethnic grouping, and, like so many, the fine network of horizontal lines about the eyes which gave the impression of someone used to working outside, in the harsh conditions of his native region.

His English was excellent, with only a light trace of the vowel pattern of African English. "How very charming! And cosy. Though perhaps a little decadent for our conservative values."

"We're old friends, don't forget," Awina answered in the same bantering manner. "You should know the link established between prisoner and gaoler. Victor's in military intelligence," Awina explained to the embarrassed Vee. "A spy, in other words. Vee's on our side, aren't you, darling? We don't keep secrets from each other, do we?" She leaned forward and drew Vee's crossed arms away from her chest. "And you don't need to keep secrets from Victor, either. He's a good man."

She stood, the white foam clinging and sliding over her dark flesh. Victor held out the huge white towel, and she stepped from the tub, turning as he folded it about her and began to dry her, his long hands tracing the outline of her flesh. He kissed her neck as she leaned back into him. Vee felt herself crimsoning. It was very obvious that they were lovers. Teas-

154

ingly, Awina moved clear of him let the towel fall to the Floor.

"Come on," she said. "You mustn't be jealous of one another. You can both share me. There's more than enough to go round. Victor, do the honours, please."

She handed him a clean towel, which he held out as he had before. "Come on, Vee," Awina ordered crisply. "He's not a rival, even if he does enjoy playing maid." He held out one hand, with old fashioned gallantry. Her head spinning, Vee reached up, took it, and stepped self consciously from the fragrant water, allowing him to drape her body in the soft white of the towel. She stood tremblingly still while His hands patted her dry. She would have kept the damp towel wrapped around her, but, still with that dazzling smile, he tugged it gently from her, let it fall. Naked, she followed Awina into the large living room, and obediently sank into the deep cushions of the long couch at her side. Awina patted the cushion at her other side, nodding at Victor. "Come on, lover. Don't be bashful."

The air of unreality settled on Vee as, Victor having showered and returned as naked as his companions, all three were lounging back side by side with drinks in hand . Drinks which were soon put aside, as Awina seized Vee with eager passion, their bodies and limbs interweaving as their mouths fastened in a thrilling kiss. Then she turned, her open mouth just as feverishly seeking contact with the black figure clutching her. Hands, lips, took possession of Vee's beating flesh. Hanging over Awina's thighs, Vee found herself gazing at the exotically dark rampant prick bobbing inches from her face. Even this minute gap was closed as an imperious hand clutched at the back of her head, and Awina literally put her to the throbbing prick, whose massive dome filled her mouth as Vee stretched her jaws in acquiescence to encompass his manhood.

"Wait! There's more to this white witch! You've seen

nothing yet. Look! See?" Vee squealed as Awina suddenly dragged her forward, over her knee. A hand fell on her buttocks, where the fading marks of the cane could still be seen. "This little stick insect likes to be punished. Don't you, my dear?"

At once, Vee's mind flew back to the many times when chastisement had been carried out. She felt that same ambivalent reaction now - the clutch of genuine fear squeezing at her gut, the trembling excitement, the secret spasming of her sex at the prospect of corporal pinishment. Awina had brushed her aside, so that she fell sprawling on the carpet while the dark girl sprang up, moved to the elegant cupboard at one wall. Victor's face was alive with anticipation. Vee blushed furiously at his amused stare. "Oh, this wicked world!" he intoned piously, then added wolfishly. "How I love it!"

If Vee had hoped for a hasty spanking of love slaps to warm her bottom, she was doomed to disappointment. Awina, her lovely face transformed now with that lustful power, the dominant arrogance which Vee had recognised and shiveringly responded to so often in the past, came towards her with a leather belt. Vee gasped, thinking that this was to be the instrument of punishment, but Awina ordered her to hold out her hands. Whimpering, Vee did so, and Awina used the belt to bind her wrists tightly together.

"Remember this, little one?" Awina asked, her voice heavy with sensuality, like a lover revealing some treasured momento of their shared love.

Vee felt her muscles clench. She stared at the silver tipped swagger stick, the officers' symbol of authority Awina had so often used to beat her with. To her confusion, Vee felt herself being pushed onto her back on the carpet, at Victor's feet. He gazed avidly at the spectacle of the two lovely figures before him. Awina knelt, and with two light taps, one on each inner thigh, with the stick, like a trainer with a wild animal, made her spread her limbs wide. Gently, she laid the stick lengthways along the groove of Vee's labia, twisting it until it lay neatly centred in the moist folds of tissue. Vee gasped, bit at her lip as Awina began slowly to saw up and down as though the cane were a bow and Vee's vulva a violin.

The stick was soon bedewed with the copious fluid emitted by the prone figure, so that when Awina withdrew the stick, and inserted its silver tip between the slippery folds, they parted and absorbed the probing slenderness with an ease betokened by Vee's lifting belly and quivering thigh muscles. The slim hardness was fitted deep within her sheath. It shone with her secretions when Awina drew it forth, gently slid it in once more, and Vee whimpered, not with fear now but with hunger for more.

She was groaning, her head tossing, she had forgotten all about the once more achingly hard observer sitting over her, when she became aware that this delicious torture had ceased. She shivered. The instrument of loving was about to be put to a more familiar use.

"Up you get!" Awina unceremoniously dragged her up by her bound wrists, led her round the wide couch to its back. "Bend over!"

All the old authority, complete and careless, rang out in that tone. Vee could not imagine disobeying.

"Please," she blubbered, her buttocks clenching in dread, for she knew this would be no mere love play. "Don't hurt me~!"

Awina's deep, sensual laugh derided her craven plea. "Hold her for me, Victor, would you, please? She's an awful coward really. She'll squirm about like a fish on a hook." Victor enchanted by this diversion, his prick bobbing stiffly in front of him, turned and knelt on the cushions. He grabbed the short stretch of the belt between the tethered wrists, and held on firmly, to make sure that Vee remained folded over the high back. Her legs were parted, her thighs locked against the ordeal which the deeply clenched bottom anticipated. Yet she shrieked in agony, her body contorted, threshed in shock, at the fine rippling fire which blazed through her at the first whistling, biting cut that seared her flanks.

"Oh Jesus! No! No!" she howled blindly, the tears streaming down her face, which turned hopelessly over the upholstery. The fire burned through from her quivering behind to every fibre of her captured body. "Please, no!"

CRACK! The second blow came only after a racking interval, in which she had savoured all the scorching torment of that first stroke, and shivered in futile dread at the expectation of the second. Awina waited at each blow, watching the pale, tormented figure twisting, bucking, her legs capering, while a savagely roused Victor held on against the wretched struggles. Four more strokes fell. Six of the best, or worst, until her buttocks vividly blazed anew with the swelling, throbbing bars of her punishment, and she couldn't move, hung there in agony, even when Victor released his hold.

At Awina's furious gesture, he came round to the back of the couch. She bent down, lifted up Vee's head by seizing hold of the damp, gold hair, and whispered like a lover in her ear, "welcome home, little stick insect!" She let the head fall, stepped back, nodded.

Victor closed in, his hands seizing the throbbing rounds, parting them. While Vee stiffened and cried out in fresh pain at his touch, his penis found the soaking entrance to her cunt. He laughed softly as he slipped easily into her and thrust deeply home, embraced by the spasming walls which throbbed in welcome, contradicting Vee's protestations of suffering. He thrust and withdrew in a steadily increasing tempo even while the pale body shuddered in delight at the torment it was undergoing.

CHAPTER EIGHTEEN

Vee was standing in the angle of the wall, where it met the wide expanse of floor to ceiling windows which comprised one end of the VIP lounge. The daylight had long since vanished, so that for the most part they showed only a muted reflection of the comfortably appointed scene behind her. And, closest of all, her own image, staring back at her enigmatically. Her own image - or that of a stranger? She was still shocked at what she saw. The rounded skull, with only the shortest fuzz of blonde hair, which Awina had insisted should be whitened, so that now as she gazed at herself she seemed completely bald. Like some space invader she thought mockingly. Her neck looked even slenderer beneath that great dome, her eyes, outlined in the almond shape of the dramatic black pencil, huge, adding to that alien appearance. And above them, the perfect parentheses of the eyebrows; long, thin curves of black, far beyond the limits of her own plucked and shaved hairs.

A sudden twitch, both tormenting and titillating, at the base of her belly reminded her that it was not only her head and face that had suffered depilation. Even as she grew warm with embarrassment, her sex gave a responsive throb at her recall of Awina's giggling face hanging over her as Vee's shorn head rested between the dark thighs, while her own uplifted knees were pushed wide apart by Victor, who knelt between

159

them, smiling, too, as he coated her mound with the thick fragrant sworls of shaving foam before getting to work with his safety razor. Vee did not need to be admonished to keep still. She tried to breathe as shallowly as possible while the blade scraped over the curve of the mons, denuding it of the clustered curls. He repeated the operation three times before both he and Awina pronounced themselves satisfied at the smooth, unblemished state of the newly exposed skin. And the trickiest - and most stirring - time of all had been when he extended his area of spoilation to include the sparser stray curls running down the sides of her cleft. Delicately, he used his thumb and fingers of his left hand to stretch and open up the brown shaded labia, down the length of her vulva, until he reached the delicately darkening tint at the base of the cleft, where the tiny coral coloured bridge of flesh separated it from the fissure of the buttocks.

Vee gasped at the sudden cool touch of Awina's hand, spreading a cloud of perfumed talc over the sensitive area.

"There now! Smooth as a baby's bum. And we'll keep it that way, my little bald one!"

Still staring solemnly at her reflection, Vee raised one leg behind her, rested the foot, in its five inch, fuck-me heel, on the wall against which she leaned. The pose was provocative. Outside, against a lamp post, she would have had cars screaming to a halt, and frantic queries of, "How much?" The black leather micro-mini rode up to her thigh, showing off her legs almost to the crotch. They looked good, she told herself honestly, in the flesh coloured tights, a last minute concession from Awina, who had wanted her to go bare limbed. Vee's pleas and the bitter end of February weather had won the day.

"But they are coming straight off when we're in the air. When the plane takes off, so do you. Maybe more than the tights!" Awina had chuckled salaciously.

The black leather jacket was open. It was too tight to fasten anyway, even across her modest bosom, which was outlined to full advantage, thanks to the expensive bra worn beneath the plain white top, whose unadorned simplicity was not reflected in its price. It cost a fortune to look that casual. And a small fortune had been spent on her in the past week. It was Awina who had come up with this transformation. And with such calm possessiveness that Vee's ideas of a predetermined destiny were deeply reinforced.

Outside, beyond the dim replica of the inner scene she could see tall rows of lamps, headlights flashing by, and the regular rushing and blur and blink of lights as the jets lifted off into the blackness. She remembered vividly the first time she had left England, from this same airport, the forest of lights that was London spinning away beneath her. She had sat, her sweaty palm tightly clasping Keith's hand, a hollow fear gripping her stomach at the thought of a new life; a new world facing them.

It was like a dream; to think that she was returning there, to that place where her life had been so stunningly transformed. It was ironic that, just as before, she had that sinking feeling - half frightening and half thrilling - of belonging to someone else, being entirely in their hands. Then it had been Keith, and how willingly she had surrendered herself, made herself his captive. Now she had once more yielded herself up, given herself over completely to another's possession. But this time it was different.

Awina, this new and resplendent Awina, was different. Before, in the rebel camp, in its own forested world, it had all been simpler. Vee had been seized and made prisoner, had been totally at their mercy. She had been a slave who had obeyed blindly to save her life. But now? This time she had submitted herself, made herself a willing victim. She recognised the thrill and even the relief which such surrender had brought. And she had to acknowledge the fundamental need she felt to be taken over, to yield up every ounce of independence.

It was like coming home somehow.

The tenderness was there, expressed in those wonderful sexual moments shared by both of them. But the possessiveness was there too, the utter dominance, taken for granted. Awina had made that very clear from the first night when she had caned her - and then stood and watched as Victor had fucked her. The coupling, just as much as the exquisitely painful beating had proclaimed Awina's possession of her. She had given her to him. Vee's body was hers to dispose of as she chose.

The whole week had proved that. She had been taken out only in the embassy car, and then only to be clothed, her head shaved, her body pampered, and all to proclaim Awina's ownership. Nowhere was this ownership more plainly displayed than in the three-way sessions which took place nightly. Victor would arrive after dinner. The girls had had the earlier evening to make love, and his arrival would signal the start of more boisterous games in which she was invariably cast as the victim. Always she was bound and beaten, usually by Awina, but once or twice by Victor. And although she still couldn't face the pain of the beatings without trembling, she could no longer hide from herself that she enjoyed the way they underlined her abject submission. And when Victor took her after each caning, her body betrayed that excitement all too plainly.

Once Vee had woken in the grey morning and turned in the wide bed to see Victor and Awina in the final throes of frenetic lovemaking. Propped on one elbow and buffeted by their threshing bodies, she had been deeply aroused but also shocked to feel a sharp stab of jealousy. Not because it wasn't her being pounded by Victor's potent masculinity but because it he who was bringing such tempestuous pleasure to - her mistress. And she was shocked again by the surge of erotic excitement she derived from framing such a notion.

She wondered if this wasn't what she had sought all along - to belong to someone, to abandon herself to another's domination and welcome its expression whether in pain or pleasure.

Wasn't this the truth?

"Why not come and work for us?" Awina had declared that first evening, soon after she had welcomed Vee into the luxurious flat. "It sounds as though you need to disappear for a while. Where better than Makamba? Your spiritual home," she had grinned teasingly. She had even mentioned a salary - more than double what she could ever hope to earn as a teacher even if she were ever to qualify. "And lots of other perks," Awina told her. "Free bed - " another salcaious chuckle - " and free board, clothing and travel. You'll want for nothing."

In the next few hectic days, and nights, Vee speculated privately on the nature of her duties. To be a sexual slave? A source of sexual diversion for Awina and her lover - and anyone else she might choose to lease Vee's favours to? And if so, Vee had blushingly questioned herself, had she the will, or the desire, to say no? But it was not as a sexual toy that she was to be employed. That facet of the relationship appeared to have been assumed from the start as something separate and perfectly acceptable on Vee's part. Which was understandable,

Vee conceded, for she had indeed raised no objections along the way, even to the corporal punishment meted out to her.

And now, thinking about it, she grew hot with shame at this clear indication of Awina's intimate knowledge of her nature. A knowledge which she herself was only just groping towards.

"Don't be fooled by her howls for mercy," a panting Awina told Victor one night, as she wielded a short handled whip consisting of many bootlace-thin strands of rubber which sent dapples of glowing fire all over Vee's quivering bottom. "She loves it, don't you, little stick insect?"

Some twenty lashes had already smacked down on her buttocks and thighs and Vee was lost in a swirling mist of savage pleasure.

"Don't you, little stick insect!?" Awina had persisted.

"Yes!" Vee had sobbed.

The short pause in the beating had allowed Awina to get her breath back and she had laid on another twenty with renewed vigour.

Her 'job' - the work she was to be paid such handsome wages for - was, in Awina's words, to be 'a spy.'

"Since we won our glorious victory," Awina had told her on another occasion, the sarcasm evident in her tone, "we've been given all kinds of goodies. "She nodded at her own and Victor's naked bodies. "You see our black northern asses everywhere in government these days. And in the armed forced - look at our gallant leader, Mavumbi. Second only to the Chief of Staff - and of course our beloved Prersident himself. But there is a lot going on underneath the surface. We must be vigilant. There are even rumours of plotted coups. Of a purge to get rid of all our black faces again. There is even a strong belief that a counter coup might take place. That Mavumbi himself and certain army officers might take over."

Her sneering tone faded, her lovely face scowled heavily. "If it's true, I know nothing about it. Even though I once shared his bed. Until you kicked me out of it, you and that Danish milk cow of yours!"

She grinned and Vee blushed deeply. "I had - we had no choice - it - "

"I know," Awina taunted. "I know how much you hated it. I used to hear your screams every night. Of delight!" She brushed Vee's protest aside. "Never mind. I think our general will do what serves him best. At the moment he is content with his share of the pot. But we have to know these things. Don't we, Victor?"

"But how can I - help?" Vee enquired, her heart quickening.

Awina grinned, winked. "You'd be surprised. A pretty girl like you. And a white. You know our menfolk's attraction to white meat." Vee stared at her in mounting horror. "You just keep your pretty little eyes and ears open." She sniggered. "And maybe your legs, too, if you get the chance. Don't worry. It will be easy. You're a natural, isn't she, Victor?"

So that was it! She was to be used as a prostitute for VIP's! But Awina reassured her. "You'll have some sort of liason role, with us. You just attend parties and things. Like I say - keep your ears open. Pass on anything we need to know. Don't worry, little bald one. I'll keep you busy most of the time." She flung her arms around the troubled figure, wrestled her to the floor and stretched her lithe frame over the supine Vee. Her actions, more than her words, did much to comfort Vee, and helped to drive cloudy speculations about the future from her mind.

She was amazed at the ease with which papers were obtained and travel documents got ready. Painfully, she agreed with Awina's directions that she should simply lie low until the flight, contact no one. She lay on her bed one afternoon - Awina was busy in the last flurry of diplomatic activity before they left - and fought against her powerful urge to pick up the phone and let David know what was to happen. The change that had come over her, the hasty plans and the hectic sexual activity which occupied her for so much of the time, had been good for her, she acknowledged. But it had not stopped her private thoughts and regrets altogether. And although already it seemed a world away she vividly recalled her one and only loving with her 'brother', and - her body blazed at the outrageous thought - his wife.

To her disgust, she found her vivid imagination working fertilely, seeing their newly discovered bodies making love to each other. She found, even more disgustingly, her own fingers sliding up her nylon leg, bunching up her skirt as she caressed the moist silk of her pulsing crotch. However, somehow she had resisted at least the temptation to get in touch, if not the urgent need to touch herself. And the diversions on hand with Awina's return were powerful enough to block thoughts of anything but the immediate present.

Suddenly, with a jolt that brought her shooting upright, with a strange little wiggle, and a scissoring movement of her thighs, one of those diversions made itself felt in the departure lounge of the airport. The fiercely tingling electric buzz pulsated deep within her vagina, and she gave a few agitated, short steps, a glow of colour rising to her cheeks. She glanced across pleadingly, and saw Awina's deeply dimpling smile. She was holding the small black plastic object in her hand, making no effort to hide it, and pointing it at her, with a wicked grin. Her thumb pressed, and Vee gave a smothered gasp, did another shuffling little step, and prayed that no one else was observing her too closely.

The deep pulsing died, but she could feel the intrusive smoothness blocking her narrow passage. At the same time, because of the involuntary nipping of her buttocks at the electric charge, she felt the even more intrusive presense of the heavy steel balls, two of them, which were jammed in the even tighter orifice of her anus. Awina crooked a finger, beckoning her, and Vee went over to her, with mincing little steps, like a model on a catwalk.

"Just testing, little stick insect. Making sure you're still with us."

The device, which Awina had produced the previous day, was a cigar shaped plastic object, with tiny raised pimples over its surface. It was about three inches in length, and at one end fanned out into a circular disc - a safety device which was to stop the instrument from disappearing within the vaginal passage. This disc fitted over the entrance, resting on the outer labia and showing only a small dark shield a few centimetres across. The electric charge it gave off was activated by a remote control as small as the device fitted to a car key ring for locking the doors. Awina and Victor had had a lot of fun testing out the range of this instrument. The rousing throb against her most sensitive flesh made it both thrilling and something of an ordeal for Vee, especially in public places, for it was virtually impossible for her to keep still when it was in operation.

The added refinement of the insertion of the metallic balls into her anus caused her even more distress. They were joined by a piece of cord, and a longer length of the same cord dangled like an obscene little mouse's tail from the puckered little hole to enable them to be withdrawn - a sensation which made Vee shudder and gasp with a feeling she could scarcely classify. The prospect of being thus fitted throughout the eight hour flight to Makamba was daunting. Especially as, already in the VIP lounge, Awina was demonstrating a devilish delight in tormenting her.

"Please!" Vee begged, in genuine distress. "I can't - I won't be able to walk if - if you keep - "

Her pleas merely whetted Awina's sadistic appetite to see her, so literally, squirm. All the way out to the plane, and after they were seated, Vee in the middle between Awina and Victor, the dark girl kept zapping her for long squirming seconds before her thumb eased its pressure, and Vee slumped back in quaking relief. Once the meal had been served, and they were reclining beneath their blankets in their first class seats, Awina subjected her to such a steady electronic burst that soon Vee's hands were clenched into knotted fists on the arm rests, her pale shorn head rocking from side to side on the pillow, her face twisted with emotion. Her knees jerked up, and also moved from side to side so vigorously that they threatened to dislodge the blanket completely. Red faced, she gazed helplessly at the smiling figure on her left, no longer caring what an observer might think of her outlandish behaviour.

"Oh God!" she gasped. "Please stop! I can't bear it!" And indeed, the insustently humming purr, the friction on the sensitive walls of her palpatating sheath, and the area above, where her enflamed clitoris beat madly, was driving her to distraction.

She almost wept with relief when the tingling discharge ceased, and she slumped in her seat, her thighs still shaking. Then she felt her own throbbing arousal, still unappeased, felt the intrusive heaviness of the object, and the unpleasantly clinging wetness of the strip of silk at her crotch.

"Take Vee to the choo," Awina grinned across her at Victor, as though she were referring to an infant. "I think she needs seeing to." She nudged Vee. "You can take your toys out. We might be buggering up the plane's instruments. Victor will give you a hand with your balls!"

She blushed for shame, and again when the smart cabin attendant looked at them with a knowing smirk before they locked themselves into the small lavatory. And she actually cried at her humiliation when Victor gently teased out the two coated and pungent spheres from her backside. But the tears were for relief, as well. When the remote control vibrator had also been removed and hastily rinsed then stowed in her handbag, she slipped off her tights and wet knickers and added them to the sex aids.

Victor was sitting on the lavatory, trousers round his ankles, and his brown cock thrusting upright like a soldier on parade. Vee climbed aboard, straddling him and lowering herself with a groan onto his hot, beating memner, which sank at once to the hilt in her well lubricated passage. "You can't beat the real thing, eh?" he grinned, his lips brushing her exposed ear.

Vee grunted, the short band of leather skirt like a belt round her waist, her buttocks jouncing as she rode him wildly to the climax already sending its fluttering cohorts in advance of the conquering hordes.

CHAPTER NINETEEN

There was none of the tiresome waiting in line at Immigration and Customs which had been such a feature of her former arrival in Makamba. This time they were whisked through in minutes. Just as well, for Vee felt as though she were naked, with nothing other than herself under the brief leather mini-skirt. She hardly dared nod her head for fear of revealing too much. When they climbed into the back of the government Mercedes, she tugged desperately at the front of the tiny garment. Her bare bottom and the backs of her thighs clung stickily to the leather of the seat, and she pushed her hand down desperately between her thighs, glancing in an agony of embarrassment in the rear view mirror. She felt the stinging soreness of her sex. The sensitive walls of her vagina were irritated by the hours of having that diabolical instrument inserted. And then, after the strenuous coupling with Victor in the toilet, when she had once more settled down exhaustedly under the blanket in her comfortable seat, Awina had insisted on toying with her vulva, squeezing and teasing under the fragile concealment until Vee was once again in a twisting frenzy of excitement, this time unrelieved, so that she was glad when, at last, in the dazzling blood orange of a magnificent sunrise, the plane banked over the vast bronze waters of the great lake and skimmed in low for thr airport runway at its shore.

The dream-like sensation, heightened by her sleepless night, gripped her again as she stared out of the car windows. There it all was - the brightly burnished sky, the vivid colours of the plants, the clustered banana fronds and tall Indian corn, the chocolate huts, the bright splashes of colour of the women's dresses, the splendidly sculpted bodies of the youths and men, half naked, or seen through the carelessly worn ragged clothing.

"Good to be back, eh?" Awina said, catching her look. She slipped an arm around her, pulled her close, and kissed her ear, ignoring the furtive glances of the driver.

"Yes," Vee murmured shyly. Her heart was thudding,

remembering all that had happened to her here. And Keith was still here, making even more of a success, one of the leading lights of the large international company which employed him. Would they meet? she wondered. Did she want to see him again? The hollow guts, the speeding pulse, answered her all too clearly. But she was still so unsure about her role here. She had fallen in so readily with Awina's plans, and already become such an intimate part of the bizzare set up involving Victor, that she felt almost a prisoner once more, as if nothing could happen to her that was not of their making, or without their consent.

It was a feeling that was confirmed from the moment of their arrival at the well appointed bungalow, in its high hedged, beautifully kept gardens, which was Awina's residence. It was on the gentle slopes of a hill on the northern edge of the capital, part of the diplomatic quarter and one of the exclusive white areas in the bad old colonial days.

"Come on. Bath time," Awina said. A maid in the pastel shaded overall, complete with headscarf, which was a universal iniform for household servants, called out a cheerful greeting, scuttling ahead of them.

"This is Memsa'ab Vee," Awina announced. "Rafiki yangu." Vee recognised the Swahili phrase. My friend. That was one way of putting it, she thought wryly. Awina was already stripping off her clothes, tossing then onto the floor all around her, while the maid, whose name was Miriamu, was filling the wide, sunken bath tub in the gleaming luxury of the large bathroom.

"Come on," Awina snapped impatiently. "Get your gear off. What's left of it. Then we'll catch a few hours sleep. I don't have to report it until later this afternoon."

The young maid giggled at their nakedness, but Awina

171

acted as though she were not there. She settled into the foam, reached eagerly for Vee's tired body.

"Come here. Let's get warmed up a little. You can finish me off in bed. Then it's sleep, you hear? You sex mad white whore!"

It did not come as any real surprise to Vee to learn that she did indeed have no control over her life. Awina slipped naturally into her position as superior - it was, Vee acknowledged, simply a continuation of their roles of the previous week, in the Mayfair apartment. She gave orders as simply and directly as she had done in the days when Vee had been the hostage of the rebel army, and clearly assumed that Vee was there to obey. And Vee did so. After all, she told herself, what else could she do? She had really known when she agreed to return to Makamba that that was how it would be. That first afternoon, when the car came to take Awina to the city, she reached out, right there in the presence of the grinning houseboy and the sniggering Miriamu, and slipped Vee's silk robe off her shoulders, exposing her pale nakedness.

"You can start working on your tan," she told the blushing figure. She nodded at the long flagged terrace, where the heavy sun loungers were scattered. "Miriamu will rub the lotion on for you. She's good at that, aren't you?" The maid giggled louder. "And don't worry about Moussa or any of the shamba boys. They're all first class. You can show them your bare arse. No problem."

That evening Awina declared, her dark eyes shining with mischief. "We're having a welcome back dinner for you tonight. Just a few friends to meet you. Colleagues, you might say. And who knows? There might be one or two familiar faces among them."

172

Her words made Vee more than a little anxious. "Does it have to be tonight?" She murmured diffidently. "I'm still feeling a bit jet-lagged - "

She shrieked at the sudden violence with which Awina's arm shot out, and the vice like grip of her fingers in the back of Vee's neck. She pulled her so close their noses bumped.

"Hey, little stick insect!" the African hissed, through closed teeth. "Don't forget who you are, baby! You're mine, right? You belong to me, understand?" The fingers tightened again, so that Vee whimpered. She nodded. Awina flung her back onto the bed, and delivered a resounding slap across the top of her thigh. The handprint stood out, a livid brand of burning red. Then she smiled, turned to the large wardrobe and selected a very skimpy dress, with a strap to tie at the back of the neck. It was made from a thin silk, with a multi-hued print of flowers. She tossed it at Vee, who was still sprawled on the covers, tremble lipped, massaging her throbbing flesh. She was given no underclothes to go with the dress, and she knew better than to get some for herself from the drawers where her woown clothes had been laid. When she put it on, its soft caress of her body seemed to emphasise the nakedness beneath. It was scooped low at the back, and the gathered bodice dipped to reveal a generous amount of cleavage. She guessed that, from the side, an onlooker would probably get a fairly comprehensive view of an unfettered breast, but then she had a sinking feeling that they would be getting that, and more, before the long night was out.

Once more, Awina made her up personally, with that chalk white visage, those dramatically huge eyes, etched in black, the long stark curves of the eyebrows. To complete the sensation of servility, Awina produced a necklet of dull metal.

It was about an inch thick, and fitted Vee's slenderness like a choker. Awina's nimble fingers fastened it on her.

"Isn't there a leash?" Vee could not help asking.

Awina chuckled good naturedly. "Of course. But I thought we'd keep that for later." How much later? Vee wondered, but, wisely, she held her tongue.

Vee grew more and more nervous as she saw that the guests were all male, and all from the northern tribes. One or two smiled and said, "It's good to see you back again, Mrs Green." She realised they had been members of the rebel force, and blushed embarrassedly at failing to recognise them.

"You know what these whites are like," Awina said sarcastically. "They say they can't tell the difference between one black face and another. Or black cock," she added, to Vee's mortification. She turned to Vee with a cruel smile. "But you'll have a chance to prove me wrong later, sweetheart." The words terrified Vee so much she was hardly able to concentrate on what was said to her, or to enjoy the sumptuous meal to which they sat down on the long veranda.

The time passed in drinking and chatting, until the edge of Vee's fear was dulled a little. It was like any elegant dinner party anywhere, she acknowledged. Not that she had been to may of those since leaving Makamba. But then, when they had moved back inside, to the comfortable living room, Awina called for attention.

"Now in honour of our guest's return to our country, I think we should give her a chance to stroll down memory lane and meet a few old friends. Right?"

Vee's limbs turned to water, her bowels seemed to melt. She rose nervelessly when Awina plucked her up, dragged her forward.

"Let's make her comfortable first. Here, little stick

insect. You asked for a leash. Here it is." She produced a chain about a yard long, with a large ring fastener at one end, which she clipped to the metal round Vee's neck. She used this to propel her over to the long, low coffee table. "But first we must make her feel really at home. And you know how to do that, don't you?"

A deeper cheer went up as, with a swift tug, Awina sent Vee tottering forward on her high heels, her shins banging painfully against the rim of the polished table. Hands grabbed and she was flung face down, stretched over its surface, her feet kicking in the air. The shoes were gone, and in a trice the flimsy, short skirt of the material was whisked away from her bottom, baring the pale cheeks to everyone's view. The long legs kicked out helplessly, to her audience's cheering delight. Awina stood at her head, holding the chain, exerting such pressure that Vee could not move to lift herself free of the gleaming surface. She ceased struggling. Weeping softly, she laid her cheek down on the cool wood, her behind clenching as she awaited what she knew would be a painful thrashing.

But it was to be a prolonged and tormenting interlude.

"Do the honours, would you, Victor?" Awina asked, hauling tight on the leash. The tugging at her neck prevented Vee from turning, not that she had any wish to do so. She therefore had no idea of what her instrument of chastisemnet was to be. It turned out to be the whip with its many rubber thongs. And Victor's first strokes were so gentle to be almost a parody of a flogging, so that Vee was even more tense. mocked by these gently stinging stroked that fell on her quivering backside.

"Oh, come one!" Awina cried. "That's no good, is it, Vee, my love? She likes to have her arse whipped properly.

175

Why do you think these whores have such tight arses? They like to see their cheeks blush. Put some back into it, man!"

Victor apologised. The next blow was heavier, stung sharply, and Vee flinched. She gasped. The stinging spread, and with it the stirring in her belly which shamed her with its strength. Then the blows became harder still, falling with an audible hiss, and her belly and hips squirmed more violently, her limbs sawed the air, and she began to whimper, then howl. The pale skin was covered with a myriad of thin red lines, as though a cat had been scratching at its surface. The severity of the blows increased again, and Vee yelped, her shorn head lifting, until she felt the tug of the metal circlet holding her down. Her bottom was afire now, the crimson glow more general, darker, her writhing movements more frenzied. "Please! Stop! Oh - ow! No!"

She was sobbing wildly, and Victor was genuinely short of breath when the whipping came to an end, once more at Awina's nod. Vee hung there until she was dragged upright by the chain. Head down, blinded by her tears, she stood, legs slightly apart, and massaged the throbbing cheeks.

"That's better. Now she really does feel at home, eh, Vee?" A vicious tug on the chain. "Eh, Vee?"

"Yuh - yes," stammered the wretched figure, shuffling miserably.

"Now for the bit you've been waiting for. Let's see if she's forgotten her old friends."

There was a roar as Awina pulled Vee over to a long couch, like a Chesterfield, which had been dragged out from the wall. Vee, who had been lost in her shame and misery, now looked about her in fresh alarm. "Oh, please - don't!" she begged, as hands thrust her down, spread her limbs wide.

"Just a minute! She can't enjoy it dressed like that.

She's not used to it, are you, lamb?" Awina's voice rang with mockery. Her fingers gave one tug at the nape of the slender neck and the dress fell from the heaving breasts. The silk was whipped down over the legs and she lay naked, thighs held open for the invasion to come. She gasped as suddenly her vision was cut off. A large velvet mask was fitted over her eyes and tied securely behind her head. She felt her tears soaking into the softly clinging material. She waited tensely in what seemed to be a sudden quiet. The hands at her ankles and wrists were withdrawn. Only that pressure of the chain at her neck remained.

Automatically, her knees jerked together, were drawn up towards her chest, at the feel of a hand fondling at her sex. Fingers probed with clumsy gentleness, uncertainty, and she felt the quiver of response at their stirring touch, the novelty of her blindness, the merciless publicity of her humiliation, peversely adding to the thrill she felt. I can't help it! she sobbed to herself as she felt that flowering, unfolding sensation of the moist lips of her vulva at this stranger's touch. Stranger? A familiar face, Awina had taunted. Who? She stared up, into the blackness, visualising her unknown assailant - lover? - her white body, stretched out, bathed in the lamp light, ready, throbbing with urgent desire.

There was a pressure on the upholstery, it moved as someone took his place, then hands no longer gentle grabbed at her, seized her thighs and pulled them roughly open, and up, to fit around a thrusting body which was still clothed. she felt the rub of cloth on the insides of her limbs, then the stab of a prick, the smearing wetness from its helm as it jabbed at the crack of her vulva, stabbed over the bareness of her mons, gained a fractional entrance to her slippery divide, funneling to the beating entrance of her sheath. Frantically now her hands scrabbled between their pressing bodies, met large, unsure hands, then guided the thick, sturdy column of his penis properly into her. Her reddened buttocks, the soreness ignored now, shuffled and lifted. She felt his hardness prod and slide firmly into her and the fierce grip of her welcoming sex as they went into the heaving drive of the fucking. Her legs came up, folding him in, her feet slid along smooth cloth, her heels dug into his plunging form.

She began to grunt, pulled along on the inexorable ride, the tingling darts spreading until the final, rushing, rutting madness took her into the orgasms, and she impaled herself on his hardness, mashed herself up into him, her head flung back, the cry of release deep in her throat, her tender skin chafed under the collar by her movement, its painfulness entirely unnoticed in the splendid savagery of her climax. Seconds later, mercifully he too, spasmed and pumped his come into her before he collapsed, crushing her, his breath thundering in her ear.

Thought came only when she felt the brutal withdrawal, the cold, stinging emptiness, the dragging out of her, the seeping dribble of his discharge. Overwhelmed by her public shame, she sobbed blindly, further soaking the velvet which clung sealingly to her and for which she was grateful now, cutting her off as it did from the scene of her degradation.

Now the cheers, the laughter and sighs of release which rose all about her reminded her of just how cruelly public the coupling had been. Not for the first time, she was stunned by the perfidy of her own flesh, which could take away all such considerations from her, blot out her very mind itself in the force of physical sensation. Nothing, not the sounds of the onlookers, the biting mockery of Awina, the tug and rub of the chain at her neck, or the stinging reminders of her punishment from her reddened buttocks, could be more painful than her own disgust at the depravity her own physical appetite was capable of. She felt at these moments that no words of condemnation, no blows, could be hard enough to punish her fully.

The after tremors of her climax were still pulsing faintly when she felt the tug at her neck again, and Awina's voice close to her ear. "Come on then. Who was it? Who was the old chum you've just got so well aquainted with again?"

The shame was complete now, Vee thought, as she shook her head helplessly. She had no idea, not one clue. She relived the plunging invasion, the feel of that ramrod cock hammering at her, and, sobbingly, she admitted to herself that she had no inkling who had just fucked her. Victor? Who else? Any one of a hundred others who had been in the rebel camp? How on earth could she possibly tell, she who had been serviced by scores in her time - faceless pricks, she lashed herself now. Mavumbi? Surely not? Such a big man, a bwana mkubwa, would not stop to put on a public exhibition like this? Besides, he was big literally. That very process of trying to recall brought fresh tears of scalding shame to her blinded eyes.

She could not stop her crazily spinning brain. Who? Her huge sergeant? It was the memory of him which had led her to the start of her present throubles. For hadn't Waynes's hunking frame reminded her powerfully of her rebel sergeant? But, like Mavumbi, the size of his body, as well as his member, surley ruled him out as her unknown lover?

Crazier thoughts occupied her helpless brain. Gerard? Dragged back from God knows where, forced like her to parade himself in this degrading spectacle. Keith? Her brain seemed to slip gear. Would she really fail to recognise her own husband in sude intimate circumstances? Would he really take part in this animal like charade? "I don't know!" she suddenly

179

howled, tossing and twisting her blind head like some tortured animal, jerking the chain that tethered her. "I don't know!" She collapsed, her entire frame shaken by the depth of her anguished weeping.

Awina, her conscience cut by this naked display of grief and shame, acted quickly. She pulled off the soaking blindfold. "Never mind!" she said, a hint of the remorse she felt in her clipped tone. "Say hello to your old chum."

Vee, the make-up weirdly streaking her face, her eyes swimming in tears, stared up, slowly made out the smiling, embarrassed features, the thin shape of - Edward! Their youthful guard, and one time husband of Katya, who had been given to him after the initiation. "We - we never - did it," Vee muttered foolishly, sprawling open limbed on the couch.

"You could have fooled ne!" Awina answered crisply now, having recovered her poise after her momentary lapse. "Let's say you just made up for a hell of a lot of lost time, eh?"

CHAPTER TWENTY

Vee sat in the back of the car, and fingered the heavy earring which dangled from her right ear. It was a perfectly plain circle, of the same dull metal as her necklet. The fact that there was no matching companion made it feel odder still. "Like a boy!" Awina had giggled, when she had first fitted it to her. But Vee knew she was not joking when she told her, "No, there's only the one. In your right ear. That's the mark of a slave, my dear."

And Vee had felt that little shiver, that frisson of both dread and erotic arousal at the forthright expression of her status. For that was just what she was. The three weeks she had spent here had convinced her. A pampered slave, in many ways.

180

A luxury bungalow, with all the comforts of modern civilisation. Servants, and a priviledged lifestyle far in excess of what she had been used to back in Britain. But a lifestyle of utter subservience, subjected to a regime which included severe physical punishment and complete sexual domination by her lovely partner. Owner would be a more truthful term for her, Vee admitted.

As now, for example. Here she was, sitting alone in the back of the car, with Edward as her driver and her watch dog. Delivering her to the figure who still inspired a quivering fear in her that was turning her insides to liquid. She had met Mavumbi at one of the many intimate evening functions at the bungalow. She had been paraded naked in front of him, he had watched her being beaten, though he had not laid a finger, or anything else, on her personally. She had a feeling that was to be rectified in the immediate future, for she was on her way now to his army headquarters, being delivered at Awina's bidding for his personal pleasure.

"Make sure you please him, little stick insect. We want you to make sure he will want to make use of you again. We want you to become part of the scene at his little soirees. And make sure you please his friends, too. Be hot for them. As I told you, keep your ears open as well as your cunt, my sweet. It will take some time, but eventually you will hear things. Things that might be very useful to us. Don't forget, that's what you are paid for. You are not a whore. You're a government servant."

No, not a whore, Vee had thought, but certainly a slave. As you knew all along, from the moment you accepted Awina's offer, her conscience argued mercilessly. And doesn't it turn you on, you little perv?

At these moments, though, when her fear took over,

she found herself wishing profoundly that she had not sold herself into this bondage, for all the hectic pleasures she undoubtedly found in Awina's arms.

She studied the back of Edward's head. His eyes caught hers in the mirror and he smiled reassuringly. Poor boy. He probably had a massive hard on right now, his balls aching for her. But they had not so much as kissed after that public coupling on her first night. It was a revelation of the sadism in Awina's character that she had appointed him as Vee's minder, her shadow. And with smiling instructions to both of them not to indulge in any sexual play whatsoever. "Not a quick grope or gobble, kiss or cuddle, feel or fuck!" She admonished them poetically. It was a testament to her power over them that neither of them had made a move to disobey her.

They talked though, Edward had plied her with eager questions about Katya, but Vee had to confess that she knew nothing of her. It still hurt to recall the young couple's hysterical grief when she and Vee had been so suddenly uprooted, flung into the back of the Land Rover and told they were on their way to freedom. A freedom which the wildly sobbing and newly pregnant Danish girl had all at once not wanted. Her distress had matched that of Edward himself, who had been forcibly restrained, and punished severely, Vee learnt, after the hostages had departed.

"Her parents made her have an abortion," Vee told him. "I didn't even say goodbye to her properly. And I haven't heard since. I wrote a couple of times." Her voice tailed off, not wanting to hurt him further. But it saddened her a little - Edward now seemed philosophically resigned to the situation.

"Yes. It would have been difficult," he said. "I am married now. To a girl of my tribe. We must have a child."

And life goes on, Vee mused. She hoped Katya would

find her happiness. She still felt the strong tremor of desire when she recalled the girl's Nordic beauty. But now she had other considerations to occupy her. She even had a new name, for Awina had stated that she should assume a new identity.

"We've decided." Awina informed her, while Vee secretly wondered who the 'we' was that her mistress constantly referred to, "that it would be better if as few people as possible know who you really are. Fortunately, there are only a handful of people, all of them in our department, who know the truth. And they won't say anything. We've even thought of a new name for you. New papers. Everything." She grinned mischievously. "You can keep the same initials. From now on you're Vicky Waters."

Victor laughed. "We put a lot of thought into it. Victoria Waters. Because many men - and ladies - will fall for you. Or refresh themselves by plunging into your turbulent surface."

"Or you might be known as VW," Awina mocked. "A very popluar ride for very many people."

"What's the saying in English?" Victor tool up the taunting. "A good goer, isn't that it?"

Vee stared about her with mounting anxiety. Deeply conscious of her nudity beneath her short, flowery dress she had alighted outside the guard office inside the military compound and, after a final wave at Edward, had followed the soldier, who led her past hordes of staring army personnel, through a maze of corridors, to an office where a uniformed female was sitting at a desk. Curtly directed to take a seat, Vee obeyed, crossing her legs and hastily smoothing down the thin material over her thighs. She was uncomfortably aware of how incongruous her brief mini and five inch heels seemed in this martial atmosphere. Nor could she ignore the hostile contempt in the glaring stare of the girl at the desk.

"Follow me," At last, Vee had been sitting for over an hour and she rose with some relief, in spite of her uneasiness. Again, she passed through a chain of corridors, across an asphalt courtyard, then through a gate guarded by a sentry. The female, whose ample breasts strained against the khaki shirt, and whose broad behind stretched the denim slacks she wore, paused to chat to the sentry, who turned and treated Vee to a slow, insolent stare, from her shorn head to her pointed toes. They both laughed, then he nodded them through.

The change in scenery was startling. They were now in a large and well tended garden, with neat gravel paths running at angles through its billiard smooth greenery and vivid flower beds, brightly in bloom even though it was the hottest period of the dry season, just before the short rains of April. The building they headed for was long and low, with white walls and a red tiled roof, in the style of the old colonial administration buildings. It had a wide veranda running the length of its frontage, with a newly painted white wooden railing. Vee followed her guide up the steps.

It was clear that this was some kind of officers' mess. The girl led her into a small reception area, where a white coated steward came forward. The girl muttered something and left without another glance at Vee. "This way, madam," the steward murmured politely. She followed him into a lounge, with deep arm chairs and couches. One or two men in uniform were scattered about, chatting or reading. She blushed as she felt all eyes turn inquisitively in her direction. She sat at the steward's invitation, keenly regretting the fact that she was not wearing underwear, and striving to make sure she did not advertise the fact as she settled herself in the deep cushions. She was certainly showing enough leg, that was for sure.

"A drink, madam?"

She ordered a soft drink and sat sipping, sneaking surreptitious glances around her. Once again, she found herself wondering what would happen if she came across someone she had known formerly. So often she had fantasised about bumping into Keith again somewhere, though it seemed that as her movements were to be restricted it was extremely unlikely that that would happen. She wondered if Awina's joking speculation would be true.

"Even if you do meet your ex-hubby, he won't know you. Can't you see just how completely different you look now? I think we'd better fix it for you to see him again, just to prove my point!" How Vee's heart had raced at those words, even though she told herself that Awina was not being serious at all.

Her musings were interrupted. "Are you all right, madam? May I be of any assistance?" She looked up in alarm. The speaker was a tall figure, dressed in an impeccable drill uniform, complete with shining leather belt and Sam Browne. His complexion, a deep golden toast hue, showed that he belonged to the predominant central tribe which had formed the bulk of the civil service and practically all the other important posts in both government and the private sector after independence. It was their superiority which had sparked off the revolt among the northerners in which Vee herself had become embroiled. An almost full scale war had been waged until, with behind the scenes help from former colonial powers, a compromise had been reached and the northerners given a larger and more equitable slice of the many profitable pies in all sections of the society.

"I'm fine, thank you. I'm waiting for someone." Vee blushed and squeezed her thighs tightly together, desperately afraid that if he sat down opposite her he would see that she had no knickers on. Not for the first time, she cursed Awina for making her wear such an abbreviated dress. But she was saved from her quandary by a bellowing roar, which she recognised at once.

"Get your bloody lecherous eyes off her, you bastard, Mulinge! Find your own white meat!"

The voice was Mavumbi's. He came bounding across, his black face shining, his great bulk straining the smart uniform. Vee saw the pained look on the other's face, who could not disguise his comtempt.

"Sorry, sir," the unknown captain answered stiffly. "I was just making sure our guest was comfortable." He stood to attention and clicked his heels, bowing his head towards Vee with old fashioned courtesy. He turned away at once.

"We know what you were after, you horny bastard!" Mavumbi roared. There was a chorus of laughter from the group around him, who had followed him in and who were all, like himself, northerners. It seemed that this little exchange was a microcosm of the divisions which split this society, in spite of the peace which now officially existed between north and south. The newcomers were rowdy, as though their brash display was a challenge to the other members of the mess, who kept themselves conspicuously apart.

Vee struggled awkwardly to her feet, all too conscious of the several pointed stares at her limbs as she did so, And they had plenty to look at, she reflected uncomfortably. She stood, blushing and ignored, while Mavumbi bellowed out orders for drinks. He had not greeted her, scarcely glanced at her. She waited, trembling, recalling the many times he had summoned her to stand naked before him before being ordered to carry out some sexual task. Often he made use of both her and Katya together, forcing them both to arouse him, with

186

mouths and hands, before he chose one of them to couple with. Now, after a long pull at his beer glass which left a ring of white foam on his upper lip, his dark eyes rested on her briefly.

"Jackson. Take her down to the gym. Get her ready,"

A young looking officer, clearly junior, stepped forward. Obediently, she followed Jackson out through a door, feeling all eyes, including those of the group gathered at the far end of the bar, fixed on her as she left.

She was led along a lengthy corridor, and through the double doors at its end. Her escort switched on the overhead lights and she saw she was in a well equipped gymnasium, with the usual equipment scattered around, its perimeter lined with the parallel rows of wall bars. Jackson directed her over its wooden floor to a small side room. It was a changing room, with benches, a row of showers at one end, and metal lockers. Frome one of these, Jackson extracted a small bundle and pushed it into Vee's hands.

"Put these on," he said.

She stared down in confusion. She thought he had given her a pair of sheer stockings, or tights, but opening up the transparent material, she saw that it was some kind of body stocking, a one piece garment meant to fit from shoulder to toes. He stood there, grinning evilly, and she stared back aghast.

"You want some help?" he growled, and his hands reached for her.

"No!" she gasped. Struggling hard not to cry, she shrugged off the dress, and stepped out of her shoes, feeling his gaze taking in every inch of her nude frame.

It was not easy to fit the clinging, gauze material to her. She had to sit on the bench, and begin with the feet, easing in her toes, drawing up the mesh, careful not to snag and cause a ladder in its fineness. She stood, smoothed it up over her calves and knees, her thighs, knowing he was watching every move and thoroughly enjoying the private show. Then she gasped anew. There was a large opening, then another, spanned only by a narrow band of the material. When she eased it into place, she saw that the area of her crotch was bare, and her bottom, also. And, as she squirmed to work the tight flimsiness up over stomach and shoulders, she found there were two more holes, through which her breasts poked.

She looked ridiculous, she thought, when at last the garment was on. The gaping holes through which these intimate parts of her anatomy showed palely looked ludicrous. The rest of her could be seen through the dark mistiness of the nylon mesh.

"Come." Jackson led her back into the gym. He glanced about, then moved to the centre of the room and manipulated some long ropes which hung from the high ceiling beams. They had large rings on their lower ends. While Vee stood in confused amazement he tied her wrists securely to two of the rings then adjusted the ropes until she was stretching high up, her arms extended above her, and her feet raised up on her toes. She had to spread her legs as far as the tension would allow her, to keep her teetering balance. The strain lifted her rib cage, sucked in her belly, and left her breasts tautened, thrusting pertly as though she were proffering them for inspection, or for some other delights.

"Don't go away," he grinned. She turned her head, and staggered, swaying. He went out and left her hanging there, alone. She could feel the pull on every muscle, and soon she was weeping softly, the tears trickling down, to fall on her breasts or her feet. In spite of her fear, she found herself hoping that they would not leave her dangling here for too long, the discomfort was too intense. But it seemed a cruelly long interval before she heard noisy laughter and approaching footsteps, and her heart accelerated with renewed fear.

They roared at the sight of her weirdly covered body, even more on display in this provocative garb, helplessly exhibited. They went into the changing room, where their noisy laughter continued. When they emerged they were all dressed in white football shorts only, over which their heavy bellies hung. They surrounded the weeping figure, closed in until Vee felt their rough hands grabbing and pinching at her flesh where it offered itself through the holes in the mesh stocking. The more she squealed and tried to wriggle away, the louder were their roars of laughter. But Mavumbi soon stopped them. "That's no good. She likes something a little more robust, don't you. Mrs Green?"

So much for keeping my identity a secret, Vee thought, but then her mind was diverted, powerfully so, by Mavumbi's idea of arousal. He was holding, appropriately enough for their surroundings, a canvas gym shoe. With a loud splat, he brought it smartly down on her left buttock and Vee screamed shrilly. She danced at the end of her rope, her nylon covered legs capering, jerking, while the red imprint of the dimpled sole leapt vividly to life on her pale skin.

The others wielded similar instruments. But two of them darted back to the changing rooms and returned with stout belts. They stood, one on each side of her, and took it in turns to crack the leather across her cheeks, and as she twisted and turned, head tossed back and howling wildly, she presented them with a glimpse of the rapidly reddening target area, which they swatted gleefully, until her bottom was one blaze of pain and she whimpered pitifully for them to cease. They did so only when both men were sweating and panting with effort, and she groaned with relief when she felt the intolerable pressure on her arms and shoulder muscles ease as someone slackened off the tension of the ropes.

She sank to her knees on the wooden flor, her head hung down and she sobbed abandonedly. When a hand jerked her head up again, she found herself gazing through tear filled eyes at the head of a huge penis, its pale mushroom helm, in contrast to the chocolate brown of the impressive shaft, hovering inches away from her parted lips. She could see the gleam of emission on the slit, which soon pressed against her, smearing her lips and chin with its slimy secretion. Thick fingers dug into her temples, held her by the ears and steered her face to the thrusting invasion.

Mavumbi, his massive thighs parted, knees slightly bent, fitted her head to his thrusting loins, and she licked and nibbled, sucked at that mighty glans, finally opening her mouth as wide as she could and taking in his driving length to the back of her throat, sucking violently, his salty girth filling her so that she feared she would choke. Her nostrils flared, the breath whistled through them, her breasts shook as she fought to breathe against the solid wedge of flesh stopping her. The great column of flesh scraped against her teeth as he withdrew, and she wheezed, drawing in some precious air before the mass plunged into her again, sealing off her working passage. Her neck was pushed back. It felt like a stalk about to snap against this relentless drive.

Her senses spun, she thought she must surely faint, but then came one mighty spasm, she felt the great muscle flex and swell up inside her, and the hot gush of his semen poured thickly into her throat. She swallowed convulsively, and then again as another surge flooded her. It spilt from the corners of her distended mouth, dribbled down her chin, then his thick flesh left her, and she was hanging, the ropy slime of the resi-

190

due dangling from her gasping lips, dropping thickly onto the valley of her breasts. The pressure was once again extreme on her shoulder muscles, pulled back as they were by her slumped stance. Then the head of his prick was being thrust comprehensively into her face, and she felt the gummy fluid spread thickly over her until she was sealed in its already cooling and tightening cover.

"Be my guests, gentlemen," his deep voice boomed. Dimly, she felt her wrists being released from their bonds, then she was borne aloft, carried across the floor and draped over the cold leather of a vaulting horse, face down, her head pointing towards the floor. Her legs were spread wide, and she felt the first stabbing burn of a prick entering her from behind. The fierce thrusts drove the breath from her, battered her belly against the hard surface under her. Involuntarily, she lifted her bottom, the abused cheeks nipping to contain the stabs of the prick ramming into her. It spent itself, and was immediately replaced by another, the whole process inhuman now. The agony was intense, but, even as her dizzy brain wondered if she would be able to stand much more of this torment, she felt those secret muscles spasming and she raised her flanks, pushing up against the pistoning drive of another rampant cock, her own urgent juices adding to the stream of fluids filling her sheath and flowing liberally over the whole raw area between her sprawling thighs.

CHAPTER TWENTY ONE

Vee had no idea how long she lay there, draped over the unyielding surface of the horse, her rump raised and darkly clad nylon legs obscenely spread. She was incapable of movement, and, for a time, incapable almost of feeling, other than the numb despair which drifted over her mind like a black fog. Pain returned gradually. The fierce cramps of her belly, the ache of muscles, the raw throb of her vaginal passage, the tenderness of the swollen lips of her vulva. Then, as an underlying theme to the mainstream of her suffering, the burning sting of her bottom, whose surface was liberally crimsoned with the blows which had rained down on her.

She was still summoning up the will power to move when she heard a noise behind her and flinched in renewed dread. But Edward's anxious visage appeared, and she sobbed with relief.

"They have finished," he said. "They told me to take you."

She accepted his help gratefully, unmindful of the sorry spectacle she presented. She could feel the sweat coldly gathered under the fine mesh of the nylon, which had become wrinkled and twisted with the violent treatment she had received. With Edward's arms around her waist and shoulders, she stumbled to the changing room, fortunately still deserted. The cement floor was still wet where her persecutors had showered.

With clumsy care, Edward eased and unrolled the body stocking from her, his big hands gentle as they rolled the damp material down her hips and her long legs, dragging it from her feet. She did not register the fact of his nudity until she found herself in his arms under the blessedly soothing hot water of the shower. And now she shivered responsively at the caress of his hands as they rubbed the foamy lather over her, from her shoulders down, his palms brushing against the hard little nipples, delving into the crevices of her behind, the puffed divide of her labia, working the fragrant soap into her skin, all the way down to her feet, washing away the pain and the degradation of what had happened.

Overcome with gratitude at the sight of his woolly black skull, agleam with the droplets of water as he knelt in front of her, she encircled the round head and pulled him impulsively to her, thrusting her belly against him. His face nuzzled worshipfully, and suddenly his mouth was working, his lips nibbling, and the pale tongue lapping strongly at the swollen sex lips. His thumbs were gentle still as they prised open the long slit, and his tongue dove in, to concentrate on the uppermost folds, to peel back the gleaming inner surface which housed her throbbing, quickened clitoris. Tears of wonder and delight streamed down her face. She could not believe that a proud African male would humble himself to perform this unselfish act of loving. The young man had indeed learned a great deal during the brief time when the beautiful Katya had been his bride.

Urgency swept over her, and, with a shuddering cry, she folded down onto the wet floor, under the spattering shower, dragging him up from her belly, fastening her eager mouth around his, which tasted of her tangy sex. She reached down, found the helm of his rearing prick and steered it to her sore but now clamorous vulva. She sat on his lap, straddling him, her ankles crossed at his back, and fitted him to her. Joined to the hilt, they rocked, slowly, tenderly at first, until the moment came when they both plunged in joyous, lost abandon to the climax which came for both of them almost simultaneously.

"The filthy bastard! The animal!" Awina's anger was genuine, Vee decided, even as she wondered what on earth her mistress had thought would happen to her when she gave her to Mavumbi for his pleasure. Surely she of all people must know what a sadistic beast he could be after the time she had spent with him in the rebel force? Hadn't she tasted something of it herself when she had served him as his sexual partner? Now it seemed she had left such things far behind her. The polished Victor, and the other influential people she now ran with, were a far cry from the hulking former leader of rebellion. But it was clear he was still a force to be reckoned with, one whom they watched with great care, even though they were of his own persuasion.

"There were half a dozen of them!" Awina told Victor now, as she sat on the wide bed, cradling the weeping Vee in her arms. "They strung her up in a gymnasium. Look at her poor backside." She turned Vee as she spoke, offering the bruised buttocks for his inspection. "Then they gang-banged her, one after another."

The TLC went on, Awina waiting on her personally, not allowing her to move from her bed, until Vee was once again filled with gratitude and love for this charismatic figure who clearly cared a great deal for her. If she was a possession, she was, at least, a precious one, she consoled herself. The thought gave her much comfort. Awina even took the active role in their love making, refusing to allow her to stir, beyond responding to the passionate kisses, making her body available for the hectic caresses poured upon it.

At the end of the second evening thus spent, when Vee lay recovering from the shattering effect of orgasm, with Awina's cropped head lying exhausted across one pale thigh, Vee felt her love swelling up so hugely her throat was blocked, tears spilt from her yet again. She squirmed, made bold to pull at the gleaming dark shoulders to bring Awina up to embrace her. They lay together in each other's arms, brows touching. Awina's lips full and bruised with love, shone with the emissions she had extracted from Vee, who tasted them now as they kissed softly. Overwhelmed by the love she felt encompassing her, Vee whispered against that beloved face,

"Don't be angry with me. Promise me. But I have to tell you - I can't keep anything from you. I want to confess. Afterwards - when Edward came for me. He was so - so kind - so gentle with me, bathing me, everything. I - let him - make love." Her voice was breathless, she rushed on, "It - it was my fault. I just - needed to feel some love after - what they did to me. Don't be angry. Please. Or at least - not with him. It really wasn't his fault."

But already Vee had sensed that split second of quivering pause, the instant that Awina absorbed her admission, and she knew.

"Well, well, little stick insect." The voice was soft, and tender, still, amused almost, but Vee was already tense. "So you are still a naughty girl, eh? Still disobedient. What on earth are we to do with you, eh?"

"I'm sorry. But - please! Don't take it out on Edward. Punish me - but not him. It's the only time, I swear it. And I have told you."

"Yes. Eventually. Took you a while to get round to it, didn't it?" She slapped Vee's thigh. "Never mind. Now let's have a bath, then get something to eat. Eating you always whets my appetite. For real food, I mean! You're a sexy little hors d'oeuvres, I'll give you that!"

Vee knew better than to be fooled by Awina's seemingly casual reaction to her confession. Wretchedly, she cross examined herself as to the reason for it. You really are turned on by this slave thing! she accused herself. You knew she'd punish you. You asked for it, you kinky little cow! But guiltily, she worried over what would happen to Edward. She decided

195

she must warn him as soon as she saw him again, for she could not rely on Awina's heeding her plea for him not to be punished.

She was right to be anxious. She didn't see him again, though Awina made no further reference to the incident over the following two days. Finally, Vee plucked up the courage to blurt out, "What's happeded to Edward? Why hasn't he been here?" Her heart was thumping.

Awina smiled tolerantly. "Oh, didn't I tell you? He's had to go up north again. A new posting. He'll be glad to get back home, I expect."

Vee knew that was far from the truth, for Edward had told her how happy he was to be here in the capital, in government quarters, with his wife and new baby. Her heart sank, but she knew better than to plead or even comment on the news. Besides, what good would it do now? It was too late. Now she had her own punishment to worry about. It would come, she was sure, even though almost a week had passed since her nightmare at the gym.

One morning, instead of heading off to work, Awina stayed with her for a leisurely breakfast, after which she dug out the flowery wisp of the mini dress and tossed it at Vee. "Get dressed. We're going out."

Vee did not recognise the driver of the government car, which seemed to be at Awina's disposal whenever she wanted it. Selfconsciously, Vee pushed down the hem of the tiny dress, which came only to the top of her thighs. Awina noticed her gesture and, with a wicked grin, pulled her hand away and flicked up the slit.

"Don't be so modest. This is Christopher. He doesn't mind, do you?" Vee's face flamed as she saw the dark eyes gaze avidly at her in the mirror. "But don't crash the car, will you?"

He grinned broadly, pulled his eyes away reluctantly.
"No, madam."

"Where are we going?" Still flustered, Vee had asked
the question without thinking, realising too late that she should
not speak out of turn. But Awina seemed to be in an ebullient
mood. She patted Vee's bare thigh fondly.

"I'm going to buy you some jewellery, my darling,"
she said.

The car nosed its way deep into the crowded streets
of the city's populous Asian quarter. The small, open fronted
dukas, or shops, were dim caverns full of exotic smells. Open
tubs of spices stood about, shiny pots and pans hung from
hooks along the wooden walls. Bolts of the brightly coloured,
cheap cotton cloth were strewn about, their billowing fronds
beckoning customers to explore the dark mysteries beyond.
The girls climbed out, and Awina led Vee towards an unpretentious shop whose front boards displayed rows of watches,
gleaming chains of gold and silver, richly coloured glass that
aped diamonds and rubies and other precious stones.

Awina moved past the fawning, toothy grins of the
young assistants to an interior doorway, and a long passage
going deep into the interior of the old building. Through swing
doors that reminded Vee of a John Wayne western, they passed
into what looked like a shabby doctor's or dentist's surgery.
There were instruments that looked vaguely medical, with long
metal arms, and tiny points, like dental drills. Various bottles
and jars stood on the shelves, there were enamel basins and
clean towels set out on a long, narrow table, and, in pride of
place, a venerable examination couch, so that both the upper
and lower sections could be raise or lowered as required. Vee
stared apprehensively about her, her stomach churning with

unease.

An elderly Indian came forward.his neat and still abundant hair was swept back in thick waves from his expansive brow. A pair of granny glasses perched on the end of his nose, and his face was wreathed in a network of fine wrinkles at his obsequious smile.

"Hello, Patel," Awina said familiarly, as he shook her hand. "Here she is. Let's get to work."

The Asian turned his beaming smile in her direction. He took her hand. She felt his delicate fingers very smooth and soft, and very limp in her grasp.

"Please, my dear. Up on the couch." With a hesitant glance at Awina, who was smiling broadly, Vee awkwardly swung her behind up onto the slippery edge of the leather. With a good humoured exclamation of impatience, Awina grabbed her ankles and swung her legs up, exposing her bare flesh as far as her loins before Vee clamped her hand down, holding the flimsy silk over her mound.

"No need to be shy in front of Mr Patel, Sweety. He might well be working on your cute little slit before long."

Mr Patel was adjusting the back rest, bringing it up almost to right angles with the mid-portion of the couch, so that Vee was sitting erect, her legs stretched out in front of her.

"Now let us have a look at her," the Asian said. Awina's fingers plucked at the strap fastened at the back of Vee's neck, and pulled the silk clear of her breasts, allowing it to fall to her waist while Vee gasped, made an instinctive movement to hide herself, then thought better of it. She gasped again as she felt Patel's brown, smooth hands settle on her breasts and heft them in his palm one after the other. He took each pink nipple in turn, rolled it in a thumb and finger, tweaking them to erection, pulling them away from the pale surrounds while Vee stared in crimson mortification.

"So small," he said to Awina, with a shake of his silver locks. "I think only the thin ones will do, madam. The thick ones will be very difficult." He shook his head again. "The tits are too small."

"My sentiments exactly," Awina grinned. Trembling with alarm, Vee stared saucer eyed as the Asian went over to the bench, came back with a bottle of clear liquid and a small white plastic tray, with a short lip. It curved inward in a kidney shape. He fitted it under Vee's right breast, his fingers arranging the soft flesh, and the tray, so that it fitted tightly into her rib cage, and her breast itself rested on the plastic.

"If you wouldn't mind?" he said to Awina, who took the tray from him, and held it in place.

"I feel a right tit," she giggled, but Vee was too afraid to appreciate either her humour or her knowledge of idiomatic English.

A sharp antiseptic smell arose as Patel tipped up the bottle, allowing its contents to soak into a wad of cotton wool. Vee gasped, jerked, as he applied it to her nipple and areola, coating most of the surface of the breast. It was icy, and Vee's nipple, and the circle of pink surround, puckered, the nipple hardening and swelling Immediately.

"Keep still, please," he said crisply, as her coated her other breast. Vee felt the tingling, blushed at the stinulating effect it had on her, her teats standing up in rubbery hardness. He tweaked each nipple vigorously, but Vee felt nothing of pain.

He moved, and came back with an instrument that looked for all the world like a very large stapler.

"No!" she whimpered automatically.

Awina rammed the tray against her ribs. "Don't be

stupid. It will only take a second. You won't feel a thing."

She did not tell the truth. In spite of the local, when her nipple was pulled, then the twin jaws of the instrument closed stabbingly over it, there was a sharp and definite stabbing sensation which made her cry out. The jaws unclamped, and she felt a brief burning. Already, he was moving to her other breast, the tray held there, too, and again the instrument snapped closed over her left breast. The same stabbing sensation, and the operation was done. He produced two very fine gold rings, no more than half an inch in diameter. He opened the tiny spring clip, and, after more swabbing and dabbing at her now dully aching breasts, he inserted them through the newly pierced holes in the nipples, holes so small she had not been able to detect them until the gold rings were being fed through.

The anaesthetic was already beginning to wear off, and her breasts felt tender, the nipples throbbing. But another throbbing, of a different nature, deep within her belly as she stared at these tiny gold adornments, told of the erotic thrill the piercings and the gleaming rings gave her.

Glad that it was over, she swung her feet off the couch and slipped off, clutching at the front of the dress, but Awina's hand seized her wrist and prevented her from concealing her body.

"Wait! We're not done yet. Don't ne in such a hurry."

Vee stood awkwardly, the front of the dress hanging from her waist. She kept her arms rigidly at her sides, knowing what Awina's reaction would be if she tried to shield her breasts. "Now the chains. One from each breast, to come down to her belly. To below. To her sex." Vee felt the tide of colour flooding up, but Mr Patel was not at all embarrassed.

"They will have to be fine," he said cricically. "The

200

rings are light also. The heavier chain will be too much."

Two silver chains were selected, clipped onto the rings through her nipples, and led down to meet over her mound. To Vee's chagrin, Awina pulled at the dress, and its folds fell about Vee's ankles to leave her standing naked in the middle of the Floor.

"Wait!" Awina said again, this time to the Asian. "They must be long enough to allow this to be inserted in her hole. See? Can you fit it onto the ends of the chains?" She was holding up a small cylindrical object, smooth, cigar shaped. As she handed it to the Asian, Vee saw that two very small silver rings had been fixed to one of its pointed ends. She could now recognise its pimpled surface. It was the remote control vibrator she was already all too familiar with.

"Open your legs!" Her lips quivering, her teeth nipping the lower lip in an effort to hold back the tears she could feel gathering behind her eyelids, Vee spread her legs, trying to hold still while both Awina and the elderly Asian crouched, slid the vibrator back and forth in her oily vagina, adjusting, fastening the chains, until at last, as she could feel the vaginal walls spasming, growing ever moister with excitation at the intruder to which they clung, Awina declared herself satisfied, and she stood there, legs astride, while they stared admiringly at the two thin chains, reaching down from her breasts to disappear into her cleft, where the black plastic object lay snugly hidden.

"There," Awina grinned, "now we won't lose it will we? And we can have lots of fun without worrying about whether it's going to pop out and go shooting across the floor. Say thank you to Mr Patel. And if you're a good girl I might bring you back to have a ring fitted down below. She'd love it!" She beamed a dazzling smile at the grinning Asian and headed for the door. "Do yourself up you little slut!" She called over her shoulder, and Vee hastily scrabbled to tie the steap at the back of her neck.

It felt strange as they walked slowly through the hot, crowded street back to the car. She could feel the fine chains rubbing against her skin, feel the tug at her breasts, the rub against the crease of her belly and thighs where the chains came together, and the heavy intrusiveness of the object inside her vagina. Then, suddenly, she stopped, her hips twitched, and she gave a little skip at the pulsing charge which fired through her. Awina turned, grinning widely, and Vee saw the little black disc in her palm. The thumb moved again, Vee twitched again.

"Please!" she whimpered. "Not here." She stumbled along, nipping her thighs together so that her bottom swung, she walked in a parody of a sexily provocative sway, the silk swinging about her, while the tingling darts sent throbbing spasms of physical arousal through her until she was ready to scream at their maddening, imperious power over her.

CHAPTER TWENTY TWO

Vee was extremely conscious of her new body adornment over the following days. For a start, her nipples were very sensitive. They were tinglingly erect, and quite sore whenever they experienced the slightest touch. Clothing would catch on them, the brush of a sheet across them would make her start. And then she found she could not leave herself alone. Gingerly, her finger tips would toy with the tiny rings, ashamed of the thrill her own caresses brought her. And of course there was Awina's lingering attention. Her dark fingers plucked and played, her pink tongue flicked at the delicate gold rounds, absorbed them between her lips as she sucked hungrily at the pale tits.

Wearing clothes was not too much of a problem at first, for, once they had returned from the trip to Patel's shop, there came a period of several days when Vee did not leave the bungalow or its compound. She remained naked for all that time, Awina ordering her not to cover herself even with a robe. By now, both Miriamu and Moussa, the cook, as well as the two shamba boys who looked after the large garden, were quite used to seeing her nude, and, however uncomfortable it made Vee feel, she knew better than to disobey her mistress. Vee could not be sure if the piercing of her breasts had been part of her punishment for having sex with Edward. The only other sign of admonition had been a spanking over Awina's knee with a bundle of thin twigs which, though it brought up her behind in a roseate glow, had been positively benign, an overture to their hectic love making rather than a serious chastisement.

Awina dextrously unclipped the rings each night, and carefully bathed the nipple areas in the disinfectant lotion. She it was who carried out the more difficult task of refitting them in the morning, though she quickly became so adept that it caused Vee no more than a few seconds of fleeting and mild discomfort. Worse, far worse, was the fact that she was made to wear the vibrator, on the ends of the slender chains, and to keep it in all day, drawing it out only when she needed to go to the lavatory, and slipping it in again immediately she had relieved herself.

Before leaving for work, Awina handed the remote control to the grinning Miriamu, clearly with orders that the maid should put it to frequent unannounced use, so that, at any time of the day, Vee could suddenly find herself subjected to the powerful electric throb inside her, with its deeply stirring results. It was excruciatingly embarrassing to have to run, bent forward and clutching at her purring mound, after the sniggering Miriamu and squeal for her to "turn it off", while Moussa stood around grinning from the looped ear to ear. Miriamu had been commanded never to let the vibrator run for more than a minute or two at a time, but it was clear that she had not been instructed how many times she could amuse herself by putting it to use. Vee, very much aware of the visibility of the twin chains snaking down her middle from her breasts, took to staying close to the maid for long periods, and even volunteered to help her with household tasks in the hope that she would prove amenable.

After more than two weeks of this limited existence, with only the prospect of Awina's return home in the evening to lift her, Vee's life changed once more.

"You're going to start earning your keep," Awina declared, while Vee gazed at her anxiously. "No, don't worry, darling. No more gang bangs from Mavumbi's pack. In fact, no orgies at all, probably. Not for a while at least."

She began to accompany Awina to more and more functions, both official and private, where, she soon realised, the influential gathered. She was given a growing wardrobe of elegant clothes, for both day and evening, and even allowed the luxury of fine satin underwear. Most astonishing of all, she kept it on throughout these arrangements, the majority of which were glitteringly respectable. She was introduced as Vicky Waters. She was even awarded an official title and reason for being there.

"Vicky's seconded to the Education Ministry. Adult Education," Awina would announce, straight faced, before murmuring in her ear, "And you could teach this lot a thing or two, eh, baby?" The buzzing instrument of such torturous delight was removed from its dangling chains, though Awina sometimes laughingly replaced it with an object of identical size and shape, without the provocative little bumps and batteries. "Just a plug," she chuckled. "To make sure you don't get up to any mischief."

One morning, Awina said mysteriously, "hope you're feeling fit, stick insect." She delved in a drawer and flung a black leotard at Vee. "Get into that, sexy one! We're going to take some exercise."

They drove to a health and beauty parlour situated on the ground floor of one of the capital's most luxuriously expensive hotels. It was elitist in the extreme, as Vee soon saw when she diffidently followed Awina into its work-out rooms. Awina looked stunning, also in a skimpy black leotard which complemented her dark skin and hugged the contours of her body magnificently. Vee slid her fingers into the tight crotch of her own brief garment and eased it a little from the crease of her thighs.

They began a programme under the tuition of one of the beef-cake male staff, until Awina curtly dismissed him with a scathing remark which figuratively castrated him on the spot. Within minutes, Vee was gasping like a fish, the sweat standing out and making the leotard cling wetly to her. Exercise bikes, rowing machines, treadmills - Awina forced her to furious activity until her legs shook, her stomach heaved, and she could not find the breath even to protest. She lay on the matting, chest heaving like bellows, while Awina finally explained the real reason behind this unlooked for activity.

"Pru Dickens-Smythe," Awina said, while Vee, scarlet faced, cheeks puffing, stared up blankly. "Willowy blonde. Bit like you, but with hair - and tits!" she added cruelly. "We want you to get to know her. To become bosom buddies, in fact." She smirked. "Far as we know, she's not gay, but you never know. I didn't think I was till you got into my knickers, you randy little sod! Her grandfather owned most of the biggest tea plantations out here in the bad old days. Pru was born out here. Now her old man's back on the scene, and she's tagged along. He's very pally with Charles Kigonja. The Defence Minister. They've even let him buy one of the old family estates back, down at the coast. We need to know what's going on, if anything. And I've a feeling something is. So you're going to be our little Mata Hari. You can do what you're best at. Winkling things out, or getting in where you shouldn't! Just up your street." She waved her arms around. "This is where you can start. She comes in her nearly every day. A fitness freak. You can start with girlie chats in the showers. Who knows where it might lead?"

Awina's seemingly casual remark proved to be prophetic. It was indeed in the wafting steam and the sultry atmosphere of the various bath and plunge rooms which led off from the gym that Vee began her aquaintance with the tall girl with the mass of tawny hair. The splendidly ripe body made Vee's secret muscles spasm in involuntary desire from the moment she first clapped eyes on it in all its unclothed glory. By that time, they were already on politely nodding terms. And Pru tried not to stare when she saw Vee and Awina exchange a tender but frankly amorous liss on the lips as the African hurriedly left her partner in the changing room to go to her office.

"See you tonight, darling!" Awina called, with a last, explicit gaze and wave from the doorway.

The girl's mass of fair hair was darkened, clinging like seaweed to her shoulders and back, stray tendrils snaking down over her full breasts. Vee tried not to let her eyes linger on

206

those rich rounds, the large, tawny areas of the areolae, and the pertly erect nipples thrusting temptingly from their centre. Pru was at least three inches taller than Vee, and her figure was fuller. She made no effort to hide herself, as she began to towel the long strands of her hair.

"I bet you're glad you don't have this problem," she laughed. "I'm envious."

"No. You've got lovely hair. If mine looked like that, I'd grow it back tomorrow." Then she felt the colour mounting as she noticed the direction of Pru's gaze. There was an instant of embarrassment that was mutual.

"I see you're not keen on hair at all. Anywhere!" Pru said, with a half apologetic gurgle of laughter.

There was an awkward pause, and the tall girl went on quickly, to break it, "What a lovely girl. Your friend, I mean. The African. You two are - you know each other pretty well. I'm Pru Dickens-Smythe, by the way. Pleased to meet you." She let her towel hang at her side as she held out her hand, and Vee took it. She dragged her eyes away once more from that mouth watering bosom. Pru was looking with a curiosity which was almost amusing. "I see you like to do things naturally."

Vee stared blacnkly for an instant, then saw that the girl's eyes were directed at her breasts, and her shaven mons, which had aquired a light gold tan almost the consistency of the rest of her body. She laughed shyly. "At home - I don't bother - I don't sunbathe nude. When we're on our own."

"We?" Pru asked quickly, and Vee's blush deepened.

"I'm - living with Awina." She nodded at the door. "The girl you saw."

"Yes. I thought you seemed - well, very friendly."

Her voice carried both humour and an avid curiosity. A curiosity which she could not contain when, dressed and sitting on the hotel's fashionable terrace, they sipped their cold drinks and chatted eagerly.

"Forgive me asking, but you and - Awina, is it - are you - you know - an item? You make a lovely couple."

Vee struggled to maintain her poise. "Sometimes - I keep telling her not to make it so obvious." She paused. "I hope you're not too shocked, or anything."

"No, not at all!" The denial was a shade too quick, Vee thought. "It's fine, I reckon. In fact, it's good to see it - especially out here." She gave an impish grin.

"That's what I really call integrating!"

"You're not...?" Vee trailed the question suggestively.

It was Pru's turn to blush. "Me? Gosh, no. Not that I've anything against - being gay," she blurted. Then she said, dropping her voice a little, in a girlish rush of confidence, "As a matter of fact, I've just become involved - with a new man. He's absolutely gorgeous! We'll probably be getting together. Legally, I mean. We're planning to announce our engagement soon."

They met daily, arranging their visits to the gymnasium to coincide, enjoying the drinks and cosy chats on the terrace afterwards. Vee's natural diffidence prohibited her from trying to rush the friendship, in spite of Awina's teasing remark after the first few meetings. "Are you into her knickers yet?"

She knew Pru was becoming more and more interested, and curious, and she fed her revelations about her past, some truthful, most lies, to whet her appetite. Deliberately, she showed a contrasting lack of inquisitiveness about her new friend's life which she was sure the tall blonde appreciated. Pru was not very forthcoming about herself, made no effort to try to introduce her to her own social circle or to penetrate hers. Vee deduced this was because of her sexual persuasion, which the girl found fascinating but also a little daunting. She was like someone standing at the water's edge, afraid to dip her toe in.

The plunge was taken, or at least the first dip, one morning in the fitness room itself. Pru was going through the last routine of her work-out, which was much more intensive than Vee's. She was lying on the narrow, padded bench which fitted under the bar weights. Her feet were planted on the floor either side of the bench, and the long muscles on her thighs were standing up as she strained at the shining metal bar pressing down close to her throat. her arms bent outwards as she pushed up against the descending weights. Vee sat on the lower edge of the bench, by her knees, ready to help take the strain and slip the bar into its safety notch when Pru had had enough.

The prone figure was wearing a dove grey leotard, its thong design cut away so high at the crotch that, in her present position, Vee could see the edges of the white sports briefs peerping coyly through the jersey lining. The pretty face was puce, the cords on the long neck standing out, beaded with sweat. The outline of her breasts, lifted by her efforts, was moulded on the clinging material, so that Vee could see the distinct shapes of the thrusting nipples, and the rounds of their areolae. A long, tapering V of darkened sweat stained the leotard between the stirring rounds.

"God!" Pru puffed, rolling her eyes with a grunting laugh. "I'm knackered! Help me!"

Vee's heart bumped. Now! she heard Awina's strident voice shouting in her brain.

"Here! Get the damned bar! I can't move!"

Vee watched the knuckles tighten, saw the silver bar drop until it rested just across the bumps of the shoulder bones, thus trapping Pru's effectively in her prone position.

"What the hell are you playing at?!" Get me out of here!" The voice was suddenly shaky, like that of a child about to burst into tears.

Vee glanced around fearfully at the one or two clients working out in other parts of the gym. Then she let her hand fall on Pru's upper thigh, trailed her fingers up over the smooth skin, and in; in to the crotch of the eleotard, and the tiny peep of white where the bikini briefs showed.

The leg jumped, the knee lifted. Vee moved in, the fingers now stroking the narrow band of the grey material, pressing very slightly, revealing just the suspicion of the hollow beneath, formed by the labia.

"Don't!" The voice was now a ragged whisper, the tone one of pleading. Vee traced the long curve of the vulva. She could feel a dampness now, pressed harder against the spongy swell. Now both knees jerked, lifted, and came together against Vee's arm.

"Please!" The blue eyes carried a helpless expression. They were large, swimming with sudden tears. "I can't move."

"I know. I've got you, haven't I?" Vee's fingers caressed, bolder, explicitly, and she felt the pulsing response, the pouting swell of the girl's sex, the growing dampness, the instinctive lift and flitch of the belly to meet her. She could see the even teeth appear, gnawing at the bottom lip, the mouth slightly open.

"Oh God! Don't!" Pru groaned. She closed her eyes, the tears appeared like glinting jewels on her lashes. "I'm not - not gay!" The breasts jiggled divinely at the huge sigh, half sob, which escaped. The beginnings of a dark patch appeared in the groove which had evidenced itself under Vee's exploration.

210

"How do you know? Have you tried it? It's no big deal. All girls like it really. All that I've come across."

The tawny head arched back, the mass of hair tumbled over the red of the bench, the tear drops broke, trickled down to her temples.

"Not here," she whispered.

Vee's hand continued to move. "Come back to my place," she said thickly.

Another sob shook the prone figure. "Yes. Now please - let me up! Please!"

CHAPTER TWENTY THREE

"You knew about this, didn't you?" Pru's quivering voice, racked by her sobs, which Vee could feel passing through her own clinging body, breathed in her ear. The leather belt, which Awina was using to bind them tightly together around their waists, bit agonisingly into the small of their backs and their sides, as the African drew it in a further notch before threading the end through the buckle. The pale, naked bodies were thus pressed even more lewdly against ech other, Pru's breasts cruched against those of Vee's, their bellies, the fronts of their thighs plastered in a contact that was a cruel parody of the loving they had just experienced. Their arms were wrapped around each other, wrists hanging behind their partner's shoulders, pinioned there by the two sets of handcuffs Awina had clicked into place.

Vee didn't answer. There was little point in denying it. Pru had guessed something was wrong, from Vee's tense manner, her preoccupied air from the moment they had arrived at the bungalow and hurried to the bedroom to shed their clothes and fall in clutching embrace across the counterpane. Awina

211

had waited until the girl's third clandestine rendezvous at the deserted house, whose servants were safely hidden away in the quarters at the top of the garden.

"No one's ever around at this time," Vee had assured the hesitant Pru. By the third visit, it was Pru who was leading the way, as eager to get to grips as her new lover.

It was a relief to Vee, who had been waiting, nerves screaming, when Awina, magnificent in her role of jealous and betrayed fury, erupted on the scene as they lay there in a tangle of recently consummated love. Though not by nature as ready to play the craven as Vee, Pru's resistance soon collapsed. However robust her mental and moral strength, she was completely unfamiliar with physical violence. Besides, being caught naked in bed was in itself a powerful disadvantage. Within seconds, a viciously effective punch to the jaw, and another thudding into her unprotected midriff, left Pru literally folded and gasping giddily on the tangled bed which she had just left.

Awina's succint argument was almost equally potent. "If you don't want a word of this to get out, you'd better do exactly what I tell you, you two-timing dike bitch!" Thus it was that the two shivering girls were strapped together in their compulsory embrace in the middle of the floor. A stance which soon turned into an obscene jig of torment as they twisted and turned, fell and were dragged upright, while Awina circled and, with another thin leather belt, lashed their buttocks, the backs of their capering thighs, the backs themselves, until their pale skin was scored with a dozen vivid red lines of blazing agony. It was the first time Awina had beaten Vee seriously since she had been pierced. And although she yelped and writhed as much as Pru under the steady smacks of leather across her back and buttocks, she found she was once again helpless in that abject delight she took in being mistreated. By the end of the punishment Vee's writhings against the lush body she was tied to had as much to do with excitement as with pain.

The fact that she quickly realised the depth of her lover's treachery merely served to complete Pru's sobbing, abject surrender. She lay across the bottom of the wide bed, groaning while Awina, all tender concern now, dabbed gently at the livid weals with cotton wool and a soothing liquid solution. Vee stood suffering in silence, reflecting miserably on how ocnvincing Awina's display of righteous anger had been, for her own body throbbed abominably. And all in vain, for Pru was no longer duped. Not that it mattered. The tall girl, her hair spread out richly over the covers, lay on her stomach and listened to Awina's bluntly stated demands.

"We just want to know what's going on between your daddy and Kugonja. Not to mention your handsome groom-to-be. His company's in on it as well, yes? Tell us all, or your fiance's going to learn just how catholic his beloved's tastes are as far as sex is concerned. How about it?"

"I don't know what you're talking about," Pru wept bitterly. "I don't concern myself with - " her denial ended in a shrill yelp of pain which made Vee jump and cry out in immediate sympathy. All she had seen was Awina's hand dive deep into the cleft of Pru's striped buttocks, which bucked in the air, her long thighs scissoring at the agony the thrusting, twisting, pinching fingers had caused in the moist, soft tissue which lay hidden beneath.

"Now now, sugar," Awina admonished gently. "We're all girlies together, remember. No secrets between us, right?"

Eventually, the distraught girl stammered out a disjointed tale of possible contracts for military hardware and other matters which were being discussed without the official sanction or knowledge of the various government agencies who

213

should be most involved.

"With hefty backhanders for your old man and your future hubby, I suppose?" Awina murmured. She turned to the silent Vee. "Why don't you go and take a nice long, soothing bath? I think I ought to try and make amends to poor little Prudence here, don't you? Kiss her poor little smacked botty better. Shut the door on your way out." Mortified, Vee turned and left, painfully aware of Pru's whimper of protest as she did so.

Vee lay exhausted in the bath until her fingers and toes were wrinkled, before she heard
the sound of a car leaving. As soon as the water had embraced her stinging body Vee's hand had gone straight between her legs, her fingers rubbing and swirling around her hard clitoris as she had remembered the sensuous writhing of Pru's body under the lash. The thrilling crack of leather on flesh echoed in her mind and her body responded with wave after wave of delight as her fingers delved into the moist channel of her vagina. She was only just climbing stiffly out when Awina appeared.

"My God, you've certainly given her a taste for it! You deserve a reward, my little stick insect. And rewarded you shall be!"

"Just a little wider, my dear." As he spoke, Mr Patel pulled at the cord beside him and Vee's tethered ankles slid further apart along the smooth running rail. Her legs formed a wide V now, through which she could see his silvery hair as he bent close to her prominently exposed vulva. The young African girl, wearing the creamy surgical gloves identical to his, jostled shoulders as she too bent to examine Vee's orifice. She dabbed at the gleaming, peeled back the slit, and Vee felt the iciness of the

214

local anaesthetic. Her inner muscles tautened.

"Keep as still as you can, my dear," Patel intoned. "It won't take more than a few seconds."

Vee closed her eyes, shuddering as she felt the strange sensation of the tiny pincers closing in on the diminutive little trigger of pink flesh which her gaping sex had revealed, and which the gloved fingers of the girl had teased to life. Despite the numbing spirit, there was a kind of tingling, then she felt the pull as the pincers gripped, the minute tissue was stretched. Vee's mind flew back to that time, when, similarly opened, in the dimness of the forest hut, her engorged clitoris had been bound with fine cotton threads and left for days in that wickedly titillating condition, by the women who had conducted the initiation rites for the young females in the rebel stronghold.

Now there were, as Patel had warned, just seconds of weird sensation, then the lip of flesh was pierced, and a gold ring, as small and as fine as those adorning her breasts was inserted.

The feeling, when, later that day the slender chains leading from her nipples were clipped to that ring hidden in the upper folds of her vulva was both a heady delight and a sweet torment. The tension which the jiggling, bra-less breasts created on the chain, and thus on that throbbing source of physical sensation within her sex, kept her constantly aroused. Every movement, sitting, standing, sent a dart of feeling through her.

"Permanently on heat!" Awina mocked, and she was right. However, a powerful diversion was soon at hand.

"That lying cow of yours isn't telling us the truth," Awina declared a day or two later. Vee had not met Pru again. Indeed she had not left the house except for the trip to Patel's. "Not the whole truth, anyway. We need a new tack. I think

215

perhaps we need to reel in her young fellow. It could be orgy time again."

"I don't know anything about him," Vee blurted. "I don't even know what he looks like!"

Vee was too alarmed to notice the smirk which passed swiftly over Awina's features before she answered quickly. "What's that got to do with it? He's got a dick, hasn't he? That's all you're concerned with. Who knows? You might find you've got a lot in common." She turned to the smiling Victor, who was watching Vee closely. "Over to you, Victor. Who do you know that's involved in their set up? Can you arrange a discreet little fuck-for-all where our Vee can put her talents to full use?"

Vee's stomach was churning unpleasantly as she sat in the rear of the car. She was glad that it was dark, for she could imagine what an outlandish appearance she must present. Her hair had been shaved to the briefest of fine naps, and newly bleached to a pristine whiteness. The effect was to give her skull the bald roundness of an egg. Over her eyes and extending down to a point just above the tip of her nose, she wore a black velvet mask deeply encrusted with paste jewels. The large, almond shaped eyeholes gave her a glittering, fixed stare, like an exotic animal or bird. Her lips were painted a glossy black. Her nipples, sporting the fine gold rings and silver chains, were painted the same colour. Below her bare breasts was a tightly laced narrow waspie of shining PVC into which the thin chains disappeared, to re-emerge at her belly, for the brief garment extended only to the region of her navel. They came together over her bare, newly shaven mons, to disappear into the uppermost folds of her labia. Long satin suspenders ribboned down from the diminutive corselet to hold the sheer, dark nylon stockings in place. The exotic assemblage was completed by the spiky, five inch heels held in place by the thin patent ankle straps.

Mercifully, a long black cloak hid her at the moment, though the touch of the cold, simulated leather of the car seat on her bare bottom was a constant reminder of her deshabille, and of the strange events which she would soon be part of.

"Remember, you're doing it for queen and country," Awina had mocked, seeing her into the car. "Though I'm not too sure how you spell that first syllable of country!"

She had no idea where she was going. All she knew was that she was a part of Awina and Victor's intricate plans for detection or perhaps blackmail, and that her body was to be used as bait.

After a long ride, she felt the car leave the road somewhere in one of the fashionable residential areas beyond the city, whose lights she had seen briefly below before the car turned off up a long, bumpy gravel lane. It finally stopped before some lighted steps, leading up to what looked like one of the old, impressive colonial mansions. This impression was reinforced by the elegantly lit reception hall, with its spears and masks on the white walls, and animal trophies and skins scattered in politically incorrect profusion.

"Follow me, please." Vee had not dared to shed her cloak, but had held it about her to hide her skimpy costume. At the foot of the staircase, the maid indicated an open doorway, gestured for her to enter, and left. She went back up the stairs and closed the door above. The room was comfortably furnished, like a country house back home. She glanced around in trepidation. Another door opened.

Then the room swam about her, there was a rushing sound as though her blood was thundering in her head. She recognised the bland, hard look, the danger of that wide smile. Somehow, she managed not to cry out or faint. She couldn't utter a sound. It was Keith, her ex-husband, standing there, his glittering eyes fixed on her with that implacable coldness that chilled her even now.

'What a charming outfit. And very appropriate, I'm sure. But what a shame! Aren't I going to be allowed to get a proper look at you?" He laughed unpleasantly, let his gaze travel crudely to her exposed sex and breasts. "I mean your face, of course. I'm sure it's as delightful as the rest of you. What's wrong? Not struck dumb. I hope? Perhaps a drink might help?" Vee took the proffered glass. She raised it, gulped, choked and coughed. He hadn't recognised her! She couldn't believe it. He was here, in the room, about to have sex with her, and he didn't know her!

All at once it dawned on her with the cruelty of a blow, that Awina had known about this all along. Her jokes about meeting her 'ex', her insistence that Vee attend this rendezvous done up in the ridiculous mask. Her brain was spinning. Could it really be that Keith didn't know her? Could it be...would he actually fuck her and still not recognise her. A huge pain, from somewhere deep within, where it had rested all this time, swelled up under her ribs, tauntingly highlighted by the restricting wisp of material cinched about her waist.

How long since he had coupled with her? In all the time in Africa, from their first arrival, long before her capture, they had never made love. He had used her as his sex slave, she had serviced him with her mouth, but they had never fucked. Over four long years! She felt her vulva beating, wet, with her overwhelming need. This was the only man she had wanted, truly longed for.

Still in silence, she let him propel her through the door he had entered from. The room beyond was an austere bedroom. Comfortable but sparse. A single bed stood directly beneath a light whose shade cast the illumination down upon the covers with theatrical concentration.

"Vicky, isn't it?"

"Yes." It was easy for her to disguise her voice. Her reply came out as a hoarse whisper, entirely unrehearsed.

"Well, Vicky, I hear you're shit hot with that mouth of yours. Let's see, shall we?"

It could have been any time during their stay in Makamba, when he would return pissed from the club and order her to do just this. Except that this time he undressed himself, without a trace of reticence, stripping himself naked and stretching out on his back on the bed, his hands folded behind his head. She knelt over his ankles, her brief clothing crackling softly at her movement. She bent forward, let the rings at her throbbing nipples scratch at his shin as she stooped low, began to nibble and suck at his legs, below the knees. She let her tongue come fully out, she lapped at his skin until she felt papery and dry. She had to keep remoistening herself with her saliva as she gave those long, slow laps, over his thighs, the crease of his belly, avoiding the now tumescing, hot bulk of penis. She felt its throbbing touch between her dangling breasts, felt its satin soft texture hardening, buckling against her chest bone.

She licked on, her tongue flickered into his belly button, and over the edge of the rib cage, then to the curcular discs of his nipples, covered with fine sworls of his fair hair. She let her tongue flicker over each teat, then spread her lips and sucked hungrily, leaving twin prints, like clamps, of her dark lipstick, above and below. She felt the wetness smear across her skin as his prick leapt to a full erection, the domed helm fully exposed, thrusting up between her breasts.

She moved at last, bending low again, very gently

219

taking its leaping urgency in her fingers, stroking lightly. Her vagina was spasming at its feel, the great, veined column, the swelling, shining rawness of the head, the splendid symmetry of the balls at its root. They felt huge and heavy, warm and fecund in her grip. She lapped at their fragrant, sweat damp surface, the fine wrinkles running either side of the thick central seam. She nipped the satiny skin lightly in her teeth, pulling at it, tasting the fine hair curling on her tongue, then stretched her mouth as wide as she could, sucking in its yeasty flavour.

He moved convulsively, his fingers sliding on her head as he tried to seize her by the hair, then they moved frantically down to her ears and jaws, dragged her up and away from the massively beating prick, while his knees lifted, jabbed painfully into her breasts. She screamed loudly, in flaring agony. His fingers grabbed at her breasts, caught hold of the tiny rings, and raised her bodily by pulling on them. Her scream was cut off, she was gasping, tears streaming down into the mask at the fine torment. Still manipulating her by his wicked hold on her tits, he turned her onto her Back and laid her down in the spot which was warmed by his own body.

She did not struggle. He seized her wrists, held them up above her head and fastened them to the bed rail with steel handcuffs, whose inner surface was padded with a spongy leather. Then he grabbed her ankles, forced them up beside her wrists and, with similar cuffs, secured them to the rail also, so that she was folded back on herself, her bottom lifted from the mattress, her whole genital area on prominent display. His erection had died down, but his prick and balls still looked massive as he knelt over her, with that familiar smile, glittering like a finely honed knife.

"Pru's right. You are wicked with that mouth of yours. She swears you're the first dike who's ever had her. I think that means you and I are rivals."

Vee's brain reeled. For an instant, she forgot the painful humiliation of her trussed condition. Keith - and Pru? He was the fiance? He stood to one side of the bed.

The first cracking blow sent a line of fire biting deep into her taut, uplifted buttocks, and the bed rocked, her wrists and ankles fought against the steel restraints. She screamed, the shrill sound ringing in her brain. Clearly, he was not worried about the volume of noise she made. Somehow, that helped. He was using a short, thick leather strap, which brought up her skin in great, oblong bars of scorching pain. Wide-eyed she stared up at Keith from between her raised and spread thighs. In horrified fascination she watched as he swung the strap up again, but she had to squeeze her eyes tight shut as it swished down onto the stretched flesh of her buttocks. She yelled with all her might as the supple leather spread its burning marks across every inch of her bottom. But each time she opened her eyes after her scream she saw him, calm and dispassionate, swing the strap up once more. It only came as partial relief when he moved his target to the backs of her thighs. A whole new area seemed to burst into flame at the first caress of the leather. And Vee at last began to sink into that strange region she inhabited when put in someone else's power. The whipping was so much more powerful than anything Awina had delivered that it had taken her longer to respond, but now Vee felt the first unmistakable flutterings of arousal deep in her stretched and exposed sex. And even as she answered each lash with a scream she knew that he was working his way slowly towards that very target. He was going to whip her right across her pouting and receptive labia. With that realisation Vee heard her screams subside into strange, hoarse grunts, half of terror, half of thrilled anticipation, as the strap worked its way towards her crotch, lash by remorseless lash.

How complete an act of domination that would be!

Keith paused for just a second before he whipped her across the furiously pulsing lips. Vee whimpered, but she couldn't pretend it was in protest, it was impatience.

Then the strap was hurtling down again and an exquisite blast of white-hot pain lanced through her, and even tied as she was, she pushed up until only the backs of her shoulders rested on the bed. Her mouth opened wide but no sound came. A second lash at the soft, inviting target and Vee's head was thrashing from side to side as if in the throes of a tumultuous orgasm, while her body bucked and twisted at the intolerable heat and pleasure of the pain. It was the most exquisite of tortures, centred on the pout of her mons until it became one mass of throbbing, burning torment. And Vee embraced it all.

She lost count of the strokes. She had no idea of how many times he had whipped her, only gradually realising through the haze of her ordeal that the blows had ceased. She couldn't even see him. She thought for a moment he might have left her, but then he came into her blurred vision, she felt him lifting her head, unfastening the mask, pulling the soaking material away from her. The mascara had run smearily all over her cheeks and lay in runnels down the sides of her nose. His hand was warm, gentle at the back of her neck, holding her head up a little from the pillow. He bent close and stared at her for a long while.

"Hello, Vee," he murmured. "Welcome back."

The sobs burst from her then, like a torrent, shaking her with their ferocity.

"You knuh - knew? All the time?"

He smiled, but warmly this time, with a ghost like trace of the old Keith. Her Keith. "Pru couldn't keep it to herself. She's in a terrible state about it. She told me all about your plot - you and that bitch, Awina. I had you watched." He chuckled, ran his fingers gently through the fuzz of her hair. "It didn't fool me. Though it is quite sexy, I admit. Now. Tell me everything. From the start."

Through her sobs, she did just that, from the trouble she had got herself into in London, to the present intrigue. "I didn't know - it was you. Pru's - man. I swear! But you must be careful. They know - they want me to find out - "

Keith smiled, put his finger to her lips, stopping her. "Don't worry. We're ahead of them. No fears. But whose side are you really on, Vee? You want to help us? You want to stay on, work for us? For me?"

"Oh God, yes, Keith! Anything - I'll do it. Don't send me away again. I beg you."

His gaze held her. "I'm going to marry Pru," he said softly.

She felt a great pain well up once more, at her ribs, stopping her breath. She nodded.

"But you could stay," he said, even quieter. She nodded again.

"Of course it would mean lots more beatings - like that one."

"Yes. I understand." And she did now. Completely.

All this time, he had left her tethered, her legs and arms raised high, her throbbing, crimsoned loins fully displayed. Now, he knelt, and began slowly to massage his prick, long, slow strokes, up and down the shaft. Within seconds, the raw, gleaming helm was fully emerged, the column pulsing, rock hard. She felt its wet tip nosing along her slit, pressing against her yielding mound. He peeled back the labia, which were

223

puffy and throbbing, yet wet, slippery, her vagina urgent with its desire to feel him inside her.

She closed her eyes, the tears still trickling down into her temples. At last! After all this endless time. What did it matter what her status would be? Slave? Hadn't she longed for that? Wasn't she willing to endure anything, to take any punishment, as long as she could somehow be with him? He wanted her. He was aching, rampant, for her, right now, his prick nuzzling its way home, where it belonged. And she belonged to him. Again, at last.

"Fuck me," she whispered, drunk with ecstasy. The pain, the degradation of her trussed and folded body forgotten.

She felt that splendid helm moving the length of her oily crack, setting her alight. Then it dipped, down, down, to the very base of the cleft, and beyond, deep into that other, deeper cleft. It nosed against the hidden, tiny, puckered slit, its fluid lubricating the dry fissure. His fingers, hard, demanding, prised open her last secret stronghold, pressed against the resistance, forced a fractional entrance, smearing the hard bud with her own juices to lubricate it. She gasped at the steady, merciless pressure of his prick, pushing at the anal slit, driving hard. There was a burning pain, so fierce she cried out, the ring of muscle fiercely striving to prevent its penetration, and, finally, failing.

The great head was in, and her sphincter muscle spasmed, yielded, burning, at the slow, remorseless conquest. It yielded completely at last and she felt the terrifying, thrilling sensation of his hard column driving into the virginal tightness, filling her, burning her to the very core as he occupied each grudged centimetre. He could scarcely move at first, but, slowly, his thrusts took on a rhythm of their own, and she felt herself straining, trying to open herself wider.

She was whimpering, with shock, and shame, and an increasing excitement. Then, she felt the fingers of his hand searching between their heaving bodies, and finding the entrance to her vulva, easing in - there was a brief flash of pain as they pressed against the tiny ring which bit into her soft tissue and sent a flare of new fire through her.

Two fingers were thrust deep into her vagina, fanned out, stiffening, and pressing down, feeling his own pulsing hardness through the thin membrane, and Vee tossed her head back, her whole body jerking in uncontrolled spasms as she began to come, and the pleasure and the pain melded into one huge madness of fulfilment, and she cried out in the bursting knowledge that he could do anything to her, she would die for him, and in the instant of oblivion she would still be his, forever.

Here is the opening of our book for next month, "Submission of a Clan Girl", by Mark Stewart.

CHAPTER 1

The coffle moved quickly along the well trodden path through the forest. The six guards searched the surrounding area for hidden danger, at the same time ensuring that their captives made no attempt to escape.

Escape was, of course, impossible. The captives were well secured by metal belts around their waists which were, in turn secured to a heavy chain that joined them together. Thinner chains joining their ankles allowed them to walk with short steps but prohibited any chance of breaking into a run.

Conscious of the danger inherent in the forest, the guards remained silent, relying on hand signals to communicate with each other. The captives were kept silent by the ball gags which had been thrust into their mouths and secured behind their necks.

Looking into the faces of the captives, the leader of the men was pleased to see the look of terror in their eyes. He allowed his eyes to rove briefly over their bodies. What he saw was pleasing indeed.

Four young females. The thin garments that clung tightly to their bodies only added to the promise of the beauty that would surely be displayed once they were removed. The lightweight armour that they had worn when captured had been quickly removed as had their weapons.

For a day and a night the small procession made its way through the forest. At night a short rest was taken and food passed round. The captives' gags were removed only to permit them to drink and feed. Any signs of them making a sound were dealt with by a sharp cuff that sent stars rocketing through their heads.

The state of shock that had enveloped the captives when they had been ambushed and taken had receded with the passing of time. This had given way to a careful watchfulness for a chance to escape as they were marched away from the region of the forest with which they were familiar.

On the second day the group emerged from the forest and the outline of buildings appeared some distance ahead of them. Eventually, much to the obvious relief of the guards, they approached two large heavy wooden doors set in a massive stone wall.

A challenge rang out from high above them and, after the leader of the guards had replied, the doors opened slowly with much grinding and the party passed through.

The captives were ushered into a building, down a flight of stone steps and thrown into a dark cell. The door slammed shut behind them with an ominous thud.

The four women, still in the chain coffle, gagged and their wrists secured behind their backs, collapsed to the floor. They were too exhausted and frightened to take notice of their surroundings. All they were aware of was the dark and dampness. Being unable to talk, each sank into her own nightmare.

Four days ago they had been cheerful and excited. They had set out on what they believed was a routine hunting trip. Their quarry had been elusive and, not wishing to return empty-handed, they had strayed far from their territory. They had, mistakenly as it turned out, thought they were well away from the areas patrolled by the Urbans.

To their chagrin, they had been taken by surprise and, although they had tried to put up a fight, the Urbans' patrol had been too quick and strong for them to resist for long. They were soon overpowered, their armour and weapons taken from them. Then, gagged and their ankles chained, they were secured to the heavy chain of the coffle.

Dragged to their feet the long march had begun. The men had not spoken during the march and this had only served to increase the captives' fear. Now they huddled together, trying not to heed the terrible thoughts that raced through their minds.

They were awakened from the troubled slumber into which they had sunk by the door to their cell being thrown open with a deafening thud.

Two guards entered and roughly ushered the girls out of the cell, back up the stairs into a large hall. One of several doors leading from the hall opened and the four girls were roughly pushed through. They were dragged across the room to where an impressive figure reclined on a throne-like chair.

The man signalled to the guards and the girls' chains and gags were removed.

The tallest of the girls stepped forward and looked defiantly at the seated man.

"Who are you?" She demanded. "Why have we been brought here like criminals and, anyhow, where is here?"

"Silence wench." The seated man shouted back. "You will only speak when spoken to."

The air of authority in his voice, and the unconcealed anger, made the girls quail with fear. They had heard many stories of the terrible fate that befell any girl who was captured by the Urbans.

"You." The seated man said, pointing at the girl who had spoken. "Strip."

"I certainly will not." The girl replied, trying to conceal the fear in her voice.

"Strip, or I will have my guards do it for you."

The girl looked quickly round. She did not fail to see the lecherous grins on the guards' faces as they took a threatening step towards her. Neither did she fail to see the vicous whip that suddenly appeared in the seated man's hand.

Slowly, reluctantly, she peeled away her clothes until she stood naked facing the man, her eyes drawn to the coiled lash of the whip.

"That is better." The man said, his eyes roving over her body, now displayed. "Not bad at all. Perhaps we can make something of you, given time."

The girl, conscious that she was the leader of her party, fought down her fear and, recovering her voice, repeated her earlier questions.

She realised she had gone too far as the man's face reddened with anger.

"You were ordered to remain silent. You must be taught obedience." His voice was strangely quiet yet filled with menace. He threw the whip to one of the guards. "Ten lashes".

Before she realised what was happening, the girl was grabbed by a guard and pushed against a wall. Her arms were pulled up and outwards and her wrists locked into two clamps. Her long hair was pulled in front of her, rolled into a ball and forced into her mouth.

She looked over her shoulder in time to see the guard with the whip raise his arm. Abject horror filled her eyes as she suddenly realised what was to be done to her. She turned her head to the wall and clenched her small fists.

A sharp crack echoed round the room as the lash seared across her back. She managed to stifle a scream as a line of agony burned its path across her stretched flesh. In spite of the agony of the stroke, she vowed she would not let these men get the better of her.

The other three girls, ignoring the danger they were courting, began to surge forward shouting abuse at the men.

"Be still." The man ordered sharply. "Unless you wish

to take her place when her lesson is over."

The guard's arm rose and another livid stripe joined the first on the girl's back. The other girls shuffled their feet angrily. They knew the dangers of being taken by the Urbans but, until now, these had only been stories told round the camp fire. Now they were seeing for themselves.

The girl at the wall writhed, her fingers clawing at the hard surface of the stone, as the lash found her body again. Just before tears filled her eyes, she noticed for the first time that the wall near her hands was covered in scratch marks similar to the ones left by her own fingers testifying to the fact that she was not the first, by any means, to have been stood here and whipped.

The seated man watched closely as the punishment was administered. The girl was certainly attractive and, once she had been cleansed from the stains of her journey, he thought she might well be worth spending time and effort on.

Samantha Rema, for that was her name, felt the weals burning terribly across her back. She had never dreamed that such pain existed. Never had she been humiliated by being forced to strip in front of a man.

Crack! The sharp report echoed round the room. Samantha screamed into the gag as her breasts and stomach were thrown against the wall by the force of the blow. She felt her legs begin to shake as her wrists and arms took the full weight of her slim body. Any thought of pride or stubbornness was erased by the terrible pain in her back.

Through the mist that clouded her mind, her brain registered that she had taken four strokes. Only four! The seated ogre had said 'ten lashes', she remembered, so she still had six to come.

"Don't avert your eyes." The seated man shouted as he noticed the other three girls look away, unable to bear the sight of their leader's white back being marred by the evil thong. Not daring to go to her assistance, they had all turned their faces away from the ghastly scene.

Too frightened to disobey, they forced themselves to watch as the guard sent the lash whistling through the air. A sharp crack of leather meeting bare flesh, a muffled scream from the suspended girl and the scraping of her finger nails on the wall broke the heavy silence in the room.

Swish. Crack!

Samantha's legs finally ceased to support her and her slim arms took the full weight of her young body. Six livid weals stood out proud against the girl's white back. That none had broken the skin showed that her punisher was well versed in using the whip.

Swish. Thwack!

Swish. Crack!

Two more strokes that sent Samantha's body thudding against the wall. Her head fell back and her tear filled eyes turned towards the ceiling as the hair gag was forced from her mouth and a shrill scream rent the air.

Twice more the guard's arm rose sending the wicked lash snaking across the stretched back. The guard altered his aim on the last sending the end of the whip curling round her side and the end flicking at the dark brown nipple of her right breast.

Samantha, no longer caring that she was a leader, screamed and screamed at the agonising pain that erupted in her breast.

His duty done, the guard handed the whip back and released the girl's wrists from the manacles. She slid down the wall and curled up on the floor, sobbing heavily.

"Bring her here." The seated man ordered.

A guard grabbed the girl by her hair, sending a sharp

231

pain through her head, and dragged her in front of his employer.

"Kneel properly before your Master."

Samantha still dazed and sobbing from the whipping, drew deeply on her reserves of courage and began to rise to her feet, raising her eyes defiantly at the man who had ordered her flogging.

One of the guards, seeing her intent, took hold of her shoulders and forced her to her knees. Roughly, he kicked her knees wide apart and manhandled her until she knelt, her buttocks on her heels and her hands, palms upwards, on her knees.

"That is the position a slave must adopt in the presence of her Master." The seated man said.

He turned his head and looked at the other three girls. "Strip and kneel." He ordered sternly waving the whip at them.

The sight of the whip, and of their leader's back, was enough to quell any thought of disobeying. Soon they were naked and kneeling, immediately adopting the same posture as their leader.

"Now I will answer your questions. Not because you asked but because it pleases me to do so." The man spoke softly. His voice was still menacing yet he was unable to hide his pleasure at the gift fate had bestowed on him.

"You are now in my holding in the town of Ethra. I am the lord of the surrounding town and country. I am both a warrior and slave trader. As befits all females, except a privileged few, you are now slaves. You," he pointed at the still sobbing Samantha, "have just experienced a taste of what will happen if you forget your place.

"My name is Andreas. Normally I buy and sell slaves acquired from the various auctions. Sometimes, as with you, my guards earn a bonus by capturing any of your patrols that stray too far into my domain."

His words sent a shiver of terror through the kneeling girls. Their leader, Samantha, inwardly cursed her negligence that had led them into this terrible predicament. She silently vowed that, somehow, she would engineer their escape and take revenge on the men who had lit the furnace that blazed in her back. She also was a warrior and would take her revenge. This she secretly swore to herself.

"You will now be handed over to Highrum who will be responsible for your training. I suggest you learn fast and well. He is short in temper and will not tolerate any nonsense."

As if on cue, a huge black man entered the room. He wore baggy trousers suspended from a thick leather belt at his waist from which hung a thin cane. Above the belt he was naked displaying heavily muscled arms and torso. The very sight of him filled the girls with fresh terror.

"These are your new charges." Andreas informed him "See that they are taught well and quickly and don't forget to introduce them to your stable in the usual way. Her also." He added, seeing the questioning look in the black's eyes as he surveyed Samantha's back.

"Follow me, slaves." Highrum ordered in a deep authoritative voice.

Completely overwhelmed by his presence, the four girls rose to their feet and followed the black from the room. Outside they found two more half naked black men who manacled each girl's left wrist to a length of chain. With other men on each end of the chain, they were led along a corridor, out of the building and across an open yard.

They stopped in front of another windowless building where Highrum unlocked a heavy door. The small procession passed through into a large hallway. The door was locked behind them.

The building, they later discovered, was in the form

of a large hollow square. It was out into this square they were ushered and made to stand with their backs to a wall to which the ends of the chain were attached.

"This is the training stable. Here you will be taught the duties of a slave and all that is required of you to please a Master." Highrum's deep voice vibrated round the square as he stood facing them.

"There is no escape. You will obey at all times and you will be diligent and learn fast or you will earn my deep displeasure." He paused and looked at his charges. "First, however, you must be introduced to your new status as slaves."

Highrum looked carefully at the line of naked females that were now in his charge. It was his task to ensure that, in the shortest time possible, they would be sufficiently trained to be put up for sale.

"What is your name?" He asked pointing at one of the girls.

"Judy Daleson." The girl replied sullenly.

"You will address me, and all men, as Master." He shouted. "You will only be known as Judy from now on. Understand?"

"Yes." Judy replied then added quickly "Master."

"I'll have you first. Perhaps this will teach you to answer properly in future." He turned to his assistants. "Prepare her."

Two of his men released Judy from the chain and marched her towards where Highrum waited. The girl saw a thick post, a metre high sunk into the ground with another thick beam fixed across the top. The sight of this, and Highrum unclipping the long cane from his belt, left Judy in no doubt what was in store for her.

She began to struggle fiercely but her efforts against the muscular black men were in vain. In seconds she was bent over the horizontal top beam and her wrists and ankles strapped to the base of the upright.

The other girls watched in horror as Highrum first flexed the cane between his huge hands then brought it swishing down across Judy's taut bottom.

The sharp crack of rattan meeting flesh echoed round the courtyard.

"Aaaarrgghhh!" A long drawn out cry of agony followed the report of the stroke. Judy shook her head in disbelief at the pain that erupted in her buttocks. Her long raven hair swept the ground sending up a small shower of dust.

Highrum gave a satisfied smile as he saw a thin white line etched the full width of the girls cheeks. A white line that quickly turned into familiar red tramlines.

Samantha cursed quietly under her breath as she watched the cane bite into her colleagues's bottom nine more times. Judy writhed as each cut into her. She was ashamed at the way she was unable to control the screams that each stroke wrung from her tortured body.

At last her ordeal was over. The assistants released her bonds and dragged her back to her position at the wall where they made her kneel with her knees wide spread. Fear of another beating forced her to maintain this embarrassing position.

"Your name?" Highrum demanded, pointing at the next girl in line.

"Jacqueline Master." The girl answered. She realised that she was to take Judy's place and thought that by answering as the man wanted she would please him and he would go lightly on her.

She was soon disillusioned as, once secured in place, she felt the rattan lashed across her tender buttocks ten times. Sobbing with pain and humiliation she was returned to her place, kneeling with her knees spread and her face and short blonde hair soaked with her tears.

The third girl, the long brown haired Stephanie Lang, was next to receive her ten strokes. She writhed and screamed with each stroke, her long hair sweeping the ground as she shook her head from side to side as the pain in her bottom increased with each stroke.

The guards returned Stephanie to the wall where she also was made to kneel, spreading her knees wide.

Highrum pointed the cane at Samantha. "Now you." He ordered.

Samantha, not believing she would be caned on top of the whipping she had received, hesitated a moment too long for Highrum's liking. "Five extra strokes," he said, "for slowness in obeying an order!"

Samantha, choking down the hatred that welled up inside her, shrugged off the guard's hands and walked to the post. A deep moan escaped her lips as the pain in her back was rekindled when her arms were pulled to the base of the post and secured.

Crack! Again the report of the rattan striking bare flesh echoed round the courtyard. Ashamed of the way she had screamed under the whip, Samantha gritted her teeth as a line of fire erupted in her buttocks.

The cane lashed her bottom as another searing stroke was laid on. Again she remained silent. She was a leader of a troop and would show these men that she would not give in to their domination.

Crack!

As the pain built in her buttocks, Samantha bit her lips hard to hold back her cries and swore to herself that she would escape from this hell-hole at the very first opportunity.

Thwack!

Escape and take revenge on the man who was thrashing her and on he who, no doubt, had ordained the beating.

Crack!

Samantha writhed in pain. She tried to rub her thighs together and clench and unclench her buttocks. Anything to ease the terrible pain in her bottom. She felt a surge of pride as she realised she had now taken five strokes in silence.

Thwack!

The sixth stroke added to the fire in her bottom and drew a shrill scream from her lungs.

Crack!

Thwack!

The punishing rod lashing her bottom sent new waves of pain through her cheeks. Now the strokes were falling on previous ones making the agony even worse.

Swish. Thwack!

Swish Crack!

The two strokes in quick succession, aimed at the soft area just above the join of her thighs and buttocks, sent two more screams echoing round the courtyard. Whilst her body wriggled and writhed in pain her brain, which was somehow keeping count informed her that she was two thirds of the way through her ordeal.

Highrum, who had been watching the girl's performance under the rod carefully, sensed there was still a streak of defiance showing in the writhing body. He gripped the cane tight.

Crack!

An even sharper report echoed round the courtyard as Highrum put his full weight behind the stroke. A shriller scream was forced from the suffering girl as a thin line of red showed over the darker weals.

The thin sheen of moisture that had, until now glowed

in the sunlight, suddenly turned into heavy beads of sweat that flowed from the beaten body. Rivulets flowed down her pendant breasts to drop from her nipples forming puddles with the tears on the ground around her.

Determined to break the girl, Highrum laid on two more vicous strokes that sent thin lines of red creeping over her writhing buttocks.

Despite the pain and the fog that seemed to cloud her mind, Samantha realised Highrum's intentions. This knowledge added fuel to her determination. He would not break her!

Thwack!

Thwack!

Smothering a sneaking regard for the girl's courage, Highrum lashed the rattan across the writhing buttocks for the last two strokes making each draw a thick line of red to mark its path.

Samantha never could explain how but she managed not to scream as these last strokes sent sheets of pain through her cheeks.

At last her ordeal was over and she was returned, shaking and sobbing violently, to the kneel beside her friends, moaning as her heels dug into her tortured buttocks.

Under Highrum's instructions, the guards led the four girls from the courtyard. Stumbling, trying not to jar their throbbing buttocks, the girls were led into the building and into a wash room. Here, several older women took charge of the girls and ordered them into a large sunken bath where they were ordered to scrub themselves clean.

At first the hot water aggravated their weals, especially those on Samantha's back, but gradually it had a soothing effect and the girls began to find it not unpleasant. It was a relief to wash away the dirt of their journey and the ordeal of their beatings and feel clean again.

Much to their dissatisfaction, they were not allowed to languish in the bath. They were ordered out and made to dry each other. Then the guards marched them out, along a short passage and pushed them into a cell. The door was slammed shut, the sound echoing ominously round the walls.

As soon as they were sure they were alone, the four girls came together seeking solace in each others' arms.

Eventually they disentangled themselves and looked round the cell. The only light, which came from a barred window set high in one wall, showed that the cell was unfurnished save for some rugs on the floor and a bucket in one corner.

For some time they were silent, each enveloped in a feeling of doom, until Samantha called them together in a corner farthest from the door. Here, they began to talk in whispers, trying to console each other.

As the leader, Samantha soon exerted her authority. They would escape as soon as the opportunity presented itself. In the meantime, they would be docile and obedient and try to please Highrum and his minions. In this way, Samantha explained, they would hopefully lull their tormentors into slackness and at the same time avoid being beaten.

Little did they know then that, not only was escape impossible, but the beatings they had received were very mild compared with what the future held in store for them.

TITLES IN PRINT

Silver Moon

ISBN 1-897809-08-5	Barbary Pasha *Allan Aldiss*
ISBN 1-897809-14-X	Barbary Enslavement *Allan Aldiss*
ISBN 1-897809-16-6	Rorigs Dawn *Ray Arneson*
ISBN 1-897809-17-4	Bikers Girl on the Run *Lia Anderssen*
ISBN 1-897809-23-9	Slave to the System *Rosetta Stone*
ISBN 1-897809-25-5	Barbary Revenge *Allan Aldiss*
ISBN 1-897809-27-1	White Slavers *Jack Norman*
ISBN 1-897809-29-8	The Drivers *Henry Morgan*
ISBN 1-897809-31-X	Slave to the State *Rosetta Stone*
ISBN 1-897809-36-0	Island of Slavegirls *Mark Slade*
ISBN 1-897809-37-9	Bush Slave *Lia Anderssen*
ISBN 1-897809-38-7	Desert Discipline *Mark Stewart*
ISBN 1-897809-40-9	Voyage of Shame *Nicole Dere*
ISBN 1-897809-41-7	Plantation Punishment *Rick Adams*
ISBN 1-897809-42-5	Naked Plunder *J.T. Pearce*
ISBN 1-897809-43-3	Selling Stephanie *Rosetta Stone*
ISBN 1-897809-44-1	SM Double value (Olivia/Lucy) *Graham/Slade**
ISBN 1-897809-46-8	Eliska *von Metchingen*
ISBN 1-897809-47-6	Hacienda, *Allan Aldiss*
ISBN 1-897809-48-4	Angel of Lust, *Lia Anderssen**
ISBN 1-897809-50-6	Naked Truth, *Nicole Dere**
ISBN 1-897809-51-4	I Confess!, *Dr Gerald Rochelle**
ISBN 1-897809-52-2	Barbary Slavedriver, *Allan Aldiss**
ISBN 1-897809-53-0	A Toy for Jay, *J.T. Pearce**
ISBN 1-897809-54-9	The Confessions of Amy Mansfield, *R. Hurst**
ISBN 1-897809-55-7	Gentleman's Club, *John Angus**
ISBN 1-897809-57-3	Sinfinder General *Johnathan Tate**
ISBN 1-897809-59-X	Slaves for the Sheik *Allan Aldiss**
ISBN 1-897809-60-3	Church of Chains *Sean O'Kane**
ISBN 1-897809-62-X	Slavegirl from Suburbia *Mark Slade**

Silver Mink

ISBN 1-897809-13-1	Amelia *Josephine Oliver*
ISBN 1-897809-15-8	The Darker Side *Larry Stern*
ISBN 1-897809-21-2	Sonia *RD Hall*
ISBN 1-897809-22-0	The Captive *Amber Jameson*
ISBN 1-897809-24-7	Dear Master *Terry Smith*
ISBN 1-897809-26-3	Sisters in Servitude *Nicole Dere*
ISBN 1-897809-28-X	Cradle of Pain *Krys Antarakis*
ISBN 1-897809-32-8	The Contract *Sarah Fisher*
ISBN 1-897809-33-6	Virgin for Sale *Nicole Dere*
ISBN 1-897809-39-5	Training Jenny *Rosetta Stone*
ISBN 1-897898-45-X	Dominating Obsession *Terry Smith*
ISBN 1-897809-49-2	The Penitent *Charles Arnold**
ISBN 1-897809-56-5	Please Save Me! *Dr. Gerald Rochelle**
ISBN 1-897809-58-1	Private Tuition *Jay Merson**
ISBN 1-897809-61-1	Little One *Rachel Hurst**

*UK £4.99 except *£5.99 --USA $8.95 except *$9.95*